## Praise for Dawn Kurtagich

"Dawn Kurtagich really is the queen of darkness . . ."

—Josh Winning, author of *Heads Will Roll*

"Scary stuff!"

—R. L. Stine, author of the Goosebumps and Fear Street series

"Kurtagich is one of my favorite writers."

—Evelyn Skye, *New York Times* bestselling author of *The Hundred Loves of Juliet*

"Dawn Kurtagich has an amazing mind. Creepy, but amazing."

—Christopher Pike, bestselling author of the Thirst series

"Kurtagich's horror imagery is satisfying and affecting."

—*School Library Journal*

"Kurtagich's writing is evocative and fearless."

—Cat Winters, author of *In the Shadow of Blackbirds* and *The Raven's Tale*

## Praise for *The Seventh Sister*

"*The Seventh Sister* is a raw, primal, spore-choked love letter to the mysteries of the forest. Kurtagich's writing is smooth and sinuous as liquid gold, her descriptions imbued with a horrible beauty. Equal parts terrifying and heart wrenching, this gothic folk horror fairy tale is something to be savored."

—Viggy Parr Hampton, author of *The Rotting Room*

"A sensory fever dream that's like *Yellowjackets* meets *We Have Always Lived in the Castle*. This is easily my favorite Dawn Kurtagich book yet—a piercingly emotional and atmospheric folk horror that perfectly captures the love and ache of sisterhood. This story crawled inside me and took root, and I'm certain it will never let go."

—Josh Winning, author of *Burn the Negative*

"Hauntingly beautiful and delightfully unsettling, *The Seventh Sister* is a masterclass on folk horror. Kurtagich lures you deep into the forest island of Beltane and keeps you there with lichen-covered fingers until you can almost taste the mold and mushrooms. Dark, enchanting, and powerful, *The Seventh Sister* will have you whispering 'All hail Daudir,' just to be safe."

—Saratoga Schaefer, author of *Serial Killer Support Group* and *Trad Wife*

"Stitched together with earthy, primitive magic and the hum of raw dread, *The Seventh Sister* brims with verdant darkness. Eloquently beautiful and harrowing, in equal measure. Kurtagich's sisters bewitch completely."

—Paulette Kennedy, bestselling author of *The Witch of Tin Mountain*

"A beautiful, twisted folk horror woven from bits of bone, roots, and trauma. *The Seventh Sister* spreads through you like an invasive ivy, leaving behind the scent of rot and loamy earth and a dreadful longing to belong."

—Tanya Pell, author of *Her Wicked Roots*

"Kurtagich's *The Seventh Sister* is a spectacular, gruesome, and compellingly woven tale of sisterly love and folk horror. A story of forests, faith, and feral girls that unfolds elegantly and irresistibly. A compulsive read."

—Angela "A. G." Slatter, award-winning author of *The Cold House*

"Eerie and propulsive, *The Seventh Sister* masterfully weaves sisterhood and folk horror into a heartbreaking, twisted tale. All hail Daudir."

—Tatiana Schlote-Bonne, author of *The Mean Ones*

"*The Seventh Sister* creeps into your brain as steadily as moss over stone—I stayed up way too late to finish this gorgeous, grotesque story of sisterhood and survival."

—Hannah Whitten, *New York Times* and *Sunday Times* bestselling author of *For the Wolf* and *The Foxglove King*

"Dawn Kurtagich has rendered a tender effigy of a novel, a beguiling totem teetering between belief and mania, faith and fury, horror and absolute wonder. *The Seventh Sister* isn't just a beautiful book—it's a bible. Read it and share in our awe."

—Clay McLeod Chapman, author of *Wake Up and Open Your Eyes*

## Praise for *The Madness*

"Sharp and relentless, *The Madness* has a bite that won't let go."

—Kiersten White, *New York Times* bestselling and Bram Stoker Award–nominated author of *And I Darken*

"Fiercely feminist and fantastically eerie, *The Madness* is Welsh gothic at its most intoxicating. Dawn Kurtagich really is the queen of darkness, drawing beautifully on Bram Stoker's *Dracula* to deliver a story that's smart, fresh, and frightening in equal measure. This book wraps itself around you like a wraith and refuses to let go."

—Josh Winning, author of *Burn the Negative*

"If you thought Mina Harker deserved more credit, more power, and more agency, this *Dracula* remix is for you. *The Madness* zeroes in on the original's undercurrent of sexual violence and puts its targets—young women—in the starring roles, arming them not only with wooden stakes and arcane lore but also with love and solidarity. Kurtagich's vampires, like Stoker's, are vicious, calculating predators, but this time the prey bites back."

—Amelinda Bérubé, author of *Here There Are Monsters*

"In *The Madness,* Dawn Kurtagich has created a stunning *Dracula* retelling—creepy, insidious, and visceral. This book will haunt me for a long time—in the very best way."

—Amy McCulloch, author of *Breathless*

"Exquisitely dark, disturbing, and clever as hell! Kurtagich's hypnotic retelling electrifies and relentlessly propels the reader forward with one cliff-hanger after another. If you think you've heard this story before, think again. *The Madness* is a tour de force of feminist horror."

—Paulette Kennedy, bestselling author of *The Witch of Tin Mountain*

"*The Madness* is genuinely chilling and endlessly compelling. Welsh folklore, small towns, and secrets—this story is gothic horror at its finest."

—Emily Lloyd-Jones, author of *The Bone Houses*

"I devoured *The Madness.* A modern interpretation of *Dracula* cast with familiar characters, the story is deferential, referential, and yet wholly its own terrifying achievement. Kurtagich's writing is lively and gorgeous. This original spin on a familiar tale is guaranteed to keep you turning the pages until the sun comes up."

—Joshua Moehling, author of *And There He Kept Her* and *Where the Dead Sleep*

"Kurtagich has taken *the* classic horror novel and dragged it into the twenty-first century in this fabulous, feminist, and fierce retelling. Mina Harker was one of the most passive women in literature, representing Victorian virtue until she is attacked, and then is considered soiled because of it. The Mina of *The Madness* is intelligent, flawed, and fiercely relatable. She takes matters into her own hands, and forms a band of badass women, reimagining Stoker's boys club in a manner that will leave you pumping your fist in the air with triumph."

—Ann Dávila Cardinal, award-winning author of *The Storyteller's Death*

"A retelling with teeth, *The Madness* is exquisitely timely and elegantly told, reimagining vampires into our current world with rich imagination."

—Hannah Whitten, *New York Times* bestselling author of *For the Wolf*

"An atmospheric and immersive read! This feminist take on *Dracula*, focusing on victim experiences and with spot-on commentary about the parallels between men and monsters, is as fast paced as it is carefully wrought. With bone-chilling imagery and deep characterizations, this is a fantastic reimagining of the classic *Dracula* tale."

—Wendy Heard, author of *You Can Trust Me* and *Hunting Annabelle*

"*The Madness* is a mesmerizing indictment of female exploitation sculpted from the decaying bones of a classic. An intricate and empathetic reimagining that haunted me in more ways than one. My new favorite thriller!"

—Isabel Agajanian, author of *Modern Divination*

"Dawn Kurtagich's official debut novel! My reading experience of *The Madness* consisted of the investigation of mysterious psychic trauma . . . strong female protagonists, and a labyrinthine Welsh castle, all of which are drenched in the pervasive echoes of Bram Stoker's *Dracula*. I especially enjoyed the mixed-media storytelling including bits of letters, texts, and message board discussions—so interactive and immersive! *The Madness* checks a lot of boxes for thrill seekers and horror hounds!"

—Sadie Hartmann (@mother.horror)

"A propulsively dark Welsh gothic reimaging of *Dracula*, which centers on the compelling and lushly drawn women of the tale. Dawn Kurtagich masterfully weaves local folklore with a malevolent conspiracy of powerful men to deliver a novel that is viscerally creepy and unforgettable."

—Danielle Paige, *New York Times* bestselling author of the Dorothy Must Die series and *Wish of the Wicked*

"A chilling Welsh gothic that sinks its teeth into you. Darkly haunting and fiercely clever, this is Mina Murray like you've never seen her before!"

—Mia Kuzniar, bestselling author of *Upon a Frosted Star*

"*The Madness* is everything a great horror novel should be and more—a creeping tale that gets its claws into you and doesn't let go. It's a story about pain, trauma, and ultimately hope, and needless to say, it belongs at the top of your TBR pile."

—Gwendolyn Kiste, three-time Bram Stoker Award–winning author of *The Rust Maidens* and *Reluctant Immortals*

"Edge-of-your-seat storytelling plus assured writing make this chilling take on the *Dracula* story a compulsive read. Five stars from me!"

—Juliet Marillier, author of the Sevenwaters and Blackthorn & Grim series

"*The Turn of the Key* meets *Underworld* in this gloriously chilling, feminist take on *Dracula*. Set against a brooding Welsh backdrop with lush imagery hiding its darkly beating heart, *The Madness* will stay with you long past the final page. Truly stunning!"

—Kat Ellis, author of *Harrow Lake*

"Writing an original story about vampires is a monumental task, but Dawn Kurtagich has done it. With spare prose and a feminist twist, meet the newest vampire classic. Part thriller, part horror, and 100 percent compelling."

—Samantha Downing, international bestselling author

"Darkly evocative and thought-provoking, Kurtagich is one of my favorite writers."

—Evelyn Skye, *New York Times* bestselling author of *The Hundred Loves of Juliet*

## Praise for *Teeth in the Mist*

"Dawn Kurtagich breathes life into Faustian lore."

—Hypable

"Kurtagich delivers a creepy, atmospheric tale of subjugation, female self-empowerment, and redemption."

—*Publishers Weekly*

"Kurtagich's writing is evocative and fearless. *Teeth in the Mist* abounds with atmosphere, mystery, and horror and gleefully plays with the Faust legend in ways both modern and classically gothic."

—Cat Winters, author of *In the Shadow of Blackbirds* and *The Raven's Tale*

"Delightfully disturbing . . . an eerie, atmospheric, satanic spooky story."

—*Kirkus Reviews*

"In *Teeth in the Mist,* Dawn Kurtagich weaves genres, time periods, and sets of characters with deft fingers. Connecting all is the mysterious Mill House. Readers will be fascinated, perplexed, often freaked out, and always wanting to turn the next page."

—Juliet Marillier, author of the Blackthorn & Grim series

## Praise for *And the Trees Crept In* (*The Creeper Man*)

"Will haunt readers with its raw emotions, palpable pain, and consistent character voices . . . Frightening and compelling, this gothic will easily sweep fans up into its creeping sense of hysteria."

—*Kirkus Reviews*

"*And the Trees Crept In* is a hauntingly immersive tale of insanity, terror, and what happens when you're not even safe in your own home."

—Hypable

"Kurtagich's horror imagery is satisfying and affecting—her descriptions of the day-to-day decay the girls face are as rich and scary as the monstrous man who scuttles around on all fours and the teeming mud pits that are waiting in the woods. A great next read for teens who enjoy being scared."

—*School Library Journal* (starred review)

"Kurtagich evokes an all-pervading atmosphere of horror with dark imagery and language evoking rot, decay, and death . . . This unique novel is for teens who enjoy being immersed in a dark, complex horror story."

—*VOYA* (starred review)

"Kurtagich has created an incredibly assured, claustrophobic horror with a fractured and troubled teen narrator that will have you gripped to the very last page."

—BookTrust

"Horror fans will be caught by the gripping cover image, and there's plenty to scare them here, even during the second reading that the surprise ending might encourage them to undertake."

—*The Bulletin of the Center for Children's Books*

"Dark, twisted, and terrifying, *And the Trees Crept In* will keep your stomach in knots from page one. A must-read for horror fans everywhere!"

—Susan Dennard, *New York Times* bestselling author of *Truthwitch* and *Windwitch*

"*And the Trees Crept In* should come with a warning label: Best read in the light of day, with lots of smiling people around, and candy canes and unicorns and cute babies. A beautifully written, gorgeous nightmare of a novel."

—David Arnold, bestselling author of *Mosquitoland* and *Kids of Appetite*

"An enthralling, unsettling fairy tale that will have you turning pages long into the night."

—Michelle Zink, author of *This Wicked Game* and *Lies I Told*

"A fight for survival, an encroaching forest, a cursed manor, and dark secrets . . . Kurtagich's terrifying take wrapped my heart up and squeezed until I was as cold as the dead things haunting its pages."

—Alexandra Sirowy, author of *The Creeping* and *The Telling*

## Praise for *The Dead House*

"A haunting new thriller . . ."

—EW.com

"Kaitlyn/Carly Johnson is troubled. Suffering from dissociative identity disorder, Carly is awake during the day and Kaitlyn owns the night. The personalities leave each other notes to help smooth the transition; they lead separate lives. When the parents die suspiciously, Kaitlyn/Carly is moved to a psychiatric hospital and then a school for troubled teens. When a doctor integrates the personalities, Kaitlyn emerges; she believes that other forces are possessing her and trapping Carly. Then other teens go missing or are killed. This book will pique readers' interest on multiple levels. Told through diaries, police interviews, psychiatrist's notes, emails, video transcripts, and newspaper articles, this unique format puts the reader in the position of investigator. Finally, there is the horror component, which will keep many readers anxiously waiting to see what comes next."

—Library School Connection

"A horror tale made creepier by the integration of diary entries, grainy pictures, interview transcripts, newspaper clippings, doodles, stills from video recordings, and other media, Carly/Kaitlyn's story is told as 'found footage' pieced together by followers of 'the Johnson incident,' which remains an unsolved mystery. Kurtagich maintains the creepy and dark tone through to the end, where readers are not given a neat a tidy ending—ghosts still haunt, pieces of the story remain missing, and life goes on despite the terrible tragedy at the prestigious Elmbridge High School."

—*Voya* (October 2015 print issue)

"Kurtagich's debut is a taut, psychological suspense novel centered around disturbed teenagers Carly and Kaitlyn Johnson and the horrifying series of events that culminated in a deadly fire at a residential high school. The timeline is recreated through a series of police files, diary entries, transcribed video footage, and newspaper stories, revealing that Carly/Kaitlyn share the same body, with Carly occupying the daytime hours and Kaitlyn the night. The two communicate via a series of notes, and, although Carly's therapist believes she suffers from dissociative identity disorder, it's not clear which girl is the primary persona and which is the alter ego. When the Carly personality disappears from Kaitlyn's consciousness, she embarks on a grisly quest to find her in the 'dead house' that is her mind. Not for the faint of heart, this is a gory and grimly compelling story, made more so by the novel's visual elements. Readers will be left wondering if the supernatural elements are real or all part of a troubled girl's damaged mind."

—*Booklist*

"This creepy boarding school novel meshes real-world issues with a paranormal mystery in a fun but scary debut . . . Fans of horror novels will appreciate the creepy photographs scattered throughout, and the multiple perspectives are smoothly integrated . . . a worthy addition to high school horror collections."

—*School Library Journal*

"I do love an unreliable narrator (or two), and this endlessly twisty psychological horror manipulated from the off. A Buzz Book of the Bologna Children's Book Fair in 2014, this is Orion imprint Indigo's biggest debut title of the year."

—*The Bookseller*

"Insightful characterization and a detailed exploration of the importance of the emergent identity to the teenage self."

—*Publishers Weekly*

"What an evil and original story. You can't stop reading Kaitlyn's diary. But is she real? It's a mystery inside a mystery—and the shocks keep coming. Scary stuff!"

—R. L. Stine, bestselling author of the Goosebumps and Fear Street series

"All I could think when I finished *The Dead House* was that the author, Dawn Kurtagich, has an amazing mind. Creepy, but amazing. I loved it."

—Christopher Pike, bestselling author of the Thirst series

"Full of twists, buried secrets, and enough disturbing corpses to please the most discerning horror lover, *The Dead House* is a thoroughly engrossing read. Diary entries, psychiatrist records, and transcripts from the investigation keep the pages turning late into the night. This is a harrowing tale, cleverly told."

—Kendare Blake, author of *Anna Dressed in Blood*

"Kurtagich weaves a terrifying and mind-bending tale reminiscent of H. P. Lovecraft. This is one of the best horror debuts I've read in a long time!"

—J. R. Johansson, author of *Cut Me Free* and The Night Walkers series

"*The Dead House* is a seamless blend of the supernatural and the psychological. Creepy, compelling, and compulsively readable."

—Victoria Schwab, author of *The Archived* and *Vicious*

"Spine-chilling, gruesome, and mysterious; an exciting debut . . . difficult to put down, and even harder to forget."

—@TheBookbag

# THE SEVENTH SISTER

OTHER TITLES BY DAWN KURTAGICH

*The Thorns*

*Teeth in the Mist*

*And the Trees Crept In (The Creeper Man)*

*Blood on the Wind*

*The Madness*

## The Dead House

*The Dead House*

*Naida*

# THE SEVENTH SISTER

DAWN KURTAGICH

This is a work of fiction. Names, characters, organizations, places, events, and incidents are either products of the author's imagination or are used fictitiously. Otherwise, any resemblance to actual persons, living or dead, is purely coincidental.



Published by Thomas & Mercer, Seattle

www.apub.com



EU product safety contact:
Amazon Media EU S. à r.l.
38, avenue John F. Kennedy, L-1855 Luxembourg
amazonpublishing-gpsr@amazon.com

ISBN-13: 9781662526992 (paperback)
ISBN-13: 9781662526985 (digital)

Cover design by Olga Grlic
Cover image: © Elise Ortiou Campion / plainpicture; © Rémy Penet / Unsplash

Fleuron: Ramosh Artworks

Printed in the United States of America

*This one's for Kat.*

*Never have black-cat and ginger-cat energy looked so good.*

One berry swallowed by a little black robin
Grew in its belly and made two red bobbins.
A girl in green sewed three large dresses
And gave them to the sisters with the violet tresses.
The violet sisters ran through the hallow wood
Stumbled into a run, where five mushrooms stood.
Six times they circled, chanting out a bray.
But the fae took them captive and turned them into hay.
The blackbird came with his family of seven,
Gulped the stalks down and sent the girls to heaven!
—Ward nonsense poem, written by Juniper

# AUTHOR'S NOTE

The idea of children moving freely through a wild, unstructured landscape has always stirred something deep in me. It echoes my own childhood—those long, loose hours beneath dappled trees, the dry hum of summer dust, the strange magic of freedom and threat coexisting in the same sunlit places. The sense that the world was porous and anything could slip through. Magic, danger, a doorway.

*The Seventh Sister* is, in many ways, a return to that space.

At its heart, this book explores the pull of once-inhabited landscapes; the way memory and myth begin to blur when we revisit the sites of our own becoming, whether physically or emotionally. It peers through a fairy-tale lens at the jagged terrain between childhood and adulthood, where wonder curdles and mystery darkens. In that sense, it is a sister novel to *The Thorns*, cut from the same bloodline but with a different face.

The atmosphere of *The Seventh Sister* was shaped, too, by the films that live rent-free in my imagination: Lucile Hadžihalilović's *Innocence*, Peter Jackson's *Heavenly Creatures*, *My Brother Tom*, *Stand by Me*, *Now and Then*, Terry Gilliam's *Tideland*, *Pan's Labyrinth*, *Where the Wild Things Are*, the '90s *It*, *Bridge to Terabithia*, Lee Hae-young's *The Silenced*—all stories that crack open the liminal space between the fantastical and the sinister, the sacred and the unsafe.

What draws me to these tales is not just nostalgia, but disturbance. The children in them often return to places they once ruled like wild monarchs, only to find the kingdom changed—or themselves changed beyond recognition. That lingering question—*did the magic leave, or did I?*—haunts the edges of this book. And maybe, too, the quieter truth: that the old myths were never about escape, but about knowing which paths not to take. To sit in adulthood and remember how the woods once whispered your name. Some places remember you. Some stories, once entered, do not let you leave unchanged.

I hope, in some quiet way, this story leaves you with the scent of earth on your hands and the hush of something ancient just out of sight.

With love and unease,

*Dawn Kurtagich*
July 2025

N
W
E
S
Guardian Rock
The Castle
The Lake
(don't go in alone)
Daudir's Place
The Hollows
The Hemlock
Ernest's Cabin
The Dock
Beltane House
(keep inside after dark)

# PROLOGUE

The flesh is a putrid, yellow-tinged gray, speckled with a purple so dark it looks black.

Like mold.

Like spores.

Like mushrooms waiting to bloom beneath skin.

The held breath in the air tastes like sorrow. Like grief. Like a reckoning.

*Press down, cut hard.*

It's the only way. Like a lover, she hopes the knife is sharp enough to sever nerves, sever bone.

To sever the enduring love between sisters.

# 1

***September 2024***

An envelope.

Crumpled. It looks beaten down from a long, wearisome journey.

Inside, a single dried juniper berry.

It rolls into my palm, and I quake with horror.

Nausea rises in my throat, and I rush for the toilet at the back of the shop, knocking piles of dusty books from their precarious piles, and an antique clock with them, barely making it in time to lose my morning coffee, viscous as oil, all over the toilet seat.

Through the acidic pant of my lungs and the sour squeeze of my stomach, I realize:

The envelope was unaddressed.

Unsealed.

The unassuming top flap had been neatly tucked into the bottom like a bitten lip.

Flirtatious.

The only person who knows I am here is Matthew, the young university graduate I reluctantly hired when he stumbled, dripping rainwater, into Curioscuro, my antique shop, as an undergraduate ten years ago.

And Ivy, of course. Ivy knows.

But no one else.

A pulse of doom ticks in my jugular like a discordant clock as I get to my feet and stalk unsteadily back onto the shop floor. Ignoring the spill of expensive first editions currently crumpled underfoot, I step over the foxed pages and crouch to retrieve the envelope and the tiny husk of a berry.

The envelope is crumpled, stained in one corner, the texture all wrong in that charming way of distant pen pals. Mottled and soft in places, hard and pristine in others. It smells of mildew and loam and worming creatures deep in soft, fertile wood.

*No,* I think. *No, it can't be.*

Not after this long.

I stare at it for what feels like a lifetime, visions flitting behind my eyes like hauntings.

Summer rain pounding a plastic roof, corrugated, draped in verdant, spongy moss. Storm winds thrashing at thin panes of glass, the window buckling under the fury. Muddy feet balancing on logs slippery with morning dew. Spring dips, naked and exhilarating, in the algae-ridden lake. Taste of fungi, juniper, and elderberry wine.

Bones jutting from skin, mushrooming outward, marrow vivid as cardinals.

I tilt my hand, let the berry roll back into its haunted paper casket, and make to tuck away the envelope flap again.

A tiny scribble catches my eye. But I don't need to read it. I already know the message. It screams, loud as a death knell.

A whisper. A plea. A command.

Beltane is calling.

# 2

***March 1999***

The sky is the deep purple of fresh bruises on the day the sisters meet Granny Alys.

Glimpses of a jungle island peek through choppy, whitecapped water.

Clementine Ward stares over the lip of the boat at the encroaching tangle of green, breathing in gulps of salty air that feel like drowning. Beside her, six other Ward girls stare forward with the same eerie intensity.

Juniper, the eldest at sixteen. Stern, rigid. As unmoving as an oak. A velvet bow in her hair, blustering in the wind. The vivid purple of royal grapes.

Hazel, next in line. Fourteen and flirtatious as the dawn. Polished orange shoes on her pretty feet.

Ivy and Holly. At eleven, the twins believe they know more than most adults ever will, and are vicious with it, knotted and complex and secretive as a vine. They wear matching green shorts the hue of pine needles.

Willow. Eight and eerie, she clutches a string of ocean-blue beads strung three times about her neck, a weeping noose.

Poppy. Three. The jewel of their family, precious as a ruby, dressed in a rouge onesie, asleep in Juniper's arms.

Clementine came in the middle, nestled between Hazel and the twins. Thirteen and terrified of the way the world has suddenly tilted sideways, sliding them from their known axis and into this . . . abyss. She must protect them. She must keep them safe. Her sunny-yellow corduroy dress belies her grief and her desperate yearning to put it all right. In her hand, she clutches a fast-disintegrating, once-yellow stuffed rabbit. His terror-stricken eye hangs by a thread, horrible as a murder.

Seven girls, rigid as iron, colorful as a kaleidoscope. Vestiges of a system their hedonistic parents implemented when a new child arrived. Assigning a name and a color was the most Hillary and Peter Ward ever did for their children.

Purple, orange, yellow, green, blue, and red.

A little Ward rainbow.

Hand in hand, they need no words to communicate their fears. They do not know the man driving the boat, or the silent boy who sits beside him, still as a shadow. These strangers could be taking the girls anywhere. Anywhere at all.

Will her sisters survive this? Life on an island seventeen miles out from the mainland? With a grandmother they have never met? Clementine wishes she could wrap her sisters in wings of gossamer, hide them from the world like so much precious silk. Would that she had the power to turn the universe soft for them so that no hard edges could ever scrape at their shine. She carries their fears, their hearts beating safely in her yellow pocket.

Clutching her stuffed rabbit in her lap, she turns away. She has seen enough. The knot of tangled green drawing ever closer like some sort of garish maw is enough to stir a hungry trepidation in her belly.

"Ripples in the fabric," Ivy whispers.

"Frays in the yarn," Holly replies.

They are eerie, the twins. Even more so than the others. Hair as pale as the rest, yes, but their eyes are almost colorless, as though empty enough to draw in what the world would prefer to hide.

Ivy reaches over the edge of the boat, leaning toward the water as though ready to pluck a secret from the ocean. The man driving the boat lurches forward and yanks her arm away with a force that makes Clem's eyes flash.

"Keep your 'ands in ze runabout," he growls, his voice heavy with a French accent.

He continues to grip Ivy's arm, fingers constricting like a boa, perhaps expecting her to cry out. And when she doesn't, he releases her with a grunt. Clem eyes him with all the vitriol in her cells, and the twins stare with a cool intensity even as the mark from his grip fades from Ivy's skin.

He mutters something in French, the tips of his ears burning red, and Clem feels an acidic pleasure. If he touches one of her sisters again, she will bite down on his hand until she draws blood, and when he screams, she will bite harder. She won't stop until she feels bone part from socket, cartilage stuck between her teeth. His nose is big enough. Perhaps she will bite that off instead.

She draws Holly and Ivy to the sides of her, tucking a twin under each arm like a hen, and watches the man with a vulpine gaze. She takes in his sun-leathered face and thin, severe lips, which are ringed with the lines of someone prone to scowling. A man that grinds anger between his teeth.

He glances at them once, then hunches back over the motor, again muttering a garbled string of French under his breath.

Ivy picks up the stuffed rabbit and holds him to her chest, and an unexpected glow radiates through Clem at the sight. It warms her terror away.

Everything is going to be okay.

She will make sure it is. Anytime a fissure erupts, or a divide appears, Clem will scramble to bridge the gap, to sew closed the gulf like a seamstress desperately fighting the erosion of use. She will be the one to mend fences, to draw her sisters close, to preserve the precious magic of their intimate sisterhood. And if she is offended or upset by their careless antics, or even if the tiniest sliver of discontent begins to rear its head, she will sew that up, too, tight as a stitch in flesh.

This time, she will keep her family together.

❋

The shadow boy inches away from the man by the motor and closer to Clem. He wears a sheepish smile that irritates her. Now, in the sun, he glows golden, hair transmuted from flat brown to a multifaceted walnut, skin from a pasty gray to a subtle gold.

"I'm sorry about my dad," he says, scratching his faintly tanned arm. The little hairs there are a stark, glistening blond. His accent, she notes, isn't French. English Canadian, maybe? "He lives on the opposite side of the island to your grandmother," he adds, "and he doesn't see people much."

So.

This boy knows something of Granny Alys, then. His knowledge is possibly worth pardoning his association with the man that Clem is going to debride one day. His father. She would hate someone to judge her based on an impression of her parents, so she forces herself not to withdraw as she normally would. Not to hide away in the tunnels she keeps deep within, a secret space only she knows.

Normally, she wouldn't speak to this boy, wouldn't open her mouth before one of her sisters did first. But she is all garbled up inside with questions and anxiety, knots that need tending and can't be ignored.

"What—" Her voice breaks, and she tries again. "What's she like?"

"Who?"

"Our Granny Alys."

Each of her sisters turns to look at him, a sudden onslaught of blue and gray eyes. Hazel leans forward, placing her chin in her hands and smiles, orange nail polish gleaming.

"Oh. Oh, um." He scratches his arm, watching the island draw close. "Well, I don't really know. She and my dad mostly talk to each other in French." He glances at the angry man and back, dropping his voice. "I only come to Beltane for a week or two in the summer. Only rarely during spring break. The rest of the time I'm with my mother. In Toronto," he adds.

Clem nods. It doesn't sound like he's given much of a choice in the matter of his location either. Tossed wherever the adults decide, like a paper boat on a river.

"I know she's strong," the boy says when Clem doesn't offer anything up.

"Strong how?" Ivy asks, almost accusatory.

"In what way?" Holly adds, pressing, suspicious.

Clem knows that the twins want him to prove himself. Either that or to be entertaining by faltering. By sputtering and moving away. They can sniff out weakness like wolves. Clem hopes he proves strong instead.

"Well, living at Beltane all alone, for one."

The twins' mouths twist, unimpressed.

"And," he says quickly, "Ernest brings the supplies and stuff," he says, nodding at his father's back, "and helps with repairs and such. But she chops her own wood, and she gets her own water from the well. Which she dug herself, years and years ago."

Clem notes two things.

1. His father, the sister grabber, is called Ernest.

2. Beltane is the name of the place they are going. She wonders if it's the name of the island, or the house.

"So, yeah," the boy finishes, grinning. "She's a strong, independent woman."

He looks pleased with himself, and Clem tries very hard not to laugh. The twins have no such restraint, and they snicker like snakes, mockery thick in the air.

"*Jadirja'autau,*" Holly sneers, using their secret language.

*Idiot.*

Ivy's eyes flash predatory, her grin turning wicked. *"Klohamonem."*

*Lame.*

Clem tightens her arms around their shoulders and whispers for them to stop.

The boy's cheeks flood the same red as the tips of his father's ears. He seems bewildered at how the mood has turned so sour, clearly unused to a life of siblings. He bites his lips and blinks hard, sitting back with shoulders hunched. A wounded dog.

Clem hasn't had many friends. She doesn't need them, with her sisters. But something about this boy is interesting to her. Endearing. He is so radiant with obvious loneliness that it makes her feel desperate with sympathy.

After a long silence, he pulls something from under his long jacket sleeve. A bracelet strung with plastic buttons.

Juniper catches Clem's eye, and a tiny smile quirks the corner of her mouth. This boy can't possibly know that, at this very moment, Clem has a pocketful of buttons and more stashed in her yellow case.

"What's your name?" she dares to ask, hurrying to rid herself of the pity gnawing at her insides.

He doesn't answer right away, searching her face for some of the twins' cruelty. Finding none, he says, "François-Henri." He says it the French way. *Frans-wah*-en-*ree*. "But people call me Henry."

He hesitates, then holds out his hand to Clem, and she gets the impression that this is a peace offering of some kind. A truce. A partnership.

Juniper, Hazel, and Willow are all watching now, too, their interest piqued. Clem glances at Ivy on her left, then Holly on her right, and when neither twin gives a sign of protest, she takes Henry's hand and gives it a firm shake.

"You'll have to learn all of our names if you want to be my friend," she warns him.

"Of course." His grin stretches from ear to ear. "I'd love to know all about you. About you all," he adds, making an effort to smile at every single Ward. Even Poppy, who is utterly oblivious in Juniper's arms.

Henry has none of the longevity of offense her sisters harbor when slighted, and that, Clem finds, is refreshing. And maybe a little foolish. He is so much more golden than Clem initially thought him. Not a shadow, then. Perhaps more a ray of sunshine.

He turns his radiant smile in her direction last, and she returns it without thinking before a stone hammers into the pit of her stomach, and she flinches away, staring out with clenched teeth at the cold gray sea.

# 3

***March 1999***

The man, Ernest, leads the girls through trails choked with plants and ivy, through narrow, twisting tunnels of green. Everything here feels damp in the way of infection. Warm, too, like being uncomfortably close to a thermal air vent. It's almost like the forest itself is breathing.

He cuts a path with unnecessary violence, slicing through leaves with a machete Clem didn't notice on the boat. It makes her uneasy. She has heard the tales of men taking girls away and cutting them into tiny little pieces, burying them in walls or soil or feeding them to pigs until not even kneecaps are left.

The boy, Henry, stays by Clementine's side, and she wonders why, of all the Ward girls, he has chosen to befriend her. It is a comfort. Surely a boy like him, a golden boy, not a shadow boy, isn't capable of cutting her down to her smallest parts?

Then again, she does not have the best experience in her judgment of character. She didn't think her parents, as neglectful and hedonistic as they were, would leave them alone in the world either. They were fixtures, like the wallpaper or the roof over their heads. She had not expected them to vanish.

Hillary and Peter Ward should not have had children. Peter, wealthy from a textile factory he owned and oversaw from afar, spent his life indulging his wife, the only real thing he cared for. The couple dined out daily and attended soirees nightly, Hillary's crystal-beaded dresses glinting under lamps and streetlights, her silks and satins shimmering with what Clem thought was magic.

They traveled for months at a time—France, Egypt, Dubai—leaving their children in the care of an au pair, Penny, an endlessly kind and patient young woman who came over from England and lived with them in their giant Upper East Side apartment since before Clem was born. Lapsed Roman Catholics, Hillary and Peter Ward refused to prevent pregnancy, a leftover compulsion from Hillary's stern religious upbringing. They were distracted and self-absorbed, and Clem had yearned for their love more than almost anything else. A love continually denied.

Her love of them broke her world in two.

"It's hotter here," Clem murmurs, scratching at her arm.

"I know," Henry says. "It's the semipermanent warm-water eddy spun off from the North Pacific Current. I mean, that and other stuff, like the rock here and something about maritime winds. It creates a humid subtropical climate, so basically it feels warmer sooner. It also means the island gets its fair share of summer storms."

Clem glances at him. "You know a lot about it."

"I did a project at school. We had to pick a place and talk about the climate."

"So, you picked here?"

He shrugs like it's nothing. "Yeah."

Clem ought to push Henry away, she knows. Deny his friendship for his own sake. But she still craves love, craves kindness, craves the softness of esteem, of connection. And when it is given, even a little, she clings to it like a person drowning, and despises herself for it.

The girls follow the path, ever inclining upward, in order, oldest to youngest. Juniper, then Hazel, then Clementine, then the twins, then Willow, who carries a babbling Poppy.

The house rises, incongruous, from the tangle of forest like a white mountain, a huge Second Empire Gothic made from wood and stone flooded with white lime wash. It gleams like a brilliant marble, glaring against the moody sky. Steep gables reach for the battered heavens, pointed arches haughty and proud. Gingerbread detailing gives it a charming facade, while the wraparound porch breathes an air of calm and space despite the tangle of green pressed so close to its skin. Two striking gables, all peeling white paint and green mossy stains, scratch at the gunmetal clouds.

It is familiar. So very, very familiar.

Plucked out of their childhood, in fact. Even the clapboard siding seems to be made from their wildest childhood fantasies, taken almost directly from a dollhouse their father had commissioned when Juniper was only four. It is, in fact, *exactly* the same. A life-size version of a stunning white toy mansion they were allowed to play with on Christmas mornings alone. The rest of the year, it stood, pristine and untouched, in the playroom. Taunting them. Teasing them. Inspiring their wildest and most lasting imaginary games.

Here, between forest and sky, between sisters and sea, the house they will call home beckons like a flaming beacon to a moth. They all feel it—Clem can tell. The way Juniper blinks hard and stares; the way Hazel leans forward as though drawn; the way Holly and Ivy go still and eerie as porcelain dolls; the way Willow cocks her head. The sudden stillness of an otherwise motile Poppy.

Life has many twists and turns, and none of them were ones that Clem could have predicted would lead to a future without their parents. A future away from New York. But as they stand on the cusp of this white building, they all breathe in Beltane and know that they were headed here all along.

As they draw closer, the house's imperfections begin to lift from the idyll. Peeling paint reveals warped wooden panels. Cement here and there beside the lime mortar—a recipe for mold—sloppily applied with fingers, the marks crude and amateur. Flaking corners of gables where black rot has already taken hold.

Still. It is perfect.

"How do they keep it white?" Willow whispers, staring up at the highest points.

"Maybe Granny Alys has a really tall ladder," Ivy offers.

"Like a beanstalk," Holly says, matching her twin.

"Or she leans out the windows," Hazel says, grinning. "With a ginormous paintbrush."

Poppy shrieks a laugh. "Beanstalk paintbrush!"

A woman comes out of the house, but Clem doesn't manage to catch a glimpse before Ernest is towering over her, blocking her like the mountain blots the sun, speaking in a fast string of garbled French.

His body language is aggressive, and Clem has an urge to defend the woman she's never met without knowing why. She glances at Henry for an explanation, but he looks as perplexed as she feels, and she realizes he doesn't speak the language either.

"*Wengihatau haresem taugi'emdos shehadosjinid?*" Clem mutters to Willow, using their secret language.

Willow shakes her head. *"Ja diraunitau kni'auwen."*

Juniper tells them to shush and goes back to trying to pick out the meaning of the heated discussion. Poppy lets out a piercing scream, and Ernest turns sharply toward her, startled into silence. The woman behind him is . . . smiling. Calm as a clam, she stands before the towering man like it doesn't bother her in the least to have his saliva flecks on her cheeks.

She steps around Ernest, ignoring him completely, and opens her arms in greeting.

"Girls," she says, and her voice is charmingly graveled. "At last."

Does . . . does she expect them to run to her? To embrace her? Or are the open arms . . . metaphorical? The girls do nothing but stand and stare.

Ernest grumbles something under his breath, another garbled French string of expletives, and stomps away. Henry glances at Clem and then follows his father, head lowered, shoulders slumped. She is sorry to see him go, but this is not his place. It is time for the Ward girls to meet the woman who is their oldest living link and determine the new order of things.

Granny Alys is not what Clem expected. She supposes she might have imagined that a female version of their father, slightly aged, would be waiting for them. Rigid, put together, cold, and untouchable. Obsessed with their grandfather, no doubt, who would be tucked safely away here somewhere in a state of aging decay.

But the woman in front of them is . . . earthy. Alive. Energetic. She stands barefoot before them in faded, mud-stained denim overalls, her long white hair caught messily on the top of her head. Strands escape in Medusa-like waves. She looks like she popped straight up out of the earth, like one of the plants Ernest cut down on their way in. Her blouse is cotton, frilled at the sleeves, but by no means pristine. Vines and tiny yellow and blue flowers are woven into her hair like a nest made by a bird particularly fond of spring. On a younger woman it might look charming. On Granny Alys it looks out of place, like her insides and outsides are mismatched.

She is, for lack of a better phrase . . . of the soil.

The constant shifting of the trees around them is making Clem queasy, and she just wants to get inside.

Clementine stares at the woman's feet, so brazenly and dirtily on display.

None of the Ward sisters have ever been particularly fond of shoes—not like their mother. When not out partying the night away, their father, too, had taken to walking about their spacious New York apartment in his socks. Their mother, when she could be bothered to notice, forced their toughened feet into stiff leather shoes that shone like oil slicks, one in every assigned color. But the moment she looked away, the shoes would be thrown down the garbage chute, hidden in trash cans, stuffed in boxes bound for the attic—and never worn again.

Until the next shiny pair appeared.

Clementine wonders if this is where the tendency originates. Here, with her father's mother, this strange, keen-eyed lady surveying them now. Is it a legacy of sorts? A link back to this wild place their father once called home, and which has now drawn them back like some sort of nexus? Can barefootedness be genetic?

Clem has an impulse to make a doll replica of the strange woman standing before them, to hem her likeness into a poppet. If only she could bring it to life, her very own homunculus to control and command.

"I'm so terribly sorry for your loss," Granny Alys says right away, letting her arms fall, and she looks like she really means it. Her eyes do look sorrowful, something in them heavy and heartsick. Clem is suddenly acutely aware that this woman has lost her son. "Peter was always a romantic. When he fell for your mother, he fell particularly hard." She smiles in a sad way that makes Clem want to cry. "It is in the nature of a Ward to fall all the way."

Juniper steps forward, brusque, as though cutting through the sentiment—or denying it. She has always tried to be the most practical, but it is a forced parade, all for show. She offers her hand to the old woman after an awkward moment. "Juniper," she says in the formal way Penny taught them.

Suddenly Clem finds herself missing their au pair and all the lessons she imparted. Whatever will she do now that Penny doesn't work for them? Live with them? Look after them? How will they get in touch with her? Where will Penny even live now?

Clem clutches a hand to her chest and wonders how much more aching it can take before it cracks right open.

Granny Alys's mouth quirks in a way that might be amusement or sadness. But she takes Juniper's hand and holds it. Clementine sees that Granny Alys's hands are swollen at the knuckles and joints, fingers bent out of shape like gnarly twigs.

Juniper looks as confused as Clem feels. *Shaking* hands is the right response, not holding it still. But Granny Alys holds Juniper's hand like it's something delicate and precious, like a benediction.

"I expect you've had to carry the weight of the whole family for a very long time," she says softly, possibly so that only Juniper can hear. But Clem has cunning ears and catches every word.

Juniper blinks at her, and she doesn't deny it. Clem feels a little betrayed by that. Hasn't she helped to carry them all as well? Haven't they all carried each other?

"You won't need to do that alone anymore," Alys says, almost like she knows that their parents weren't much in the way of carers.

Juniper blinks even quicker now, and then Granny Alys is turning to Hazel.

"How beautiful you are, Hazel," she says, and Clem notices how Hazel didn't even need to give her name.

Hazel's skin *is* beautiful when it flushes, like it's doing now, and she curls her hair around a finger when she says, "Thank you, Granny Alys."

It's Clem's turn next, and she can feel herself curling inward. Can feel the stubborn way she does not want to let this stranger in, to disrupt the intimate dynamics of the Ward ecosystem. She can feel herself scowling even before Alys steps up to her.

"Clementine," Alys says softly. "I think we'll be friends, eventually."

That's all she says.

She doesn't ask anything, nor does she offer anything other than this vague, meaningless statement. She simply smiles in the enigmatic way their father did when looking at their mother, and steps around her.

Clem feels relieved and bereft all at once. She feels both overlooked and left alone, which is, after all, what she wanted. But surely Granny Alys could have said something more? Noticed her in the way she had her two older sisters? Is she so innocuous that all she warrants is a vague hope of friendship?

Anger flickers in her breast, and she lets it grow.

"You are perfection personified," Granny Alys says to the twins. "The Holly and the Ivy, both full grown. Of all the trees that are in the bush," she says, touching Holly's head, "the Holly wears the crown."

Clem thinks she has made a terrible error here, raising one twin above the other, but Ivy is beaming just as hard as Holly is, and Clem knows she herself has made another mistake. She is losing control. Losing control of her sisters, of their love, of their minds and hearts, and she hates it.

This isn't supposed to happen.

Granny Alys gives Willow a gentle pat on the hand, murmuring her name and then saying something quietly that Clem doesn't catch, before she turns to Poppy.

Granny Alys is a firm favorite with the youngest Ward, who allows herself to be picked up and perched on Alys's hip. Granny Alys bounces her softly, and Poppy giggles. None of them have been shown this kind of attention before, except by Penny, who was often discouraged from touching them.

Again, Clem feels herself overlooked. Why was she not given some sort of praise? A kind touch or smile? Why did Granny Alys pass her by so easily? A flush of shame rises on her skin even as her brain tells her: You don't deserve this love. You don't deserve the sun. The anger she had been nursing dies away, smothered by grief and shame, and she bows her head.

"Come inside," Granny Alys says. "You'll like this house. All the best houses have strong personalities."

As the girls follow Granny Alys inside, Clem grabs Willow's hand and holds her back.

"*Wenhajatau,*" she mutters at her sister, when Granny Alys peers briefly back at them. When they're alone outside, Clem rounds on her.

"Why did you let her pat your hand? And what did she say to you?"

Willow frowns. "Weren't you listening?"

"She said it too low for us to hear!" Clem protests. "She wants to divide us."

Willow pulls a face. "Your hearing is the best of all of us. She said it loud enough for even Juniper to hear. Maybe you just didn't want to listen."

Clem is offended and wounded all at once. "What did she *say*?"

"She said everything was going to be okay. That Beltane would keep us safe now. And that I will speak for it."

A flick of anger. "That's stupid," Clem spits.

Willow smiles like she doesn't care about Clem's rage, like the sun has risen in her mind. She shrugs, then turns and skips into the house.

Clementine watches her, trying to believe that they really are safe now but unable to shake the feeling that something is very, very wrong. In moments alone, Granny Alys has managed to sow a seed of discord between Clem and her sisters, a little sapling that she fears will root and take hold, growing bigger and bigger the longer they are here.

This is wrong.

Even the door to the house looks off . . . like a mouth ready to devour them whole. Clem turns away from the building and looks into the forest instead, back toward the path that Henry and Ernest took. But there is no sign of the track. The forest has closed around them like a hermetically sealed petri dish.

Clem shivers and hurries inside, all the while feeling like there are keen little eyes on her back.

Or lots of little mouths waiting to take a bite.

# 4

***September 2024***

Matthew finds me on the bathroom floor an hour after I've opened the letter, squeezed into the space beside the toilet at the back of the shop. After a second bout of purging my morning coffee, I'm considering the berry in my palm, head against the wall's frigid tiles. Despite the cold, my body is flushed with stress, skin tingling in that horrid way of fever.

Matt opens the door slowly. "Clementine?"

It must be eight o'clock, if he's here.

"Morning," I manage, but my voice sounds far away to my own ears. The croak of a frog.

"You okay, boss?"

He's holding two t0-go cups of coffee, the Nero logo emblazoned across them in bold black, and my stomach heaves again at the sight. I shut my eyes and take a deep breath.

"Crikey! Should I be contacting the Food Standards Agency?"

I glance blearily up at him. "What?"

"Looks like your breakfast didn't agree with you. Funny eggs?" He puts the cups in the sink and places his hands on his hips as though surveying a fashion crime. As though I'm a pile of torn rayon, or a seam sewn askew.

To be fair, I do feel like a hem gone wrong, held together by a thread, a hope, and a prayer.

"Coffee," I grumble.

"Ah," he says, picking both cups up again with a shrug. "Jolly good. More for me!"

"Heard from my sister," I offer vaguely, by way of explanation.

"She called?"

*Called,* my mind sneers. More like bellowed across the ocean. More like reached across with a jagged fingernail and hooked it beneath my skin, right in the hollow of my throat.

Scents and sensations lick at me, memories vivid as burns. Summer, thick and humid on my skin, smell of Sitka spruce and maple sap heavy on the air. Henry's skin, the golden brown of late July, sweat pooling at the hairline, taste of salt and algae from the lake. Sultry nights, windows thrown wide, a long-limbed boy sneaking into my bed, tangle of limbs beneath the sheets. Kiss of earlobe, collarbone, inner wrist and hollows.

"Has there been a bereavement?" he says, in a softer voice.

I realize I've been staring into space for longer than is socially appropriate. He looks slightly bamboozled. I don't blame him. In the ten years he's worked at Curioscuro, he's never once seen me less than composed. He invited me for drinks one Christmas in my first year, and I—stupidly—agreed. I was feeling lonely, I think, in this new city. New country. A foreigner displaced. He was kind and open. Soft in a way I needed. I hadn't yet firmed up my barriers, hardened my armor. One too many drinks and I slipped: mentioned the seven of us. He'd been surprised but delighted, having come from a big family himself. But I shut it down when he began to pry—and never went for drinks again.

He wasn't to know that only four of us remain. Me, Juniper, Hazel, and Ivy.

It was a stupid mistake. I was asking for it.

I close my hand around the berry and think about flushing it down the toilet, then get to my feet and slip it into my pocket. I brush down my jeans, tuck my hair behind my ears, and brush down my jeans again.

"No, no. Nothing so dramatic," I say now, noncommittal, passing him and going onto the shop floor. I pick up the pile of dusty books I knocked over on my headlong scramble for the toilet—books just arrived from Geneva—and carry them to the cabinet where they'll be displayed behind locked glass doors, unlikely to sell for many years, if ever.

I add, "It's just the eldest."

*One, two, three, four, five, six, seven. "You're the biggest, Juni—you should be seven!"*

Fuck.

"Oh, that's nice," he says, following behind.

I shake my head, distracted. Catch sight of the broken clock on the floor.

I can smell his damn coffee.

Look down at my hands. Don't know what I meant to do with these books.

Where to put them.

Train of thought vanished like a whisper, past overwriting present.

The foxing of the books' pages is now mold on Victorian wallpaper, unspooling in spirals. Is now: mushrooms growing through a torn cotton nightdress. Is now: bones woven with flowers.

"We used to do little things," I murmur, memory ensnaring sense. "Leave little—"

*Sacrifices,* my brain insists, attempting to force the word through my clenched teeth.

I manage to bite it back, straining, swallowing it down like gritty mud. Putrid. Foul.

"—*gifts.* We played games of leaving gifts. It was stupid. Childish. The rule was to leave as many gifts as your number." *Stop talking,* I command myself, even as the words keep snowballing, panicked. *Stop now.* "One of us, I don't remember who"—*you do*—"pointed out that it made more sense for Juniper, the eldest, to be seven. Seven is the highest number, we reasoned. The biggest. And *she* was the biggest. So, she should leave seven gifts, which would be easier for her than—"

*Say her name. Say it.*

"—for the youngest. It made sense to us at the time."

Matt has a deer-in-headlights look on his face, like he can't believe I've strung so many words together in one go. Like he can't believe I'm a real person capable of this kind of intimate revelation. "Right," he says. "So, the seventh sister called you."

A chill fingernail scritches a jagged line of mossy anxiety from the nape of my neck to the back of my knees.

Seven sisters.

And only four left.

Colorful buttons strung from branches on silk ribbons; bones carved with whorls and lines; the stink of acrid char. Leaves threaded through seven sets of white-blond hair. Trees with roots and hollows so large we crawled through them like ants in an ant farm. Like bees in a hive.

Clementine Ward does not leave things undone. There isn't so much as an unopened envelope on my doormat. Whether local election leaflets, junk mail for government-sponsored free solar panels that will cost an arm and a leg to maintain, or my latest electricity bill—not one single envelope is left unopened, unread, and unsorted.

"Yeah," I mutter, remembering the glass cabinet and the books in my arms. "So, um, I'll be gone for a while."

Hadn't meant to say it. Was determined *not* to go. To leave *this* unsorted. This one small thing.

"Not too long," I add, unlocking the cabinet awkwardly with one hand, tomes clutched to my chest with the other. "You can handle things?"

He shrugs. "Of course. No problem."

I try to smile but only end up grimacing. Already, I can feel the spores in my teeth.

# 5

***March 1999***

The interior of Beltane really is exactly like their toy house, with minor differences that are easy to ignore. The ceiling in the main entrance is disproportionally high. The dollhouse didn't have the stained glass windows and transoms, nor the plethora of potted plants. The wallpaper is a faded version of the one in their toy, and several pieces of furniture are in the wrong place.

The air inside the house is crisp, but stagnant. It has the faint smell of crushed leaves and wood sap, a scent that would be cloying if it were stronger. And under that: the odor of a stranger.

Clem doesn't sense malevolence in the house, not exactly. It's more a wariness, like a cat sizing her up. The innards of the rooms off the corridor are mantled in dark, full of suspicious shades and silhouettes.

She clutches her stuffed rabbit tighter, his familiar softness easing some of the fear.

Their heels clip over the wooden floors, somehow offensive in volume beside Granny Alys's bare, cushioned feet. She leads them through the entrance hall and into a spacious dining room paneled in wood, a rickety chandelier hanging over the table, draped in dust. It is the only one Clem has seen in the house so far.

The table faces a wall that is almost nothing but glass, an enormous window overlooking dizzying trees that sway like ocean waves. They make Clem faintly nauseated. In the dismal light, they're too alive for comfort. She turns her back on them, trying to find her sea legs.

Here, notched into the doorframe, inches of growth, year after year, a life recorded. Each new milestone, noted with pencil, reads: *Peter, age 4. Peter, age 7.* Peter, age ten, twelve, fifteen, seventeen.

Clem runs her fingers over the cuts, imagining her father, all knees and elbows, standing with his back pressed to the frame while Granny Alys tracked his growth.

A faded emerald green sofa sits against one wall, beneath a moth-eaten tapestry dotted with berries, beetles, and mushrooms. Several pools of wax and half-burned candles litter the sideboard, and Clem wonders if this house even has electricity.

The brass handles of the sideboard have patinaed where Granny Alys's hands have held them, year after year, decade after decade. Clem wonders if she has been heartsore, all this time alone, or if it was a kind of haven.

"The house," Granny Alys says, turning to face them, "is called Beltane. The forest is called Beltane. The island is called Beltane." She pauses and regards them seriously. "Beltane will keep you safe."

Clem would like to ask what she means, but Granny Alys continues on without pause.

"The house, the forest, the island—all of it is yours to explore and enjoy as you see fit. I have only three rules." She holds up three gnarled fingers.

She lays out the rules in the solemn way of funerals.

1. Always return to the house before sundown.
2. Always eat dinner at this table at seven.
3. Never stray past the boundary after dark.

She silently waits for the girls to process this information.

"What about school?" Juniper asks. "And what about other mealtimes?"

"School is a problem for the fall," Granny Alys says, smiling. "And other mealtimes are yours to do with as you see fit. The kitchen is through there." She points to the next room. "Ernest delivers food and other supplies every three months, and the forest provides plenty of nourishment in between. We're stocked until September."

Juniper steps closer. "And . . . the only rules are that we're home before sundown, we eat here at seven, and we don't go past the boundary after dark?"

"Those are the only rules."

"So, we can scream inside?" Willow asks, grinning.

Granny Alys nods. "You can."

"And we can run around inside?" Ivy asks, joining in.

Granny Alys smiles, the skin around her eyes crinkling. "You can."

"And we can swing off the chandelier?" Hazel challenges, smirking.

Granny Alys turns sage eyes on her. "As long as you obey the three rules, especially to eat dinner here once a day at seven, you can."

The laugh rises in Clem's throat but dies there. No one else is laughing. She scans the room, pulse quickening, suspicion prickling at her skin. Is this a joke? A test? Is Granny Alys mocking them? What will happen if they do something wild?

She feels watched. The window is so big in this room. Clem wishes they could hang some curtains, but there are no curtain rods to attach them to.

Granny Alys catches her looking. "I'd prefer you keep the windows in here bare. It's good to let the forest watch sometimes."

Clem's skin crawls, but she isn't exactly sure why. Holly twists her lip with an air of challenge that Clem recognizes and fears. Holly has always been the braver twin, the one who pushes boundaries, the one to draw Ivy along into schemes of her own invention.

Perhaps sensing this, Hazel whispers something in Holly's ear, and Clem knows it's trouble.

Holly, grinning, pulls out a dining room chair and steps up onto it, waiting for Granny Alys to screech at her to get down. Alys does nothing but watch with mild amusement, so Holly climbs up onto the table, shoes scuffing the wood. She stands there with her hands on her hips, staring the old woman down while Hazel gloats. But Hazel's smirk falters when Granny Alys stands, placid, hands clasped in front of her—and does nothing.

Clem tries very hard not to laugh. She doesn't like it when Hazel stirs trouble, and it looks like Granny Alys is not easily broken. Maybe Hazel has met her match.

"There will be time to show you the house tomorrow," Granny Alys says, ignoring Holly, who is beginning to look foolish. "I expect you'll want to see your rooms, unpack, and lie down." She glances back toward the entrance. "Ernest will be along with your bags in time. Let me show you the bedrooms."

There's a sense of being devoured as they travel deeper into the bowels of this huge, nebulous mansion, as though Clem will be digested long before it releases her. She would let it, too, if not for her sisters.

She has so many questions. Why have a mansion on an island? Who owns the island? Who built the house? What about school? Why are there no rules except the three? Why do they have to eat at the table facing a window that has no curtains?

The mystery of it is almost enough to entice her into feeling good about her grandmother.

Almost.

Holly's step falters in front of her.

"What if I don't follow?" Holly whispers, a cunning defiance in her face, traces of her earlier embarrassment lingering in the blush of her cheeks. "What if I don't obey? What if I just stand here in the entrance hall and wait it out?"

"Wait what out?" Clem asks, her voice low.

Holly presses her lips together. "I don't know."

Then she follows on, and Clem releases her breath.

The others are already far enough up the winding staircase that if they didn't follow, they'd lose sight of them, a prospect that jolts a lightning bolt of fear into Clem's legs, and she urges Holly to catch up.

Unlit sconces along the walls give a whiff of the Victorian era. Were it not for the darkened bulbs tucked into the tops, Clem would believe they'd gone back in time. The stairs go on for a long time, around and around in a wide, dizzying helix, until at last they come to a landing that opens up to the left and right onto two long corridors.

Granny Alys turns left and leads them along the dim hall. It's so dark in this part of the house, it almost reads as night; the shadows lurk like secrets. Twisting forest wallpaper, which Clem can make out when she gets close, guides them along, broken by more unlit wall sconces.

Juniper is shown into a bedroom, then Hazel, and each of her sisters closes the door behind them. When Clem's turn comes, she, too, closes the door, choking back the feeling of being excluded. This is not how it was supposed to go. Her sisters were supposed to make an enemy of Granny Alys, just like her. They were supposed to forge their bond even tighter by locking hands, not widening the gap by locking horns. They were not meant to give in to Granny Alys's strange, magnetic charm.

Clem's room is bright and airy, mostly white, but with hints of buttermilk and eggnog yellow in ribbon and lace trim. She doesn't remember seeing any purple in Juniper's room, or orange in Hazel's, so this must be a coincidence. Besides, she tells herself with stubborn pride. She prefers canary yellow, not this pale imitation.

A square tapestry occupies one whole wall, the pattern the same tangle of eerie forest as the wallpaper out in the corridor, only this one seems to be from later in the year, holly with rare yellow drupes almost glistening with cotton realism, smatterings of white that suggest snow among the foliage. Hint of bone and mushroom.

When she looks behind it, she finds a door, just big enough for her to crawl into. She opens it and discovers a small space. Likely for storage, but it reeks of magic. She closes it and untangles herself from the tapestry, refusing to be charmed.

A Winchcombe triple wardrobe stands in the corner, exactly like the one in the dollhouse. She used to put a little doll version of herself inside and shut the tiny doors. The doll was a slip of a thing she made herself with cloth and wire. She'd close her eyes and imagine she was in the cupboard, alone in the dark. Like a womb, shutting the whole world out.

She takes a tentative step toward it, then another. When she opens the door, she relishes the long, slow creak. It smells of mothballs and florals. Like dusty potpourri. A music box sits tucked into the very back.

She retrieves it and thumbs away a film of cottony dust. A leaf-patterned mosaic made from green pearlescent stone adorns the lid; opening it reveals a ballerina hugged by a twisted vine. It reminds Clem of Hazel's classical beauty. But it remains still, and Clem realizes she hasn't wound the level. She does it slowly, anticipating a soft, lilting lullaby. One that might ease her into sleep. Instead, though the wings spin and twirl, only a dull plucking noise emanates from the comb like melancholy raindrops.

Annoyed, she shuts the box and shoves it back into the deepest recesses of the wardrobe, feeling cheated and even more alone. Clem has always been the quiet one. The sensible one. The one who needs the others more than they seem to need each other.

How is she going to keep her sisters safe if they're separated by walls?

# 6

***March 1999***

The dollhouse wasn't electrified, so it comes as a surprise to Clem when, in the evening, the house hums with evidence of electric wiring gone wrong.

Bare bulbs hang from ceilings in place of the dollhouse's miniature chandeliers, ominously flickering, threatening to blow at any moment. The dangling drop bulb in the corridor sways ever so slightly, hinting at a crooked dance of shadows over the stairs. Clem wonders if the walls might be breathing.

Her sisters don't seem to notice, which sets Clem's teeth on edge.

At seven p.m., they gather in the dining room, hand in hand, awaiting instructions in silence, the smell of garlic permeating the air. Poppy tugs on Juniper's skirt.

"Hungry," she whines.

None of them have eaten since well before the boat ride, late in the morning, and no one seems to have thought that seven children require sustenance. Clem longs for a soda more than anything. A cold grape soda, or even a cherryade.

Granny Alys rounds the corner carrying two plates in each hand. Clem stands on her toes to see what's on them, but can only make out a mess of black, gray, and green. Her stomach turns sour at the sight.

"Choose your seats," Granny Alys instructs, in a way that implies an important decision and the establishment of a permanent order.

Juniper takes the seat at the head of the table, farthest from the kitchen. Hazel sits to her right, and Clem to her left. The twins sit beside Clem, and Willow and Poppy next to Hazel. This is the order they kept at home. Since Peter and Hillary never dined with them, the opposite chair to Juniper's was always Penny's.

Now it seems Granny Alys will sit there, a new, yet similar, paradigm that Clem finds acceptable.

Granny Alys brings out another round of two plates per hand, until everyone has been served. Clem is pleased to note Poppy's food has been cut into small pieces on a plastic plate.

Clementine inspects her own dish. Giant mushrooms in what looks like a butter, garlic, and parsley sauce. Beside the mushrooms: broccoli and an unknown large flat leaf fried in batter and a dark sauce.

Granny Alys bows her head and murmurs, "I thank the eldritch God of the Wood for all He provides."

It takes a moment for the words to sink in.

Clem glances at Juniper, whose lips have thinned. Hazel smirks, and the twins stare at Granny Alys with open intrigue. Juniper shakes her head in a way that Clem knows means not to ask questions, and none of them do. When Granny Alys picks up her cutlery and begins to eat, Poppy follows suit first, her little fingers grabbing the cut-up mushrooms and plowing them right into her rosebud mouth. Willow giggles when Granny Alys doesn't scold the girl, and does the same.

Clem glances at Juniper again, wanting to silently ask about the strange prayer, but Juniper is smiling now, so Clem also uses her fingers in lieu of the cutlery, daring herself to challenge what Granny Alys said about no rules except the three she laid out before.

Granny Alys does not scold them.

Does not warn them to behave like ladies.

Does nothing but eat her mushrooms with a serene smile.

Only Hazel and Juniper eat with their forks, and not a single Ward child complains about the taste. Except for an initially bitter overlay of fleshy mushroom, the food is, in truth, quite palatable.

When the plates are empty, the girls awkwardly rise to their feet. They wait for a cue from Granny Alys, but she simply watches them with another enigmatic smile, so they tentatively wander away.

"I'm so glad you're here," Granny Alys says quietly.

Clem suspects she is the only one who heard it.

The sisters explore the house silently, in a line. Eldest to youngest—Juniper, Hazel, Clem, the twins, Willow, and then Poppy—they tiptoe up the creaky staircase, and along corridor after swaying corridor. Juniper shows them her bedroom, which is much like Clem's, only bigger, and with a second, smaller room off to the side, with a washtub and jug on a white vanity. There is no toilet, and no running water, but the little window—about the size of a melon—looks out on the overgrown vegetable garden and a stone well.

"That must be where the water comes from," Clem says when she sees it.

"How can a home have electricity," Hazel says, her tone slightly petulant, "but not a flushing toilet? Where are we meant to . . . you know . . ."

"Poop?" Ivy and Holly say at the same time.

Clem grins, and Willow and Poppy burst into a fit of giggles.

"Pee," Hazel says, flushing pink. "Everyone pees."

"Everyone poops too," Ivy says, deadpan. Holly smirks.

"Poop, pee, poop!" Poppy shrieks, before Juniper claps a hand over her mouth. *"Mooomeeeemoooo!"*

After a moment and a stern look, she releases Poppy's lips.

"Granny Alys said no rules," Willow reminds Juniper.

"Except to be in the house before sundown," Ivy says.

"And to eat at the table," Holly adds.

"At seven o'clock," Ivy says.

"Every day," Willow says, nodding.

"We don't know her yet," Juniper says, lifting her chin.

Clem folds her arms across herself, discomfited. "You think she's lying?"

Juniper smiles, but Clem can see it's sad. "People sometimes say things they don't mean. Or they change their minds. Or they think they mean what they say, but then later on they find that it wasn't true. It's not necessarily a lie."

"We could always test it," Hazel offers.

"Could pee in the corridor and see if she gets angry," Willow suggests, grinning.

Hazel rolls her eyes. "Why are you so interested in *pee* all of a sudden?"

"Let's see your room," Juniper interrupts, speaking to Hazel, and the girls all coo in agreement.

They traipse across to Hazel's room. Another lacy bedspread, another frilly canopy. More heavy furniture. Hazel's window, like Clem's, looks out onto the forest.

"The trees are so close," Holly says, peering out.

"One storm and we could find a branch in bed with us," Ivy adds.

They share a look.

"These trees are old," Juniper says. "The roots probably grow right under the house. They're too strong for any wind to blow over."

The inspection continues, and Clem is glad of it. She wants to feel connected to her sisters again, to see the spaces they will now inhabit, to absorb them into her memory, seep into her cells. The seven of them, bound by love and loneliness.

The twins share a room. Two single beds on delicate wooden frames have been placed against a wall, each on opposite sides. In the center: a large round rug in shades of cream, pink, and pale green. Neither of these beds has a canopy, and Clem wonders if it bothers the twins at all.

"She must have known we were coming," Clem says, trailing her fingers along the foot of one of the beds.

Ivy sits on the mattress and crosses her legs. "They would have told her, right? The social workers?"

"But how long in advance?"

Juniper goes to the window. "I don't know. It could have been weeks, I suppose. It took long enough for them to tell us what was happening."

Hazel sits at one of the matching dressing tables and combs her fingers through her hair. "But getting the beds—*all* the beds—over that stretch of ocean? How?"

"I suppose that grumpy man did it," Willow says.

"Ernest!" Poppy yells. "Ernest, Ernest, Ernest!"

Juniper lifts Poppy onto her hip. "Maybe we can ask Granny Alys. What do you think of that?"

Poppy nods, putting her thumb in her mouth.

"Does Poppy have her own room?" Clem asks.

Juniper nods. "She does. But I think maybe tonight she'll stay with me."

Poppy's eyelids are heavy, and she rubs them with a saliva-wet fist.

"I think it's bedtime," Juniper adds.

"But we haven't seen my room," Willow complains. "Or Clem's. Or Poppy's."

Juniper adjusts Poppy on her hip. "It's late. There's time in the morning, sprout. Poppy's tired. We all are, I think."

Clem has never owned a watch. There was never a need, when the big clock in the apartment's entrance kept them continually abreast, and when Penny kept them rigidly to schedules. Now, though, she wishes she had asked for a watch for one of her birthdays. She could run down to Beltane's entrance hall right now and check the grandfather clock there, but the idea of being alone in this big old house without the blanket of her sisters nearby is so horrifying that she immediately discounts it. If Juniper says it's late, it must be. Reluctantly, they all disperse.

When Clementine shuts the door to her bedroom, closing out the eerie dark of the corridor, she feels oddly uncomfortable. It isn't just that the room is strange, or that the house is strange, or that it smells of a stranger they ought to know. It's that, back home, she shared a room with the twins, and before they were born, she roomed with Hazel. She hasn't slept in a room by herself in her entire life.

Grief inches across the floor and over her feet, enveloping her in a cold, wet caul. She shivers and glances toward the bed.

Old blankets, thin quilts, pillows that look too flat.

Strange bed.

Strange covers.

Strange walls.

Strange shadows.

She changes into her yellow nightie in a rush, then hurries to the bed and climbs in, pulling the blankets up to her chin. It's freezing cold, even though it's March already, and she shivers so hard her teeth clatter in the silence like alarm bells. No lamp on the bedside table, no stuffed rabbit to comfort her—she forgot it in the dining room. Only her lone suitcase, which is sitting beneath the window like a yellow block, is a friend.

When she begins to cry, she is grateful, at least, that her teeth stop their chattering.

# 7

***September 2024***

Ernest has changed in the years since I left Beltane.

His hair, once a deep brown, is now mostly salt rather than pepper. The lines around his mouth have deepened and solidified, like a stone carving, and he wears a spray of dandruff on his stiff shoulders like a dusting of cornstarch. His skin is still weathered and dark, but there's more of it bunched under his eyes, seemingly sucked out from his now hollow cheeks. Not exactly the lipo I'd go for, but who am I to judge?

He still looks severe.

"'Ow did you know to come?" he asks, accent as thick as it ever was.

He handles the tiller the same as the first day he brought all of us across this stretch of dark water, gripped in a white-knuckled fist, like he has a grudge. I find myself wondering if this is the same boat and just how safe it is.

I pull out the envelope and hold it up for him to see.

He grunts and makes no further comment.

It's obvious from the crumpled state of it that I've opened and closed it more than a dozen times. I'm not sure why. Maybe I hope I'll wake up from this nightmare each time. Maybe I still can't believe it's real.

I frown at the island. I can see the house . . . it stands starkly white, right at the edge of the cliff. That's different. I don't remember being able to see the house from the water as a child. Where has the foliage gone? It's as though a quarter of the island has fallen into the ocean. But maybe it's only my memory that has corroded.

A whisper in my mind:

*The daughters of the Forgotten God come home.*

My body quakes anew, and I stare around, wide-eyed, searching for danger. My heart is threadbare in my chest. I don't have a drum inside; I have a quivering moth, fragile wings beating up against my ribs.

I crumple the envelope anew and stare, dead-eyed, at the encroaching horizon.

I can hardly believe my eyes.

*Henry* is on the dock when Ernest and I arrive.

I can't help but stare as he bends down, grabbing the rope from his father and then pulling us in, shirtsleeves rolled up from forearms grown thick and ropey with muscle.

I know it's him immediately. Same walnut hair, same dark eyes, same upward tilt to his mouth so he always looked optimistic. Same golden energy.

But why is he here?

I manage to shut my mouth before he looks up after securing the rope, setting an uninterested frown onto my face. Ernest is already off the boat, a box in hand as he strides down the dock toward a rickety metal cart waiting for him at the end.

God. The cart . . . it's like traveling back in time, the fact that they still use carts to unload supplies. Then again, Beltane was never a hub of innovation.

"Clementine Ward."

I blink up at Henry. The clouds are sharply luminous behind him in the painful way of island summers, and another chill kisses my skin.

I feign a casual tone. "François-Henri d'Aboville."

There is a moment where we just look at one another, digesting time as a physical thing, acknowledging it between us; the years stretch like a gulf, but it isn't wide enough to eradicate the memories we share.

He offers me his hand, and I take it, surprised when he lifts me out of the boat with speed. I stumble into his chest, and swallow when I have to look up at him.

"Sorry," he murmurs.

"Don't rip my arm off."

He chuckles. We blink at each other. He's still holding my hand, our arms pressed between torsos.

I'm the first to step away.

The first to let go.

As always.

I rub my now free hand on my jeans, then realize it looks like I'm wiping away his cooties or something, and hurry to stammer, "Wow, it's—it's an island day, huh?"

"Plenty of those around here."

He was the one who first told me about the strange weather system here, I recall.

I nod, staring at my feet. A breeze, warm and salty, plays around us. I have so many questions: What is he doing here? Does he live on the island too? With his father? In his own cabin? Why? What did he do after . . . everything?

But those are answers I have no right to, so I meet his gaze again and ask, "How is she?"

He shrugs, but looks less than happy, tucking his hands into his pockets. "Same as ever. Stubborn."

I snort a laugh. "I'll bet."

A pause. "I rarely see her."

The silence grows between us again. Too many days shared. Too many traumas unexamined.

Her letter burns a hole in my pocket like giant hogweed.

Ernest stomps back down the dock and shoves between us, reaching into the boat for another box.

"He hasn't changed much," I mutter, rubbing my shoulder as he passes and strides away again.

Henry's grins have become grimaces. "Sociable as ever."

"He still lives on the other side of the island?"

Henry nods, watching his father with an expression I can't read. "He doesn't cross over by boat much anymore."

I hesitate, then blurt, "And you?"

"I have a place in Warrenton. Come over now and again when he needs help. Mostly it's me that ferries the supplies across these days. Less often than before, though. Usually at midsummer and before midwinter. It's only Juniper and Ernest here, after all."

So lonely. So isolated.

I can almost smell my childhood, feel the way Granny Alys and the seven of us ran around Beltane, flowers threaded through our hair in the spring, fire roaring in the inglenook in winter, feet bare and dirty.

So loud, so full of life.

The memory of it is a haunting.

The island is a mausoleum.

"You married?" he says, and it almost feels like an assault. "Kids?"

It gets my back up. "No. *You?*"

My retort is blunt.

"No kids. An ex-wife. It, uh, it didn't work out. I wasn't much of a husband."

I nod, wishing the ocean would just swallow me now and get it over with. I turn to look at the trees, at the path I know is waiting for me.

For the first time, I wish it wasn't just me facing this alone. But how could I possibly wish for Hazel or Ivy to be here too? I could never willingly pull them back to the mania of the past. Never remind them that we are incomplete. Four out of seven might seem like good numbers, but it isn't. When you've lost as much as we did, adding three sisters to the mix is one grief too many.

Henry hesitates, then leans forward and opens his mouth to say something I know will be uncomfortable.

“Better get this over with,” I say quickly, and stalk down the dock after Ernest.

The sooner I answer the call, the sooner I can leave.

“Wait,” Henry calls, and I turn back, frowning.

“What is it?”

“You’re not the only one who got a letter.”

# 8

***March 1999***

Clem wakes to the mournful howl of wind.

She stares at the window.

A storm.

It's just a storm.

A clatter at her window jolts her out of her stupor; something white, flashing in the night. She pulls the duvet over her head and waits. But the clatter persists, so she braves a peek. The flash of white returns, identifying itself as a shutter, banging outside. Relaxing enough to venture from under the covers, she goes to the window, opens it, and strains to catch the offender, hair whipping about her face. But the second shutter catches a brutal gust that nearly smacks her back into the room, just before it breaks off the house entirely.

Clem regains her balance and slides the window down, now soaked. She'd had the horrible sensation of something unseen suddenly racing toward her from the dark.

She climbs quickly back into her bed, feeling safest off the floor, and, shivering, uses the canopy curtains over the bed to dry her face.

This storm is like nothing Clem ever experienced in New York. The apartment walls had been solid, sturdy, and so thick that only the familiar noises of traffic and human voices reached them. But this . . . this is something else entirely.

Clem has never heard wind like this. It rips through the trees outside like banshees, screaming through the single-glazed window and blowing the remaining shutter free. At one point it sounds as though stones are falling from the sky, and the windowpane rattles like it will shatter, tilting the scant moonlight into something sinister.

Clem does her utmost to sleep through the squall. Maybe storms like this are normal here, and she'll need to get used to them.

A creak from the hallway startles her again, until a muffled "Shhh! Be quiet!" unclenches her jaw. She gathers the quilt like a cloak around her shoulders and hurries to the door.

A familiar shape, small, like a Victorian ghost in a white sheet, is moving away from her, in the direction of Juniper's room. Willow. Clem hurries to follow.

By the time she arrives, all her sisters are already gathered in a pile on Juniper's bed. She hates that, were it not for the storm, she might have been left out. But no. One of them—perhaps Ivy, or Holly—would have come to collect her. They aren't whole unless they are all of them together. The Spectacular Seven.

Juniper has lit a candle on her bedside table, and the warm glow makes the whole room feel so much safer than the rest of the house. As though light is a protector. Juniper smiles at Clem and gestures for her to climb up. Clem's heart swells, and she rushes to clamber onto the bed beside Holly.

"It's scary," Willow whispers, and Poppy whimpers.

"I don't like it," Ivy says, taking Holly's hand.

Hazel leans out so she can see the small window. "You think the house will hold?"

Juniper tugs Hazel back and replaces the blanket over her shoulder, tucking her close.

"Did you know," Juniper says, "that back in the old days, Italian witches would go to sleep and let their spirits leave their bodies to wander about at night?"

Poppy shoves her thumb into her mouth, watching Juniper with wide wet eyes.

"Their souls would leave their bodies in the form of a mouse that crawled out their mouths. Some witch souls wandered away from their bodies as sleek black cats, which is why people act scared of black cats today."

Willow snuggles closer. "Why would they do that?"

"To be free. To explore without being told no. To spy on people. Lots of reasons. Unless the witch's spirit was back in their body by cock of crow—that's before the rooster cried—they'd be doomed to be parted from their bodies forever, wandering the spirit realm alone."

Silence falls between the girls, so that when a gust of wind *ooooooo*s through the room, Poppy shrieks and then begins to whimper.

Juniper pulls her close, kissing her head. "It's okay, little sprout."

Silence falls again.

"One berry swallowed by a little black robin," Juniper begins, and raises her brows, looking at each of them.

"Grew in its belly," continues Hazel, "and made two red bobbins."

"A girl in green sewed three large dresses," Holly says.

"And gave them to the sisters with the violet tresses," Ivy says, grinning.

Willow licks her lips, a tentative smile creeping across her face. "The violet sisters ran through the hallow wood . . ."

Juniper takes Poppy's hand and helps the child plod through the next line. "Stumbled into a run, where five mushrooms stood."

Juniper tickles Poppy's belly until she's giggling so much she can hardly breathe, before continuing. "Six times they circled, chanting out a bray."

Hazel pinches Poppy's cheek. "But the fae took them captive and turned them into hay!"

Ivy and Holly together chant, "The blackbird came with his family of seven," and then glance at Clem with two wide grins.

"Gulped the stalks down," Clem replies, smiling, before they all yell:

"And sent the girls to heaven!"

They fall into a spell of giggles over the silly nonsense rhyme that Juniper wrote for them years ago, the one they sang at home in random moments when seeking out one another. The final half line always yelled in unison, no matter who began the rhyme.

Their laughter comes up short when a noise in the hall rings through the room, and a moment later, the door handle turns. Even Juniper tenses at the sight.

A glow of light enters, followed by Granny Alys, a candle in her own hand. She is barefoot still, but clean now, and dressed in a white nightgown. Her gray hair is loose, flowing past her waist like riverweed.

"I thought you might congregate on your first night," she says, closing the door behind her. The candlelight makes her eyes look strangely hollow, odd shadows eating them out like a skull.

Clem wishes she would have knocked, but then remembers what Granny Alys said about there being no rules except the three. She really meant it.

"The storm is scaring them," Juniper says, as though confiding, one adult to another.

Clem doesn't like that. A barrier, no matter how small, between any of them, is one to be broken down immediately.

Granny Alys nods. "Understandable. But, you know, there really is no need. You're safe here."

"Nowhere is safe," Clem challenges. She does it quietly, but loud enough for their grandmother to hear.

Granny Alys smiles, glancing out the storm-beaten window. As she turns her head, the shadows unspool from her eyes, and she looks like herself again. Then she turns and walks over to the chair, sitting down and placing the chamberstick and candle on the table beside it.

"I'm going to tell you a secret," she says after a while, her voice low. The shadows have shifted now, making homes in the lines of her face instead. "The forest is alive."

Poppy recoils in Juniper's lap, and Clem feels a surge of anger. What does this old woman mean by saying something like that?

But Granny Alys's eyes are warm and liquid blue with joy and perfect trust as she says, "Beltane will always protect you."

Clem glances up at Juniper, whose expression is radiating a similar fury.

"What an odd thing to say," Juniper manages.

"It's only the truth."

"What . . . what do you mean?" Willow asks, her voice cracking.

"There is an ancient being in this forest," Granny Alys says. "A forgotten god of the wood who looks after everything on this island, including any person with Ward blood in their veins."

Juniper sighs in the way their father did sometimes when he clenched his jaw. When he pinched the bridge of his nose and tried to remain calm.

"I'm sorry," Hazel says, suppressing a smirk. "Can you . . . repeat that?"

Granny Alys smiles indulgently. "There is an ancient creature, a forgotten god, who looks after the forest . . . and the Wards with it. As long as you're on, in, or with Beltane, nothing bad can happen to you. You will always be safe."

Clem can see the shift. How Willow, Ivy, Holly, and even Hazel are beginning to look enthralled. Only Juniper and Poppy, like her, seem alarmed. This woman is crazy. Clearly. And Clem has no idea how to get to the man, Ernest, so he can take them back to the mainland. Henry said that they lived on the other side of the island, but without a map, she has no idea where that other part is, or how far away.

And . . . where would they go if they *did* get off the island? There's nowhere else. Their apartment probably already belongs to a different family.

"But what is taken must also be given," Granny Alys continues, unbothered. "There is a balance."

Clem and Juniper exchange a look full of meaning, but Hazel leans forward, her blanket slipping off her shoulder.

"What does the god look like?" Her eagerness alarms Clem.

"No one has seen Him. Not in many generations. And it's best not to go looking."

There is a strange warning in her voice.

"How do you know he's still here, then?" Juniper says, and her tone is challenging, but Clem doesn't like how she's allowing the premise to stand at all.

Granny Alys ignores the question. "When He wants to find you, He will. Beltane will always protect Ward blood."

"Why are the Wards protected?" Willow asks, shuffling to the edge of the bed now.

Granny Alys leans forward so her elbows are resting on her knees, hair falling over her shoulders and to the floor. "My father used to say it's because Ward blood is gifted with magic. Sight. Witch blood, he said. We can see and feel things that other people can't."

"Just like wackos," Holly mutters.

Granny Alys ignores her as well. "Wards can see the extraordinary in the ordinary."

"Imagination is a powerful thing to have," Juniper says, and Clem balks at the betrayal. Is Juniper being won over too?

Poppy slides from the bed and totters over to Granny Alys, who lifts the child onto her lap. Poppy settles against her, playing with that long white riverweed hair.

"A powerful thing indeed," Granny Alys says, though Clem thinks her expression looks less like one of agreement than one that says *Little do you know*.

# 9

***March 1999***

The girls wake in a pile the next day, sunlight buttering the floor.

"Up," Juniper says, voice peppy. She pushes at a sleeping Hazel, who groans and goes back to sleep.

"You're squishing my legs," Willow complains, shoving at Poppy. "And you're hot as a furnace!"

She shoves Poppy again, who rolls over and giggles, then wipes sweat from her shins with an exaggerated retch. "Eugh! I'm wet!"

Clem sits up and rubs the sleep, like sand, from her eyes, watching the twins, who have slid from the bed and wandered over to the window, blocking the sun so effectively the buttery light grows muffled and chill.

"Move," she grumbles at them. "Let the light in."

But they don't. They just stand on tiptoes, noses pressed to the glass.

Juniper and Clem share a look.

"What is it?" Juniper asks, pushing herself free of the tangle that is Hazel and then going over to join them.

"Oh . . ."

Clem's heart is beginning to stutter. "What? What is it?"

Has someone come to bring them back to New York? Has the storm cut off access to the water? Is it all devastation out there?

Juniper glances back at Clem and shakes her head. "I think the well flooded. Everything's all muddy and wet."

Clem's muscles relax, her jaw unlocking. "Oh. You scared me."

"We should go help," Ivy says.

"It looks like she knows what she's doing," Juniper says. "And Granny Alys said there were no rules . . ."

A lengthy silence drapes the girls like gossamer.

"We should help," Holly echoes her sister after a moment. A tentative suggestion.

"I like mud!" Poppy shrieks, shattering the fragile discomfort.

Juniper laughs, rolling her eyes. "Okay, okay! Everybody get dressed. Meet at the landing in five. Go!"

Clem is oddly invigorated by the game, by having a purpose for the morning. She enjoys knowing what is going to happen and when. She rushes back to her bedroom, drags her case onto her bed, and clicks open the two clasps—expensive replicas from a novelty designer boutique on Fifth Avenue that her mother insisted on adding.

She is clothed in a yellow sundress and on the landing before any of the others, second-guessing her choice not to wear shoes. A moment later, Willow and the twins arrive, also in their colors, also without shoes. She should have known that her first instinct would be the same as her sisters'.

Outside, the morning air has the in-between feeling of ten thirty a.m., on the cusp of crisp and afternoon. Granny Alys looks up as they traipse over, wiping her brow and leaving a muddy smear.

"G'morning," she calls, smiling at the sight of them.

"Good morning," Juniper says, speaking for them all.

"Did you have a good night's sleep?"

"We did, thank you."

Clem notices that Juniper omits how they all slept in a pile on the one bed after Granny Alys left. Maybe Alys already knows this. Maybe she expected it.

"Weird dreams," Willow says, squinting up at the sky.

"New places'll do that," Granny Alys says. "Or maybe Beltane is just trying to tell you something."

"Why's it so muddy?" Ivy asks, kicking at the dirt, squelching it between her toes.

"The well," Granny Alys says, by way of explanation.

"It floods when it storms?" Juniper clarifies.

"Not always, but usually. When it does, the basement floods with it, and the mud needs scraping away. The water drains pretty well on its own—but I like to give it a helping hand."

Juniper nods. "Let us help, then."

"No need, child," Granny Alys says, but Clem thinks she looks pretty tired.

"No trouble," Hazel adds.

Granny Alys's mouth twists into a rueful smile. "Well, all right then. I think there's an extra shovel or two in the shed, there."

She nods to the side of the house where the doors to an old shed stand open. Juniper and Hazel both go, coming back with a shovel and a broom, respectively. Clem follows after a moment, but there aren't any useful tools left, so she takes a rake, deciding to do what she can with the tines.

Juniper shovels at the mess. "Where are we moving the mud?"

Granny Alys nods at a gap in the green, spattered with trails of mud. "Into the forest. That way. Down that there slope."

"No one ever comes to help?" Willow asks while Juniper, Hazel, and Clem get to work.

"Sometimes strangers appear," Granny Alys says, leaning on her own shovel. "They come for various reasons. Some don't realize the island's private. Some do know, but they come anyways, wanting to see the forest."

Ivy bends down and begins scraping up big slops of the mud into a pile with her hands. "Why?"

"Because the island has an old growth forest, like the Smokies. That means it has very old trees that haven't been interfered with by humans and their logging. There are insects and animals and plants here that people want to study."

"But they're not allowed?" Holly asks.

"No," Granny Alys confirms. "The Forgotten God of the Wood forbids it."

The girls glance at each other, but no more is said about the God of the Wood. The Ward sisters make much quicker work of the mud than Granny Alys would have alone, though Clem finds the rake more trouble than it's worth and abandons it pretty soon in favor of her hands. Juniper uses the shovel to carry great big dollops of mud over to the slope Granny indicated, painting the surrounding foliage even more brown in the process. Hazel sweeps a lot of it into piles for Juniper to deal with.

The twins and Clem grab handfuls, carrying it to the slope between mud-ball fights, and Willow uses her feet to sweep it along, slow and steady. Poppy is so full of mud by the time the area is cleared that no spot of red can be seen, and Clem's legs are caked up to her knees. She relishes the feeling of the mud between her toes, but less so when it dries and begins to flake.

Granny Alys, who disappeared inside sometime during the cleanup, now returns with a wicker basket, which she hands to Juniper.

"The island is so glad you're here," she says. She is washed clean, mud no longer coating her face and hair.

Clem has the uncharitable thought that perhaps it is Granny Alys who is glad to have seven new pairs of hands to help with chores, then feels ashamed of herself. Granny Alys never asked for help.

Juniper takes the basket. "What's this?"

"Food. Go. Explore. Discover what the island is all about."

Clem is so hungry she could eat a horse, and she hopes there's a pile of peanut butter and jelly sandwiches on fluffy white bread in there, as well as a gallon of lemon iced tea. Granny Alys gives them a radiant smile and then traipses back inside to do who knows what. Clem is surprised to feel a strange pang when she leaves.

# 10

***March 1999***

The forest is alive with sounds. Birds squawk, bugs hum; the trees whisper to each other above the girls' heads. They follow the path they came in on, at first not daring to stray from something familiar. Juniper leads the girls until, impatient, Willow breaks away.

"Hey!" Clem calls, alarm bells firing in her brain like sirens.

Juniper glances back and sees Willow vanish into the green. She twists her mouth, considering, then rolls her eyes and nods for the others to go after their eight-year-old sister.

Brave sister.

Wild sister.

The first of them to venture into Beltane unaided.

"What if we get lost?" Clem whispers to Juniper.

The girls are batting away fat leaves, rogue branches, and hanging vines.

"Then we get lost," Juniper says, apparently unconcerned.

Hazel, in a rare show of alliance with Clem, snaps, "And that's okay with you?"

Juniper shrugs. "It's an island. We'll eventually find our way back around. Besides, if we don't turn up for supper, Granny Alys will come and find us."

"She's an old lady," Hazel grumbles. "How do you expect her to carry you out if you break your neck?"

Juniper gives a serene smile—the perfect impression of Granny Alys—and says, "Beltane will protect us," then wanders off ahead.

Clem can practically see the heat rays coming off Hazel's head as she seethes in her dress, no doubt irritated that no one is siding with her. Clem is in total (and silent) agreement. This is a strange place, and they don't have a map.

"So now she *believes* this Beltane nonsense?" Hazel mutters. "Am I the only one who's noticed that everything is falling apart?"

She throws a scathing look in Clem's direction, demanding agreement. Clementine shrugs and follows her sisters, not wanting to lose sight of them, and definitely not wanting to admit that she, too, worries about the same thing.

They find a dark spruce-colored lake reflecting the sky. It stands like a glittering jewel in the middle of the greenery.

Willow wades in up to her knees, and Poppy hobbles in after. The twins are quick to follow, shrieking about the cold, while Juniper lays down the shawl from around her shoulders. She and Clem sit down and open the wicker basket, and, no doubt because she's hungry, Hazel joins them, apparently keeping her irritation to herself.

Clem does agree with Hazel's worries, and were they less at loggerheads, she would admit as much. But harmony is more important, and if this is what her sisters feel they need, then she has to make herself part of it. She has to support them, regardless.

Juniper draws out a clip-top jar full of what looks like iced tea—but could well be mushroom water—a tub of dark berries, a second tub of some sort of pulled meat, and a huge hunk of brown crusty bread. Last is a cloth containing a wedge of cheese threaded with blue mold, which Hazel pulls a face at and tosses back inside. Juniper laughs and takes it out again, laying everything out on the shawl.

Clem glances at the girls screaming and splashing in the lake and calls, "Anyone hungry?"

"Me!" Poppy yells. "Me! Me! Me!"

She rushes over and throws herself, dripping, into Juniper's lap.

Juniper shrieks and tickles Poppy. "You're getting me all wet, you monster!"

Poppy, finding this hilarious, rolls off Juniper and onto the shawl, raucous giggles bubbling into the air. When she's calmed down enough to sit up again, she claps her hands with evident glee. "Berries!"

The others hurry over, dripping wet, and settle on the grass.

The girls descend on the food like a pack of hungry wolves.

"I don't even miss them," Hazel says quietly, when the food has been reduced to crumbs on the shawl and the air is sleepy with increasing warmth.

"Why would you?" Juniper says, plucking a partly uncurled bracken fern from the earth and then pinching off tiny leaves one by one. "It's not like we even really knew them."

"Mom used to tuck us into bed sometimes," Ivy says. "I miss that."

"And her perfume smell," Holly adds. "I miss that too."

"Mostly Penny did it," Juniper counters. "I miss Penny so much more."

"Dad would sometimes do it when Penny was away," Hazel says. "I suppose I miss those nights. He'd tell a story, remember?"

"I think he got that from Granny Alys," Willow says, looking dreamy.

Juniper listens without comment, still pinching leaves, fingertips slowly turning green.

"The shoe thing too," Clem says softly.

"I noticed that as well," Juniper says, smiling. "That's definitely a Ward trait. Being barefoot."

"Keeps you tied to the earth," Hazel says. "But it makes your feet get ugly and old."

"Good," Willow says, grinning. "I can't *wait* to be old."

Hazel rolls her eyes. "Wait till you're forty and then say that."

"Deal."

Poppy holds up her dirty foot. "Is my foot ugly and old?"

Juniper grabs her trotter by the toes. "Absolutely." She sniffs them while Poppy flops about shrieking with laughter. "Stinky, stinky feet!"

"The shawl!" Hazel cries, trying to shield the fabric from further mud—a task Clem thinks is impossible.

Clem tickles a wriggling Poppy. "The stinkiest little girl there ever was!"

"Gonna pee!" Poppy yells, face a brilliant red, teeth white as snow. "Gonna pee-pee my panties!"

And to prove it, a moment later, Clem feels a warm wet patch by her leg. *"Ew!"*

Juniper drops Poppy's foot and Hazel jumps to her feet. "*Gross,* Poppy!"

"I told you!" Poppy yells, her hysterical laughter turning to tears. "I *told* you!"

"It's okay," Clem says, laughing. "Pee is mostly water anyway."

She very much does not feel this way, but the last thing she wants is to cause Poppy any distress.

"Come on," Juniper says, reaching for Poppy, who allows herself to be lifted, revealing a slightly yellow bum.

"We're right by a nice clean lake." She looks at the others. "How about a swim?"

"Another one?" Holly asks.

"Not supposed to swim after eating," Ivy adds reasonably.

"No rules, remember?" Willow counters.

"Except the three," Hazel agrees. "Could be fun. Anyway, I've got Poppy pee on me."

"Could be worse," Clem offers. "Could be—"

"Caca!" Poppy yells, her voice high and sweet.

Juniper's lips purse, and she's never looked more like their mother. "You can't say *caca*."

"It's poo-poo," Willow informs Poppy importantly. "That's how you say it."

Poppy considers very seriously, before screaming, "Caca poo-poo!"

"I'm gonna caca poo-poo you in the lake," Juniper says, to which Poppy giggles in hysterics and nearly rolls right out of Juniper's arms.

Before long, they're all laughing and yelling, "*CACA POO-POO!*"

Clem makes as though she's going to tickle Poppy again, and Poppy shrieks and wriggles free from Juniper, running for the water.

Juniper grins. "I'm gonna get you!"

They race her to the lake and fall on top of themselves in the bottomless murk, playing with water, playing with shadows, playing with their wild, free childhood.

When the sun begins to dip below the trees, Juniper pulls them, shivering and goosefleshed, from their reverie.

"Beltane is calling," she says.

They follow, wet and muddy, without protest. This is the new order of things.

They are home.

# 11

***September 2024***

Henry shields his eyes against the light glinting off the water and regards me carefully.

I swallow. "So, they're coming? Ivy and Hazel?"

He glances in the direction of the house, jaw working. Eventually he says, "They're already here."

Fuck.

"Right."

I turn and head into the foliage; apparently my feet have perfect memory and remember the way, even though there's an almost impenetrable wall of green beyond the small strip of sand at the end of the dock.

Was I the last to receive a letter? The ancient but familiar feeling of being an outsider in my own family rises like a heat shimmer, but I trudge on as I always have. Maybe it's not that deep. Maybe I just live farthest away and the message took longer to reach me.

Henry's footsteps fall into sync with mine, and I try not to look at him, try not to feel the warmth of his skin like a furnace. Try not to remember soggy summer afternoons at the lake, droplets of water on browning skin, the radiant explosion of laughter on the air.

Instead, we walk in silence. Him, an enigma. Me, a silent and seething resentment.

"I'm staying with my father for a while," he says at last. "In his cabin."

I don't say anything, but I'm secretly glad to know he'll be fairly close by.

"Want me to go with you?" he asks as we near the final stretch of forest before the house appears.

I don't stop walking when I say, "No."

But he does.

By the time I'm brave enough to glance back, he's already gone. I tell myself I don't regret my decision. That I don't regret treating him so coldly.

What good would leaning toward a shadow do me anyway?

I almost don't notice when the house comes into view, but when I do, a rising horror grows through my feet, up my calves, and into my belly.

The house has changed.

It is not the pristine-white, if-slightly-crumbling side of the house I saw facing the ocean. This side of the house is in the process of being completely retaken by the forest. A branch is growing from one of the top windows of the mansard roof like a crooked limb, which means that there is a tree growing in the house somewhere. Bracken has sprouted close to the siding, and has been allowed to grow so tall that it reaches halfway up the lower windows. The porch is an algae green, riddled with moss and mold, and a gaping hole in the side of the building has left jagged wooden edges like some giant fist has smashed its way through. Vines have already begun to sneak their way inside. Beltane is no longer protected from the elements. The windows on the bottom story, at least, are all intact. In fact, it looks as though some of them have been sealed entirely shut by vivid-green moss that has grown thick around the edges like nature's own grout.

I can't help but think that the house is two faced.

A house that can't be trusted.

I approach it with a sense of nervous apprehension. I haven't seen Juniper in twenty-five years. A lifetime. What will I even say? I step forward, stopping beside the left entablature, and my eyes snag on a carving in the wooden threshold before the door. A symbol. Our symbol. A childish sketch we invented one winter to keep evil out and the Forgotten God appeased while we waited for spring. My shoulders slump at the sight of it, because even though it's ridiculous to believe such a thing could hold any power, I still don't want to cross it.

Some distance off, to the left, the new skull of an elk lies in the center of a circle of leaves, each leaf held down by a lit stump of a candle. My stomach contracts at the sight of it, and I vomit into the bracken.

I could turn around and leave right now.

Instead, I ignore the macabre offering, step over the symbol and through the open doorway, into the house.

The cloying taste of something moldering lingers at the back of my throat, and I gag again. Dead animal? Rotting moss? Swollen wood riddled with mold? It could be all three.

It takes a moment for my eyes to adjust to the darkness. Movement in the center of the entrance hall catches my eye. Something is crouched there in the dark.

It's a woman sitting cross-legged. Tatted hair spills from a headscarf the multifarious colors of sunset. Long, thin arms end in dirty, long-nailed fingers, which are gathering and scattering small bones on the wooden floor.

Slowly, she raises her head, and I see that she still has small pieces of bone shoved through her earlobes. The ones I put there myself. She's added a few over the years, so that she looks like a boho witch from a thrift-store horror flick, the kind you'd see smoking clove cigarettes at a dive bar. Her eyes are the same—eerily blue, wide, and intense. Like lasers pointing into my soul.

It's hard to look at her.

She lets a hand hover over the bones, clawlike, and says, "They said you'd come."

I jerk up a brow, unimpressed. "Hello to you, too, June." I glance around, taking in the staircase strung with ivy, the walls spotty with mold and mushrooms, the dank wet air. "You never left the island?"

Juniper frowns up at me, cocking her head like a cat. "Of course not."

She rises lithely to her feet, and my knee aches with bitterness.

*"Hold her down!" Juniper was yelling for the others to hold Holly. My head was screaming, I was screaming, and the storm was screaming too.*

*"You hold her," I cried. "You hold her while I fix your mistake!"*

*"It was an accident," Hazel said, backing away. "It was an accident!"*

"It's my duty," Juniper says, peering at me. Bringing me back into the present moment. "My calling. To shepherd the Wards home."

"Enough of the theatrics," I snap. "What am I doing here?"

I am aching to go. I wish I had thrown the berry in the trash like any sane person would have done. I wish I was in my shop, handing antique books to customers who will love them. I wish I was in the back room, sitting on my small sofa, sipping tea and going through the inventory with Matt.

Juniper turns on her heel and heads for the dining room. I sigh and follow, very much *not* wanting to go deeper into this hellhole. My sinuses are already tingling.

We round the corner just as two women come in from the kitchen. They are both holding chipped mugs. Mugs I recognize. The same mugs I sipped from for years. Granny Alys's mugs.

Ivy has beauty in the way that unassuming things do. Not asking for attention. Not plastering itself with airs and graces. No lick of makeup on her delicate lashes, no blemishes to mar the perfection of her skin. She is the Ivy of my childhood, but older. Grown into herself in a way that makes me ache.

Hazel is her antithesis. Hair dyed a darker color, hazelnut brown bordering on chocolate. It minimizes the red of her scars, which she has attempted to hide beneath a layer of thick-caked foundation and too-light concealer. Thick mascara globs her lashes together like sap on branches, and old lipstick gathers in the corners of her mouth, cracked along the age lines. Her left eye is smaller, the once-clear cornea turned opaque, a white haze veiling its surface. The sight of it makes my skin crawl, and I look away.

These are women standing before me. Women that are my flesh and my blood, and who are strangers.

Ivy is wearing the smart casual outfit of a businesswoman on vacation. Next to her, Hazel is done up to the nines. It isn't quite enough to distract someone from her scar or her eye, but she does look good. Like someone who knows what they are doing from afar. Like herself, but older. So much older.

The air leaves my lungs, and for a minute I can't get it back.

"Clementine," Hazel says, smiling. "You look the same."

I laugh, the air finally coming back. "Liar. You do, though."

Hazel shakes her head, subdued in a way I'm not used to.

"You look like you're doing well," I tell Ivy, my heart heaving complex feelings into my stomach, where they roil. I am so, so very proud of her. I am so sorry to see her back in this house.

"I got the promotion," she tells me.

I beam. "I knew you would."

Of all my sisters, Ivy is the only one I stay in touch with. Not regularly, not by any means. I doubt any of us could manage anything close to a normal social schedule. But every few months I call, and we talk for a few hours. Knowing she is safe and happy is important to me. I owe her as much.

I look to Juniper again. "What are we doing here, June?"

Juniper pulls out a chair and takes a seat at the dining room table.

*There are only these rules: Be home before sundown. Eat dinner together at the table every night at seven. Never stray past the boundary after dark.*

"He's been leaving signs," she says.

Hazel, Ivy, and I exchange a wary glance.

Juniper stands again and goes into the entrance hall. She returns holding a broken branch longer and thicker than her arm.

She holds it up reverently. "See?"

We exchange another look.

"See . . . what?" Ivy asks. She is tentative in a way I wouldn't be. In a way I no longer have patience for.

"And here," Juniper says, leading the way into the formal downstairs sitting room—the one we never used. The sofas are threadbare and moldy, the floral chintz barely discernible, and the smell I associate with animal fur is more potent here. There are an endless series of bones nailed to the wall, eldritch and disturbing. A tiny cairn of bones has been built, each fragment stacked with quiet care. Juniper heads to the hole in the wall I saw from outside, crossing over the warped floorboards, spongy underfoot. They bow up in places, swollen and buckling beneath her feet, as if Beltane remembers the thousand nights of rain, water stained and weary. She stands beside it, waiting for our reaction. I see nothing but a hole caused by storm damage and decaying wood.

Juniper's face falls when we just stand and stare, confused. Her disappointment lingers like a slap on my cheek, like fungi blossoming.

"You've lost your sight," she says quietly, as though her heart is breaking.

"It's a hole," I say bluntly. "Storm damage?"

Juniper practically crumples to the floor. She bounces on her haunches, clutching her head. A small pile of bones lies nearby, just like the ones she was throwing in the entrance hall.

*The bones said you'd come.*

"You'll anger Him," she murmurs. "You'll anger Daudir."

His name descends, a collective shock wave through us.

D

A

U

D

I

R . . .

*Him.*

Almighty.

The Forgotten God of the Wood.

Hazel takes a full step back, and Ivy gasps a little breath in. The shadows in the room have grown deeper, and sentient.

*Stop it,* I tell myself. It was a stupid fucking game.

I glance at Ivy, who shakes her head. Hazel gives me a pointed look. One that says, "She isn't well."

I nod, biting at the inside corner of my cheek. What the hell are we supposed to do?

"If the God has returned," Ivy says gently, stepping close to Juniper, who is still clutching her head, rocking back and forth on her haunches, "then maybe we should go. Leave?"

Juniper goes still.

She looks up at Ivy, then rises to her feet in that same fluid way she did earlier, her smile eerie in the way of insanity.

We watch as she considers Ivy, still grinning in a serene, unsettling way, and then wanders off, farther into the bleak depths of the house.

I walk over to the pile of little bones and scatter them with a kick, ignoring the fissure of fear that has grown between my shoulder blades.

# 12

***May 1999***

The ritual begins with an innocent comment.

Granny Alys had said on their first night: *The Forgotten God of the Wood will protect any Ward. If you take, you must give in return.*

In the weeks since then, she has shown them plenty of examples. Planting a seed when a flower is plucked. Leaving a flower when a branch is taken from the wood.

The rhythm of the ritual, the hum of the routine. The magic in their muted prayer, the satisfaction in the small movements. Clem is drawn in despite herself, her skepticism shrinking each day, each week, each lonely month, until she finds herself unable to pluck a wildflower without leaving a pinprick of blood behind.

Willow is the one who finds the rock. Three times the height of Juniper, the tallest, it stands sentinel near the river, where the ground slopes gently up and then all at once into a rocky peak. It is accented in moss and water stains from generations of rainfall, chipped and shaped into something almost human.

"It looks like a giant's head," Willow murmurs, reaching out a hand as though to touch it.

Clem anticipates the cold grainy texture. But Willow stops short of actual contact.

"It *is* a head," Juniper says softly, staring up at where the indentations suggest eyes.

"Is it the Forgotten God?" Holly asks, taking Ivy's hand in sudden terror.

It certainly has the feeling of a god, Clem thinks. There is a sense of magnitude in the air around it, like a held breath, too still to be normal. Awe and terror mingle in Clem's bones, and she almost wants to run away. All of a sudden, she is sure—absolutely sure—that the rock is looking right at her. Regarding her. Studying her. Making a decision about her. She steps back, flinching.

"*Daudir,*" she murmurs, using their secret language. "God."

"No," Juniper says firmly, breaking the tension. "It's a guardian. A watcher. Daudir has them all throughout the woods, all over Beltane, and Willow—" She cuts off, turning to Willow with a wide grin, her eyes bright with moisture. "Willow clearly has the Sight. She can see them too."

Willow nods, solemn. "I can see."

A pang of jealousy burns in Clem before she quashes it. Does Juniper really believe this, or is she just playing along?

"Willow, the Seer," Clem says quickly, hurrying to agree, desperate to be a part of this revelation. To show that she, too, belongs in this game. She is desperate to see what they see.

Juniper ignores her, but Poppy steps close, hugging her leg with a discomforted little mew. Clem picks her up and holds her close, a security blanket. Comfort in the sudden cold of late afternoon.

"When a guardian is found, we have to leave an offering," Juniper says. "A sacrifice."

A ripple of energy passes between them, a current of electric interest carried from one to the other, quick as a flash.

"Or a ritual," Willow says, her expression oddly blank.

"Or a ritual," Juniper agrees, watching her. "So that the Guardian will take a message to the sylvan god and keep him appeased."

Clem has always collected, unable to let go of the items she finds. She packed as many of her collections as she could fit in the yellow suitcase. She has a collection of buttons, ribbons, bows, string, coins, and the few pilfered jewels from her mother's broken necklaces—two diamonds, six rubies, two sapphires, and three green stones she thinks are emeralds, but could just as well be moldavite or green diamonds. They glisten in her palm when she takes them out by moonlight. Penny knew about her secret stashes and called her Magpie, but Clem didn't exactly know what it meant.

Now, her sisters scatter into the surrounding woods, searching for offerings and the beginnings of their own collections. A swell of warmth rises in her chest at the idea that this is something else they are connected by. A new tether between them.

Juniper gathers a bunch of wildflowers, yellow, white, and purple; Hazel offers up her favorite lip gloss, though it's almost finished—she only has one other tube left. Holly and Ivy create a two-headed doll from twigs wrapped with vines; Willow finds the skull of a small dead bird, and she places it before the Guardian with flowers stuffed into the empty eye sockets. Clem pulls out a single strand of Poppy's hair and hands it to Juniper for inspection, as though asking to be graded while Poppy cries on Clem's hip, rubbing at her head.

"A joint sacrifice," she says, when Juniper says nothing.

Juniper nods, and places the fine strand on top of the other offerings.

Poppy's sacrifice is her pain. Clem's is the pain of having to hurt her sister.

It is enough. They all agree that it is good.

"It is good," they murmur in union, never deciding explicitly to do so.

The sky rumbles, and the light fades faster.

"Beltane is calling," Juniper says, and they turn as one and leave the Guardian—and their tributes—behind.

Clem, still holding a snuffling Poppy, is the last to follow, her heart beating out a constant rhythm that pounds with every bare step.

It is good.

It is good.

It is good.

# 13

***June 1999***

Granny Alys teaches the girls to repot seedlings, to fix the walls with old nails and a heavy hammer, to press flowers and bracken between the pages of heavy books and hang them on the wall between panes of glass. She teaches them to forage, to recognize the mushrooms that harm and nourish, the berries that are safe to eat: which can be cooked—and which must be avoided. She teaches them cooking, baking, canning for winter, how to sew their clothes when tears appear, and how to use the manual water pump in the sink, which squeaks like a dying squirrel with every pump. She teaches them the way to fell small trees with the heavy axe and split wood with the maul, how to sharpen the blades and oil the handles, how to set the grandfather clock so it always works and lets them know when it's time for supper.

She teaches them how to dance, listening to old records on a gramophone she shows them how to operate; she helps them cook stews over the fire, flavoring the meat with spices, safe mosses, and sap. She shows them how to make paints and pigments for dye from the flowers and berries, mushrooms and dirt of the forest—slapping great mounds of it into jars that they'll use to paint old newspapers and white cloth.

She sits with them at night on the wraparound porch, taking each of the littles in turn on her lap on the rocking chair, showing them how to recognize the call of the loon, the owl, and the chirps of migrating birds coming home, explaining the way that the northern spotted owl makes its home here, and needs standing snags to nest in—and so wood must be carefully taken, and only after asking permission and leaving a trinket in payment to the Forgotten God of the Wood.

Clem's favorite is when she teaches them about papier-mâché.

"You take flour and mix it with water," she said one day in the kitchen, laying out the jar of flour on the wooden table. "Then, when it's nice and gloopy, you take strips of newspaper, dip them in till they're nice and wet; then you lay them down to make shapes. Kind of like a sculpture."

"Paper machay," Willow said, reaching for the flour jar.

"Mâché," Granny Alys corrected. "It's French. Meaning *chewed up*."

Willow giggled. "Chewed-up paper!"

"You got it. Right in one," Granny Alys said, and her smile was so warm that it even reached her eyes.

Clem felt a warming in her belly then, looking at Alys. She had never raised her voice to them, not once in the weeks they had lived at Beltane—not even when Poppy spilled the pancake batter all over the floor and a bunch of it seeped through the floorboards, so they had to pull them up to wipe it clean, then nail them down again.

"Just a good chance to fix them right" was all she said.

Clem reached for one of the rolled-up newspapers that sat on the table, taking off the elastic band that held it closed. The date read two years ago.

"Why do you get so many?" she said quietly.

"I like to know what's going on in the world, even if I prefer to stay out of it."

Clem had noticed that Granny Alys read a newspaper every morning on the porch with her cup of black coffee, rocking and rocking and reading and reading. When she was done, she rolled the paper back up and added it to a pile that she took down to the cellar.

"Ernest brings them when he brings the supplies," Granny Alys said. "One for every day."

Hazel took the newspaper from Clem's hand and looked at it. "But won't they be old? Irrelevant?"

"Stories are stories no matter when they're read," Granny Alys said. "I like to know that folks are out there being themselves, causing all sorts of trouble. Makes me more grateful for what we have right here."

"Why do you keep them when you're done?" It was Juniper who asked.

"I use them. Shine up the windows, line the drawers, use them for kindling. They catch nice and quick for fire. And then, this here. Papier-mâché."

She had shown them the way to create a base, either from wire or from cardboard, and then how to lay the gooey mâché paper onto the form and mold it into something new. When she was done, it was their turn.

"What shall we make?" Hazel asked. "A heart? A flower?"

"Rabbit!" Poppy shrieked, and Clem winced with the volume.

"Perfect idea!" Granny Alys said. "Rabbits."

Several weeks before, Clem had gifted Poppy her threadbare stuffed rabbit, and now Poppy is rarely seen without it. Rabbits, it seems, have become her new favorite obsession.

And so, it was agreed by all, and rabbits were made. Masks, to be precise. Seven rabbit masks with wonky ears, each and every one hung on the stairwell wall by Granny Alys when they were dry, like prize art.

They begin living in a lunar cycle, twenty-eight days at a time, until—without really noticing—spring has burned into a sultry, humid summer.

Clem and her sisters have begun new collections. What began for Clem as buttons and ribbons has morphed into a collection of stones, leaves, sticks, and seeds. She even has a small animal bone she found on one of their treks, snuck into her pocket and sequestered safely in her Winchcombe beside the silent music box. It makes her feel powerful. It makes her feel safe.

"Henry will be here with Ernest tomorrow. Or, perhaps, the next day," Granny Alys says after supper one night. The girls have just finished their food, a green-tinged porridge that tasted of oats and pine beside a soft pulled meat Granny Alys cooked in a cast-iron pot.

"New supplies?" Hazel asks, stroking her hair, eyes turning wistful.

Granny Alys nods. "I asked him to bring new clothing for all of you."

Hazel squeals and bounces from her chair, flapping her hands like Poppy on Christmas morning. Like a banshee.

Of all the Wards, Hazel is the provocateur. Wearing clothes she knew broke school protocol, shoplifting things she later threw away, using items she knew were precious to others, and smiling through it all like a princess, all pretty hair and flirty eyes. Golden, is Hazel. Even here in Beltane, even with a muddy grin.

Clem knows how much it means, far more than any of her other sisters, for Hazel to feel beautiful. Each day she picks flowers or pretty leaves and winds them into her hair. Clem has even seen her smash elderberries between her fingers and apply the stain to her lips and cheeks.

"Do we have to help bring the supplies in?" Willow asks, slumping in her seat.

Holly and Ivy fold their arms, looking mutinous.

"You don't have to do anything you don't want to," Granny Alys assures them.

"I'll help him bring the supplies in," Clem offers, wanting to make her sisters happy.

Willow perks up. "Really?"

"Yeah."

A quiet curve touches Granny Alys's lips. "If that's what you feel like doing."

It is. Clem wants to see Henry, to ask him what he knows about Beltane. To find out if he's seen the God of the Wood. Henry has, after all, been here longest. Not continually, no, but repeatedly over the years, through different seasons. Didn't he say he stayed for the summer sometimes? Maybe he'll be here for a while, and she can learn how to gain favor with the Forgotten God on behalf of her sisters, to make amends and beg forgiveness.

They are not the girls they were last season. They no longer bathe very much, preferring to run into the rain and dance the grime away, or to sink into the algae-riddled lake like alligators. They no longer wear shoes; their feet grow tough and dirty, in order to commune with Daudir, the Forgotten God, who is Father. Who is Mother. Only their assigned colors remain as the dregs of who they used to be. Is it a tribute to their negligent, hedonistic parents? Or have they claimed the color so absolutely that it is as tied to them as much as their scent or name? Whatever the reason, this is a ritual they cannot shake.

They spend much of their time running through the wilderness, playing in the castle they made out of a large weeping elm, carving out their secret space in the hollow beneath its hanging umbrella branches. They've spent days and weeks tying on ribbons in every shade they have, so that beneath it looks like colorful rain. A fort fit for the Ward witches of Beltane.

They have grown used to the earthy tang of green leaves harvested from the wood; the sour flesh of mushrooms gathered from the bark of dead trees; the sweet, medicinal tang of sap suspended in water. Their tongues, now fluent in the forest's secret language, move like burrowing spirits, seeking the hidden flavors of root and shadow.

Clem waits on the raised dock all day, wondering if Henry will be able to tell. Whether he will think she looks different or just the same. She lets her legs dangle over the edge, watching the horizon. Minutes tick by, agonizing as a yawn.

Clem returns to Beltane before dark but is back on the dock first thing in the morning, when the sun is barely risen.

The boat is almost here. Henry stands in the small prow, waving frantically. Clem can't help but grin back at this golden boy, who seems to carry the sun with him.

"Hi, Clem!" he calls when they're close enough.

Clem's cheeks feel like they might burst from the pressure. "Hello."

Ernest doesn't say anything when he gets off the boat, just walks past Clem and secures the rope. Henry hurries over, pausing when he reaches her in an awkward guttural stop.

Clem realizes she doesn't quite know how to greet him.

"How've you been?" he asks after a moment, breaking the tension.

"Good. You?"

"Mostly at school. Boring. But it's summer break now."

"Are you staying?"

"For a couple of weeks, yes."

Clem's smile unfurls like a guilty flower. Tentative. Henry looks her up and down, and Clem again wonders if she appears as different as she feels. Can Henry sense the change that Daudir has wrought?

"You look like Granny Alys," he says, half laughing, and Clem isn't sure if that's a compliment or an insult.

"Thank you," she says, deciding she likes the idea of being more like her grandmother.

Granny Alys spends time with them. Granny Alys doesn't constantly leave them or ignore them. Granny Alys loves them.

Clem swallows a lump of guilt when she realizes that she prefers Granny Alys to her own parents.

"Get moving," Ernest grumbles when he passes them, the noxious smoke from his thin rolled cigarette burning Clem's lungs. He is carrying a large box. He takes it to the end of the dock and dumps it, heading back.

"I've got to get the cart," Henry says. "Want to come?"

"Get it from where?"

"Here, I'll show you."

The cart is stored in a shed not too far from the dock, hidden by a thick overgrowth that Henry says he will have to prune back before it gets eaten by the forest. He says it with a grin, like he's joking, but Clem wonders if Daudir really would eat it if left alone.

The cart is silver, a metal contraption with two levels and four wheels that twist, like a shopping cart.

Henry gestures to it. "Hop in, I'll give you a ride."

"Really?"

"Yeah, go ahead."

Clem climbs onto the top level and holds the sides. The bottom level is big enough for each of the twins to sit in, and she makes a mental note to ask Henry to let them have a go too.

The ride back to the dock is exhilarating—bumpy, fast. Like flying. The cart jolts over roots and stones, rattling beneath her, and she feels each jostle carry her closer to the water. Clem has never felt like this before. Usually, she keeps things locked up tight, and when she doesn't, she's sharing it with her sisters—a seventh of it for herself. This is all for her, and she wonders, vaguely, if she should feel guilty. She is becoming aware of something. A warmth in her belly not associated with her sisters.

The ride comes to an abrupt stop when Henry makes her get off before Ernest sees. Then they spend time loading the boxes onto the cart before walking uphill to the house, too breathless to chat.

Henry shows Clem the way to the cellar, and how the bulkhead doors open up and out.

"No lock?" Clem asks.

"Who's gonna break in? Deer?"

"You never know!"

He grins.

The space is vast—the entire footprint of the house and divided into five large rooms of similar size. Henry shows Clem where the meat is stored, where the grains and potatoes and legumes are stored, where the tin cans and bottles are stored, where the nonperishables are stored, and where the fuel for the generator is kept.

"The gas'll only last three months, so we keep it close to the doors," he says.

Not for the first time, Clem wonders why Ernest is the one to bring in supplies.

"How come your dad lives here?"

"On the island, you mean?"

"Yeah. Why does he do this for Granny Alys? And why does she let him?"

"I don't know the full story, but I think Alys, her husband, and Ernest were school friends. When she married her husband, they invited Ernest to stay."

"And he never left?"

"No, he did. For a long time. Met Mom, had me. But after that went sideways, he came back. I think he likes the quiet. The isolation." Henry sighs. "The supplies are a kind of payment, I think."

"Labor instead of rent?"

Henry shrugs. "Guess so."

Good deal, Clem thinks. She has an impulse to hide from him, to make him find her in the stygian dark of these shadowy rooms. But the feeling of something else in the shadows stops her. She pauses after unloading the cart to peer into the murk. Could a guardian live beneath the house itself? Keeping tabs on the sisters even as they sleep? Keeping them safe?

"Maybe we could install a lever system," Henry says, when he pushes Clem downhill back to the dock.

"Yeah," she says, imagining a giant bucket connected by a rope to a series of intricate cogs. "Or a railway from the dock to the house, so we could just ride it right into the cellar."

Henry grins, his eyes turning inward the way Clem knows hers do when she's off in a daydream.

"We could build it next summer," he suggests. "I could ask Ernest to bring in wood for the slat things."

"Okay, deal."

Clem twists in the cart and offers Henry her hand. He takes it, and they shake on it.

When the supplies, including Granny Alys's new stock of newspapers, are safely stored and the cellar closed up, Clem and Henry go in search of her sisters. She feels fidgety having been out of their presence for so long.

"They're probably by the lake," she tells Henry, leading him in that direction, wondering if he knows about the eldritch God of the Wood or not, and whether she ought to tell him.

The lake is a brilliant sea green today, reflecting blue in parts where the sky is not overshadowed by canopy. Her sisters are not here. A rising unease bubbles in her stomach, but she forces it down, clamping it shut. Daudir watches over them; she has to trust that this, if anything, is true.

"How many summers have you spent here?" she asks Henry instead, taking a seat on a small grassy verge where waterside reeds reach for the sky.

"About five of them. I started coming when I was nine. Before that, Ernest used to come to us in Toronto for a week."

He explains that his parents divorced soon after he started school, splitting his time between them. Ernest saw less and less of Henry until it was only a couple of weeks in the summer. Henry thought about refusing to come a few times, since it was so lonely and boring to be here all by himself—just free labor, as he saw it, for a man who barely liked him. But now Clem is here, and her sisters are here, and he likes it much better.

She flushes, feeling that *thing* in her stomach again. "Did you explore the island?"

He pulls up a handful of grass and presses it to his nose, inhaling the scent. "When I had a chance, yes. I know a few cool spots. I could show you."

"Maybe I've found them already."

"Then we'll compare notes," he says, grinning at her sideways.

Clem can't decide whether or not to tell her sisters about Henry and his knowledge of the island. She feels bad when she thinks that maybe she could keep this secret for herself. If she told them, though, she'd be revealing a secret that isn't hers to tell, and that isn't fair. Clem decides to let him tell her sisters himself.

"You said that Ernest pays for his house by bringing supplies, right?"

"Sort of." He shifts uncomfortably. "She lets him live on the island for free, and to use any resources that he needs on his edge. Within reason, of course. He can use the wood he needs, but he can't, like, sell it on. She pays for the supplies he brings in—both his and hers. He just has to do the delivering."

Seems to Clem that Ernest has a better deal than Granny Alys does, but she doesn't say that.

"Why doesn't he go visit you and your mom sometimes?" she asks instead.

Clem can tell he's getting uncomfortable by the way he won't meet her eyes, and how he's rubbing at his arm.

"You don't have to tell me," she adds.

"I don't think Ernest was meant to be a husband. Maybe not even a dad. He's better in the wild. I think he prefers staying out here because it's sort of, like, invisible? Because he doesn't need to answer to anyone. Like the government, you know? He's off grid. He doesn't want to be found. Sorta paranoid."

"But how can Granny Alys even afford it? The supplies and stuff?"

"I think she has a lot of family money. She owns the island, for one, so someone along the way must have bought it." He plucks another handful of grass and picks out blades, one by one, letting them fall to the ground. "I think it's just passed down from generation to generation. Probably like trust funds or stuff rich people have."

A shriek in the distance catches their attention, and Clem perks up. A moment later, her sisters come careening through the foliage, dashing aside the lyrate leaves of a fiddle leaf fig.

Hazel is in the lead, and she comes to a stop when she sees Clem and Henry sitting side by side on the bank. In her hand, she twirls a length of vine like a whip.

"Well, well," she says, coming closer, the twins trailing behind. "What have we here?"

"Henry's here for a couple of weeks," Clem says, patting the grass beside her.

Holly, Ivy, and a red-faced Poppy come to sit, but Hazel and Willow stand watchful. Juniper arrives soon after, a crown of berries on her head. She stops, goes very still, and looks down her nose at the boy at Clem's side. Clem can almost hear her thoughts, her judgment. Is this boy deserving? Is he worthy of inclusion into their world? Is he an interloper, bringing discord, or is he an intriguing mystery to be uncovered?

Clem could defend him. Could tell Juniper that Henry is a good one, full of stories and ideas—that he predates their arrival to Beltane and so, surely, has prior claim. But she doesn't. Juniper must judge for herself, and for them all.

This is how it works.

The wind blows playfully in their faces, taking a few blades of grass with it. They land in Clem's hair.

"Oh, sorry!" Henry leans forward and meticulously picks them out, gently laying them back on the ground.

He never tugs even one of her hairs.

When a slow smile creeps along Juniper's face, Clem's muscles relax. Henry has passed a test he didn't even know he was taking. While he pulled at the grass absentmindedly, Juniper was deciding whether he would be allowed to stay. And now that he has her approval, Clem knows he will be allowed into their inner world.

They spend hours together, braiding vines to make into swings, naming trees and picking leaves. Then Ernest's voice calls through the rising gloom, echoing through the boughs like a trumpet.

"I better go," Henry says.

"No!" Holly cries.

"Not yet," Ivy begs.

"Stay!" Poppy demands.

Clem grins as he stands, wiping plant debris from his legs. "I'm sorry. I wouldn't want you to get in trouble on my behalf, though."

Poppy pouts, but doesn't protest. She, no doubt, doesn't want him to get into trouble either.

They are all sad to see him go.

"You'll come by tomorrow?" Clem asks.

Henry bends down, hesitates, and then kisses her on the cheek. "Of course."

The twins tease them with *ooo*s, and *aaa*s, and Juniper smiles indulgently. Willow watches dispassionately, head cocked to the side with vague interest, and Poppy screeches, "Me next!"

As Henry lifts Poppy and plants a kiss on her chubby cheek, Clem notices Hazel scowling from the water, where she is washing her hair with nothing at all.

Of all the years Clem has allowed Hazel to take things from her, she can't help but feel good about finally having something of her own.

# 14

***September 2024***

We drift through the house under the pretense of seeking Juniper. But we are remembering. Unraveling. Scouring the silence for things we left behind. Small treasures ripped away from us that final night.

Yellow suitcase.

Bone doll.

Button collection.

I climb the groaning stairs, haunted by the memory of seven girls dashing up and down, making a race of it—bare feet on wood, laughter like wind chimes. The memory is superimposed, brilliant as sunlight, on top of this new shadow reality. It aches that three of our little troop are gone forever.

We walk in a line down the hall, Hazel, me, Ivy, and the memory of our younger selves walks with us: orange, yellow, and green. Only now do I realize that Ivy is wearing a green jacket, subtle, almost gray but most certainly tinged green, and that Hazel has an orange belt. And, around my neck, a yellow pendant.

Are we all just echoes? Trapped in the routine of our former selves, brainwashed so thoroughly that we've never truly escaped, ritual bound and memory washed, forever circling the pattern of who we were?

I break formation. Slip into my old room alone. Fingers to my neck, I unfasten the pendant and let it fall onto the dust-veiled vanity where I once braided my hair and believed in forever. Dead leaves lie scattered on the floor like careless whispers. Mildew freckles the bed-curtains like old bruises, and the scent of rot rises, familiar, and somehow sacred. I wrinkle my nose, sinuses tingling.

My little yellow case sits beneath the window, so much smaller than I remember. A sob claws at my throat. Grief—sharp, absurd—rises like smoke.

And with it, a ridiculous guilt, raw and powerful, at having left it behind. For a breath, I imagine it waiting for me. Lonely. Then I catch myself in the silly sentimentality of giving an inanimate object feelings.

Still, I reach for it.

Lift it gently.

The floor beneath is an entirely different shade, revealing the stark passage of time, a memory outlined in dust. Something rattles inside the case, and the sound startles me. It sounds alive, somehow.

I drift to the bed, but the quilt is damp with mildew. I sit at the dressing table instead, laying the case down like an offering, and click open the latches. A doll lies inside, pieced together from bone and feather, twig and thread. She stares up at me with yellow button eyes—wide, watchful, impossibly knowing.

"Mara," I breathe, and the name feels like a spell broken.

I remember the day we made her. Juniper sewed her gaze, Hazel's fingers tied her limbs, my own hands shaped her heart. But—

No.

*No.*

I shut the case. Close the memory. Fasten it tight.

"Just junk," I whisper.

Just junk.

A knock at my door.

Hazel stands on the threshold, eyeing me. I turn away just long enough to wipe my eyes, then face her like I'm whole.

"Hey," I manage.

Hazel steps over the threshold like she's bracing for a storm, hair windblown, boots caked with Beltane's stubborn clay. "She's certifiably insane," she mutters, shedding her jacket like it offends her.

"Juniper?" I ask, though I already know.

Hazel gives a sharp nod, jaw set. "She won't budge on the Daudir stuff. She's locked in. Keeps talking like it's sacred scripture. Like the sun won't rise unless we smear ash on our faces and chant in our secret tongue."

Her voice catches that old teenage scoff, the one she used to throw like a rock at any rule she didn't write.

"It's hard to believe she's been here this long," she says, quieter now, "just . . . steeping in all this make-believe."

I let out a hollow laugh, an image of a Juniper-shaped tea bag flashing in my imagination. "I wish Henry would just ferry us off this rock already. Take us all and be done with it."

She blinks. "Henry?"

"Yeah. Didn't he bring you in?"

Her brow knits, and something passes across her face—confusion first, then something heavier. "No. Ernest brought me. Brought Ivy too. Henry wasn't there."

I stare at her. The silence stretches like a thread pulled too tight.

"But . . . he was—" I stop. The room tilts slightly, my thoughts slipping out of place like books knocked off a shelf.

Hazel folds her arms. "We came in together. Ivy and me. On that broken old boat with Ernest."

The wind outside rattles the windows, trying to get in.

"God," Hazel says after a beat. "The whole thing's a farce, isn't it? Daudir. The rituals. All this theater in the woods. Juniper prancing around like she's a priestess in some lost age."

I nod, too tired to lie. "She believes it, though."

"She's the only one who does."

For a moment, something unspoken flutters between us—an exhausted kinship. Two outsiders caught in a play they never auditioned for.

Hazel leans back against the wall, glancing toward the curtained window. "We could leave, you know. Just . . . go. Leave her to her holy delusions. Or grab her if we have to. She can kick and scream all she wants."

The idea blooms for a moment. The sweetness of escape. Of salt wind and the sound of the boat motor whirring, steady and real.

Then I glance at Hazel, and something old stirs. "You did always try to take what wasn't yours."

Her eyes narrow, just a flicker. "Excuse me?"

"You heard me."

She straightens, all the softness gone. "Don't pretend to know who I am."

"I know enough," I say, getting to my feet and then stepping forward. "You talk like a savior, but you only show up when it suits you. You didn't come for Juniper. You came for Ivy."

Her mouth opens, a sharp retort forming—but then she laughs instead. No heat in it. "And you didn't come for her, either, did you? Not really. You came for Henry."

The name slices the air between us.

I flinch. Just barely. But she sees it.

"I didn't know he'd be here," I snap.

Hazel's voice turns soft and vicious. "Still chasing ghosts."

My hands curl into fists, nails biting palm. "You don't get to talk about him."

"Why? Because you still think he's yours?"

"I never said that."

"You didn't have to."

We stand like statues, the kind that crack in frost, waiting for a thaw that may never come.

Somewhere deep in the woods, the wind calls again. Or maybe it's something else.

Nuclear tension rises, dampened all of a sudden by Ivy's entrance. She stands, awkward, in the doorway.

"Clem?" she says.

Hazel curls her lip at me, and then storms from the room, almost careening into Ivy as she does.

I loosen my breath, trying to shake the stress and nausea from my body.

Ivy pretends not to notice the tension still sitting in the room like swamp water.

"Want to go for a walk?" she asks. Her voice is as brittle as leaves. She looks as misplaced as I feel.

"Sure," I say.

Outside, it's easier to breathe.

"I think Hazel's been trying to get a sense of what it's been like for Juniper here," Ivy says carefully.

"Can't have been the best," I admit. "But she chose it."

"Yeah."

We move toward the tree line, both of us gulping down the fresher air, eager for distance.

"I don't remember it being quite so . . ." Ivy trails off.

"Green?" I offer.

"Exactly."

I take a long breath. "The house has withered more than I remember, but the forest—it's always been like this."

I glance at her. Neat clothes, clean hair, an aura of stillness she never had back then. All her cunning has left her.

"The promotion," I say carefully. "What does it mean for you?"

Ivy moves a branch out of her way with the gentleness of a soft person. "I'm an accountant now," she says, like it's nothing. "Not a junior anymore. Thank you for encouraging me to go for it."

For Ivy, it's everything. In a world that once devoured her, she's carved a quiet life—and I could weep from the miracle of that.

Safe.

She is safe.

"And . . ." I hesitate to ask because I hate the question being directed at me. "Is there . . . someone?"

Ivy picks at her nails. They are short and clean and unobtrusive. Her movements are those of a person used to dirt gathered there. A tick of swiping it away, one nail beneath the next.

"There was someone," she says. "But . . . I don't know."

She glances at me, and I don't press.

She doesn't look at me when she asks, "And you?"

"Many someones over the years. I don't really do long term."

Ivy nods. "My issue is space. Laura—" She stops short, breath caught like a snag in thread.

"She's the someone?"

A long silence. Then: "Yeah."

"But you're unsure?"

A hollow laugh. "I'm unsure of everything. It's like I'm waiting for something . . . I don't even know what."

"For Holly," I whisper.

She crumples then, and buries her head in shaking hands. "I'm always waiting for her," she whispers.

"Being here is . . ." I falter.

The words curl back into my throat like smoke. This is dangerous ground. To speak the truth would be too sharp—that this place is cruel, that she should never have been dragged into its splinters, that we are already fractured, all of us, cracked along the grain in ways no one else can see.

Instead, I shake my head and say, "I just wonder what I might have been, if not for Beltane."

She nods. Wipes her face. "It changed us." Her voice is hoarse. "Changed our trajectory. I always thought it meant something that none of us got married, none of us had kids . . ."

I shift my weight, suddenly aware of the plants beneath my shoes. I don't want to follow her down this path, of imagining what we may or may not be paying a price for.

"Mom and Dad weren't the best examples," I say.

Ivy looks at me quietly. "It's more than that."

I meet her eyes, but only because I don't want to look away first. I raise my brows—half a question, half a challenge. The look I give her says, "And?"

She is the one to break. She stares at her feet, and murmurs, "'*The Holly and the Ivy*' . . ." her voice trailing away into another whisper.

We drift to safer ground—updates, anecdotes, small comforts. Her apartment.

A goldfish named Moon. A life that doesn't claw at her.

I tell her about my book piles, my glass cabinets of relics—objects holding other lives, waiting to be needed again. Carved furniture, clever hinges, hidden stories.

She scratches her arms at the mention of dust. And I remember how small she was after Holly . . . How she'd fold into herself, how she wouldn't sit, wouldn't touch. How she wiped the mug's lip before sipping.

I dig in my bag and extract my disposable wipe, offering her one. She looks at me sideways, then takes it with a small thanks and wipes furiously at her hands.

"I don't know when I became so particular," she murmurs. "I just . . ."

"You like what you like," I say.

She stops walking and looks at me. Really looks. Then smiles. "I like what I like."

As if I've given her a truth to hold. Language to use.

We keep walking, never daring to touch the wounds. No talk of partners.

No talk of childhood. No talk of what happened after. And certainly not of each other. Nothing that will disrupt the status quo.

But the subject we've skirted finally finds us.

"Juniper's not well," Ivy says, eyes on the water.

We've arrived back at the dock without planning to, perhaps because we're both questioning why on earth we've let ourselves come here. It's clear we both want to leave as soon as possible. If Henry were still here, I'd climb in the boat and ask him to ferry us away right now. I don't want to walk uphill again, don't want to carry this weight.

"She won't come with us," I say. "She's too far gone."

"Maybe she will," Ivy hedges. "If we find the right words."

"I don't know."

Ivy pockets the wipe, glancing behind us. "We should head back. Before dark."

I give her a look, and she colors.

Then I give her a one-armed side hug, pulling her into me.

"Sorry I'm so . . ." Her voice trails off again. "It's just . . . alone, I'm nothing."

I squeeze harder. "You're wrong."

She puts her head on my shoulder, and we just watch the fading sky.

"I'm sorry I've been so distant. I'm going to change that."

She watches me, but I keep my eyes on the horizon. An eddy of wind catches my hair like a promise.

Or a lie.

I've made so many mistakes.

I don't know how to unmake them.

And then Hazel's words drift back to me. *We came in together. Ivy and me. On that broken old boat with Ernest.*

If that's true, then how did Henry know about the letter? I sure as hell didn't tell him.

# 15

***September 1999***

The banisters are strung with red-and-orange autumn ivy, the windowsills padded with moss, a velvet hush against the glass. Lichen, fragrant and fresh from the trees, has been tucked with care between hearthstone and wall, all in readiness for the celebration.

The skull of an elk, which Ernest shot, and which has been sitting in the cellar for twenty years, has been hung on the formal living room wall above the fireplace, which dances with merry little flames. Proud as Daudir Himself.

Tomorrow, Poppy turns four. And Granny Alys, with a spark in her eye, has declared that a party is just the thing. Here, in this room where memory and myth mingle, the party will unfold.

"Technically," Holly had said, all sly delight. "Tomorrow is at midnight."

Granny's smile stretched, gleaming like frost in moonlight. "Then we'd best begin. Midnight is only seven hours away."

The twins had shrieked and spun, clapping like birds taking flight. A party. A *real* one, for them. Not one observed from the quiet upstairs, or peeked through staircase slats, while their parents laughed elsewhere.

Poppy, thrilled without knowing why, let out a gleeful scream and ran shrieking through the rooms, trailing joy in her wake like ribbon.

The air tingled with something electric. Expectation. Wonder. It passed through them all.

Hazel has been making flower chains for hours, braiding the last garden blooms and dried bundles from the storeroom into curtains, into her hair, into the canopies of their beds. She drapes them from the mantel, humming, skimming across the floor like a breeze. Her hands are reverent. Every petal touched is a secret kept.

The rabbit masks—papier-mâchéd last week—are dry now, strung with twine, and ready for the night's dances. Hazel made a snide remark about them looking more like hares, but surrendered to the moment after Poppy's wails of "*My wabbits!*" split the room like thunder.

Juniper and Granny Alys swung into action and adjusted two of Granny's dresses so they fit the girls, white ones with lace edges and long sleeves. A big iron pot of rabbit stew flavored with cloves, nutmeg, and cinnamon has been simmering on the fireplace for an hour, watched over by Willow and Poppy, an ever-babbling sentry.

Clem has been sewing buttons into the eyeholes of the rabbit masks as a surprise—a pair in each of their colors. She's also sewn white ones into her old mask, the one from spring when Granny Alys first showed her how. It's not perfect, but it's infused with her enthusiasm. White is all colors at once, she remembers. A small thing she learned in school—another world now, half fogged and far away.

They are the Ward rainbow that makes up their grandmother. Granny Alys, like Beltane, has become her home. Clem no longer fights this fact. Granny Alys has become, in the last six months, one of her favorite people. Clem can't even count the number of times she has stayed up late talking to her, Juniper and Hazel joining them most nights, the four Wards talking of all manner of things on the porch as the heat of summer bled into autumn and the rains began again in earnest. Those nights gave Clem a particular feeling in her lungs, like she might burst with the happiness of it, but also, somehow, like she wanted to cry. She doesn't understand the contradiction of being so happy that it makes her sad.

As a gift to her sisters, Clem also raids her ribbon stash and winds some of the prettiest samples into the ivy on the banister, bringing more pops of color into the space. By the time midnight has come, even a cake has been prepared by Juniper, while Granny Alys ties off the last of the stitches on the twins' dresses.

They gather in the dining room, five hours after their simple dinner of bread and butter, and they sing "Happy Birthday" and blow out four tea candles wedged into the cake.

Poppy is *four*. Four years old already.

"Time flies," Ivy says to Holly.

"Just over a year," Holly says to Ivy, "and we'll be teenagers."

Clem winces, just a little. She doesn't like how they wish time away, skipping over their birthday coming up this November and right to the one *after*. Not here. Not now. Not in this forest where the clocks don't chase them. Here, she reminds herself, the outside world can't find them. Like Granny Alys, they are safe. Beltane watches, and Daudir protects. Newsprint ages quietly in the corner, its stories fading to myth beside the fairy tales on Granny's shelves.

As long as they follow the rules, everything will be perfect.

They cut the cake at the dining room table, the bare window like a black gaping hole that makes Clem shiver, until Hazel suggests they move into the living room. Clem readily agrees, and the eight of them feast on gritty chocolate cake on the sofas, and on the floor.

When the grandfather clock chimes the one o'clock morning hour, Granny Alys gets stiffly to her feet.

"You're going already?" Juniper asks, pretty smudges of chocolate on her cheeks. She turned seventeen last month but refused a celebration. Hazel will be next, fifteen in less than a month, and Clem knows she will want a party even grander than this.

Granny Alys gives a tired smile. "You children enjoy the witching hours. My skeleton's begun to sing with the dark. I must go hush the bone birds."

Juniper grins, and Clem does too. What a strange way to say she has creaky old joints. Clem has heard them crack when she rises to her feet or crouches in the garden. She has also seen how Granny Alys's hands shake when the day gets late, more and more now that the air is growing colder. Clem supposes that when the hairs on her own head turn white as Granny's have, her skeleton will sing too.

"Good night, Granny," Juniper calls, and the others echo her. A chorus of murmured *good nights*, blown kisses, and teary smiles.

"G'night, Nana," Poppy yells from the chaise longue before promptly falling asleep again, a glob of cake in her hair.

Granny Alys takes a candle with her and heads for the stairs, a solitary figure moving shadows as she goes.

# 16

***September 2024***

The cabin stands hunched against the gathering wind, windows glowing faintly in the dusk. I climb the path with fists clenched and breath rising in sharp bursts. The letter—creased, rain spotted, damning—is folded tightly in my pocket. I hadn't told anyone about it. Not a soul.

Yet Henry had known.

I don't knock, not properly. I just hit the door with the flat of my hand before shoving it open.

Inside, the cabin smells of pine sap and fire. Henry starts as I come in, half rising from his seat at the table, one hand still pressed around a glass of something amber. Ernest is here, too, slumped in a battered armchair by the hearth, half lost in shadow.

My voice rings out like flint on steel. "You knew."

Henry shakes his head. "Knew?"

"About the letter." I fling it at him. It spins through the air and lands at his feet.

"Clem—"

"You knew about the letters." My voice cracks, not with grief but with fury. "I never told you I got one. Not once. And you didn't ferry Hazel and Ivy across. So tell me. How the hell did you know?"

The envelope flutters like an injured bird on the floorboards. Ernest doesn't even blink.

Henry studies it, then meets my eyes. "Because I'm the one who sent them."

The words punch the breath from my lungs, even though I had begun to suspect as much.

"What?"

"Over the summer," he says quietly. "Juniper begged me to have them delivered. She's not well, Clem. I couldn't say no."

My mouth opens. Closes. I glance at Ernest, who stares into the fire like it might answer something for him.

"How did you know where to send them?"

"Juniper gave me Ivy's address."

I shake my head, trying to fit everything together. "And Hazel's?"

"Ivy gave me Hazel's address when I went to see her." He pauses, waiting for me to digest the information.

"You . . . you went to see Ivy in Chicago?"

Henry nods, taking the last sip from his glass as if bracing for something unpleasant still to come.

"And she gave me yours," he says.

I hold up my hand. "Wait. Wait a minute . . . Ivy gave you my address?"

It's like I'm still tuned to him, somehow, after all this time. Even though he isn't the same boy, but a middle-aged man, I can feel him tense, hear the strain in his voice when he says, "Yeah."

Still, I can't accept it. "No." I shake my head. "No, she wouldn't give my safety away like that. She wouldn't. She—"

He says my address out loud, three little sentences, the name of my shop, the number, the street, and the postcode, laying it in the air like a projector screen.

"It was unaddressed," I say weakly. "You . . . you came to my home?"

He shifts his weight from foot to foot, eyes darting anywhere but mine. "No. I have a friend in London. He owed me a favor."

My voice shakes at first, low and disbelieving. "You . . . you *what*?"

The words taste like acid. My vision tunnels, heat rising under my skin.

"You gave a fucking stranger my home address?"

He takes a full step back, and Ernest gets quietly to his feet, menacing in the dark.

I swallow hard as Henry stares at the floor, jaw working like he's chewing on words he can't swallow, spit out, or take back.

"You just, what, didn't tell me?" I say, quieter now. "After everything?"

Ernest speaks then, his voice dry as old bark. "Eh, this looks like Ward drama, *non*? Nothing to do with us. It's time you stop taking more than what you're owed."

My glare snaps to him. "Why are you even here? This has nothing to do with you."

Ernest meets my gaze with something unreadable, steps menacingly closer, and then walks past me, almost brushing my shoulder in the process.

"*L'arbre pourrit à partir de la racine,*" he mutters as he swings the cabin door open for me. "Out."

I grit my teeth, staring daggers into his hateful old face, then spin on my heel and storm outside. I expect him to slam the door behind me, but Henry follows, closing it quietly instead.

I head down the incline, fury pulsing at my temples. Henry stops me with a tap to my arm.

"Clem, wait."

I spin to face him. "Why? There's not much more I want to hear at this point."

Henry rubs wearily at his face. "Just . . . ignore my father. Let me explain."

"Explain how you gave away my only safety net to some stranger? Explain how my sister betrayed me by giving it away to *you*? For what? For *Juniper*?"

Henry looks back at the cabin, hesitates, then pulls me toward the rickety old shack of a shed a little farther up the track.

"Get off me," I snap, but I keep walking in that direction.

I slam through the door, needing to break something. Needing to hear the smack of noise to prove my anger is real and not just . . . not just sadness.

Henry closes the door behind us and grabs a flashlight from one of the shelves. Dust hovers in the beam of the light as he hangs it from a rusty hook in the low ceiling. Shelves sag with corroded tools and old oilcans. Everything reeks of cedar and damp rope.

I pace like a caged thing. Henry leans against the door, watching me.

"Stop looking at me," I snap, and I sound like a petulant teenager even to myself. I pause, rub my eyes, and lean my head against the wooden slats. "Why did you do it? Why travel to Chicago? Why even agree to send the letters in the first place?"

There is a long silence, so long I turn to see if he's left. But he's watching me, those dark eyes inscrutable.

"You don't want to know the real answer."

I probably don't.

"Why?" I insist again.

"I wanted to see you."

I laugh, but it sounds bitter and broken. "Right."

"I wanted answers. I wanted to know why, after everything that happened, you chose to ghost me. And I wanted to see you."

"Why didn't you come to London, then?"

"Thought about it. Almost did. Kept the letter a full month before I sent it on to Dave."

I assume Dave is his London friend. The one who now knows my address.

"You thought sending my address to a total stranger was, what, perfectly okay?"

"He's not a stranger. He's a friend. From school. He helped me after . . . you know. After you left."

We stare at each other with growing tension that morphs into something . . . more.

Time bleeds away. Resistance bleeds away. In its place, something fevered. Something urgent.

The air between us is soaked in memory, heat on summer skin, sweat in hollows—and something older, something that never died, just went dormant under years of silence and growing up.

He touches my jaw like he's afraid I'll vanish again, thumb brushing over the line where I'm already trembling. I catch his wrist and hold it there. Just hold it. The shape of his bones under skin I used to know. We're older now. Softer in some ways, harder in others. And he's looking at me like I'm still fifteen.

We shouldn't be here—not like this, not after everything. But then his mouth is sweet on my mouth, his body pressed against mine, and the years collapse like rotten wood.

He pulls away. "You didn't change," he says, voice low.

"You did," I whisper, feeling the sharpness of stubble on his cheeks.

His mouth finds mine again before I can think better of it—warm, unsure for a breath, then deepening like he's falling into something he's been trying not to want. He kisses like a man who's missed something for half a lifetime. Hands gripping my waist, sliding under my shirt like he's starving for skin. I feel it, too, low in my belly, crawling up my spine. His hands are rough, warm, and when he palms my breast through my bra, I gasp against his lips. He growls low in his throat like the sound of me does something to him. I think it always did.

We stumble back into the cluttered dark of the shed, tripping over boots and buckets, knocking into the workbench like we're drunk on the past. My shirt goes first, then his. I press my mouth to his chest, tasting salt and heat and something bitter, memories I won't face. He groans when I scrape my teeth along his ribs, going lower.

"I missed this," he mutters, pulling me back up and then dragging my jeans down over my hips, fingers fumbling with the button. "Missed you."

My skin remembers him before my mind does. I arch into his touch, gasping softly when he mouths along my collarbone, slow and hungry. It's not gentle. It's not polished. But it's real. We know how to be careful—we just don't want to be.

He pulls off my underwear, and I hear material rip. The cool air hits me before his fingers do—two of them sliding over me, testing how wet I already am. He doesn't speak, just watches me, eyes dark and unsteady.

"Clementine," he says, voice husky.

"Don't stop."

He doesn't. He slips two fingers inside me and curls them just right, just like he used to on those long summer nights. My head falls back, hips rocking up to meet his hand. The sound of it—slick, shameless—fills the shed.

I slide my hands over his chest, feel the warmth of him, the muscle, the time. He hisses when I press my mouth to the hollow of his throat. There's a desperation in him, something just beneath the surface, and I match it.

I reach for his belt, tug it open, push his jeans down just enough. He springs free, thick and flushed, and I wrap my hand around him. He swears under his breath, hips bucking into my palm. We're both panting now, both shaking.

He presses into me with a low, broken sound, inch by inch, until he's buried to the hilt. I cling to him, fingers digging into his back, my mouth open in a gasp that turns into a moan. Our hips find each other like magnets. There's no ceremony—just friction, breath, the thump of his heart against mine.

We move together like we remember how, here against the shack wall. The rhythm is raw, imperfect. My legs wrap around his waist, and I bury my face in his neck to muffle the sounds I can't stop making.

"Henry," I whisper into his shoulder, nails biting into flesh.

We say each other's names like prayers, or curses, or maybe both.

I come first—tightening around him, crying out as everything coils and shatters. A breaking. A reclaiming. He follows with a cry that sounds torn from somewhere deep, spilling inside me with a shudder.

He slumps against me, heart thudding against my ear, chest heaving. I stare up at the spiderwebs above us, threads catching light like ash in water.

For a long time, neither of us speaks.

Then I extricate myself from beneath him and wordlessly dress. This was a patch, a lovely one. A desperate one. But there is still so much unsaid. Something has changed now, though.

And neither of us can pretend it hasn't.

# 17

***November 1999***

Even the air holds its breath.

A preternatural stillness. An emptiness. Beltane—usually nosing in with creaks and pops, shifts in timber and stone, breath in, breath out, as the night settles over the island—is silent.

The house feels quiet this morning. Unusually cold. None of the fires have been lit. The kitchen is still asleep, the normal cooking sounds absent. The feeling of presence, of home, is missing from within the walls. Emptiness floats outward from the source, an infection. A ripple.

Juniper steps close to Granny Alys's bed. Takes the old hand in hers. Drops it just as suddenly. Steels herself. Takes it up again. Squeezes it between two quivering palms.

A smattering of snow fell in the night, blanketing the world in a brilliant but temporary hush and marking the beginning of real winter.

Never has a November felt so cold.

Now, even colder.

They say it looks like sleeping, death. It doesn't. Granny Alys isn't here anymore. Clem knows this. But still, she sits in Granny's chair. The one by the bed, not the one by the wardrobe. She sits, and she watches her grandmother, doing her best to pretend she's just sleeping.

She squints her eyes. Just . . . sleeping.

But the reality of Granny Alys's shell is a horror. Pale and waxy, gray verging on yellow. Skin sagging in a way it never did in life, dripping toward the bed with a waxy lack of tension only death can achieve.

No, this isn't sleep. Not even the faintest imitation.

It's a void.

An abyss.

A terror.

Clem wishes she could close up this dollhouse and reset it, fresh and new for tomorrow, all the pieces back where they should be.

Poppy comes next, sucking her thumb, dragging her blankie. Her cheeks are ruddy, eyes glistening—as though she knows what she's going to find already.

As if she found her first.

Clem hates the thought. The idea that it could have been little Poppy to find this emptiness without them by her side.

"Nana," she says, her voice choked with sleepy tears. "Nana Alys." She says it to Clem as if pointing it out. As if to say, "I found this. Can you see this? Can you change this?"

Clem opens her arms, and when Poppy clumsily toddles over, falling into them, she lifts her up and holds her close, feeling her little heart hammer against her ribs.

The others don't take long.

Hazel is the first to cry. A little chipmunk hiccup that she tries to hide.

Clem can't find tears, just a yawning emptiness. She failed again. Another connection, severed. Another love, lost. If she thinks about it too long, her skin begins to tighten, her heart to drum. Her mind pinwheels from one terror to the next. Looking around the room, she has a crazy impulse to shove her sisters away—like loss might be catching. Like it's spreading right now, unseen, toward them, dense and dangerous as a storm cloud. Her hand twitches, but she forces it to still. She tries to remember Granny Alys's voice. The cadence, the texture. It had reminded her of an old jukebox their father had for a few months when they first moved into the big New York apartment. Musical but old, scratchy with time.

They sit for a long time, none of them daring to speak. Sunlight and shadow evade one another over the floorboards, punctuated by a sniffle or soft cry. There is no language for this; not even their secret one has the syllables needed to utter this grief.

After the shadows have won the war over the day, someone breaks the silence.

"What happens now?" Hazel asks. She's wringing her hands like a washcloth, the skin twisting and growing red. "Do we call someone?"

"How?" Ivy says. "There's no phone."

"We'll have to go to the man who brought us here. Ernest. Henry said he lives on the other side of the island."

"It shouldn't be hard to find," Holly reasons.

Panic rises in Clem like a viper, poisonous. Leaving? They're leaving? She looks at Granny Alys, hoping she'll object, but of course she just lies there, empty.

Unreality bathes the moment in a haze.

"He'll have to go to the mainland and get someone," Hazel says, pacing at the foot of the bed. "Right?"

They look to Juniper, who has said nothing. She is standing with her hands folded in front of her, the corners of her mouth turned downward as though on two little strings. She is deep in her mind, wandering corridors they can't see. The silence stretches like a Slinky, and Hazel stops pacing, moves from foot to foot, her agitation growing in size.

"Well?" she snaps eventually.

"Granny Alys told me what to do," Juniper says at last, the Slinky snapped closed. "She said this might happen, and she told me what to do."

Relief. It washes over Clem, extinguishing the fiery panic in one fell swoop. Of course she did. Granny Alys would have prepared Juniper for everything.

"What did she say?" Willow asks, breathless with want. With need.

"She told me to remind you all," Juniper says slowly, looking at each of them in turn. With careful intention. With a warning. "What happens when someone dies. To remind you what happened when Mom and Dad died."

Willow's voice is small. "We . . . we were taken away."

Juniper nods. "We were taken away. The apartment was taken away. All our things were taken away. They gave us to Granny Alys because she's family. But she is—*was*—also the last family. There's no one else left."

"Who will they give us to?" Ivy asks, and Clem can hear the panic beginning to infect her too.

Juniper looks pointedly at Hazel, daring her to answer.

Hazel's eyes dart around, panicked. "Well, we can't just—"

"The state," Juniper finishes. "We'll become wards of the state. That means strangers. An institution. Foster care."

Ivy shrinks, and Holly casts out nervously for her hand, finding it and gripping tight.

Juniper strokes Granny Alys's hair again. "We'll be put in the system."

Poppy cries, snuffling closer to Clem, as if desperate to burrow into her lap and hide.

"It's okay," Clem murmurs, holding her even tighter. "That's not going to happen."

"No," Juniper agrees. "It's not."

"What did Granny Alys say to do?" Holly asks.

"She told me that Daudir wants her to remain at Beltane. And for us to remain too." She gives the girls that measured look again, like a dare, like a challenge, like inevitability.

Hazel laughs, shaking her head. "I don't believe you," she says, and her voice is also infected with the hints of something. Hysteria.

"I heard her say it," Clem says, before Hazel can work herself up, before she can drive a wedge into the middle of their family.

Hazel turns to her, eyes wide.

"I was spying," Clem says, glancing at Juniper. "Granny Alys said we need to stay at Beltane. Beltane will protect us. As long as we follow the rules."

Hazel looks at Clem like she's made out of betrayal. Like she can't believe what she's hearing. "Or what?" she spits, a challenge.

Clem's skin feels like it's being replaced with hard scales, the kind that can no longer be hurt by Hazel's temper.

"Granny Alys told Juniper what would happen if we broke the rules," she says. "Daudir is kind, but Daudir is also wild. Untamed. If you defy Him—" Clem breaks off, the edges of her imagination stuttering.

"We'll be punished," Willow says quietly. "It's true. I can feel it. The Guardian rock told me so. Months ago."

Hazel is floundering now, Clem can see. But the fight hasn't quite gone out of her yet.

"The Watchers in the woods whisper to me," Willow says again, dreamlike, filling the gap where Hazel might have had her last chance to convince anybody of something else. A moment that is quashed into nothing.

"Willow has the Sight," Juniper says, just as she said on the day they found the Guardian's face rock.

Granny Alys's words come back to Clem. *The Forgotten God of the Wood protects the Wards because our bloodline contains the Sight.*

It's true. It's all true . . .

"We have to pay tribute," Juniper says. "We have to thank Daudir for Granny Alys's life and return her spirit to the Wood. And we have to take up the mantle of the Guardian."

Hazel looks like she wants to scream, but Clem can see it: doubt. She's doubting herself. Doubting her next course of action.

*Good,* Clem thinks. She needs to accept the forest into her heart. She needs to take in Daudir and all that Daudir brings.

Juniper tucks the blanket, a white knitted affair that has come down around Granny Alys's waist, back up over her shoulders. She combs stray hairs out of Alys's face, smoothing down the waves so they fall to her side like the riverweed Clem always thought they resembled.

"We'll get some flowers tomorrow," she says. "The mahonia cultivars should still be blooming."

"It's snowing," Clem says gently.

"There will be some left. And if not, we'll get the leaves of the evergreens. Tuck them around her, make a nest, safe and warm."

"It's almost seven."

It's Willow who whispers it, and none of them asks how she knows.

Juniper nods, takes a deep breath, and gets to her feet. She kisses Granny Alys on the forehead, and goes to the door. Hazel reluctantly follows in her step: kiss, retreat.

Clem and Poppy are the last to move. Clem is tempted to stay here, fearing that movement will make this real—solidify it in some irreversible way. But Granny Alys gave them three rules, and that's all.

The least she can do is to keep them intact.

The food is simple. Bread. Mushrooms from the pantry. Cheese, dried apples, and a bottle of old homemade elderberry wine. Granny Alys pressed it with her own two feet. The handwritten label is dated three years before. Clem has an impulse to refuse it, to try to save it. It could be the last one Granny Alys made. The last bit of her left.

Silly . . .

Juniper pops the cork and pours a measure into their favorite mugs, plus an eighth in Granny Alys's.

"Daudir," Juniper murmurs, and her voice seems to expand in the space.

Even the black beyond the giant window appears to stand to attention, ears pricked.

"Watch over Granny Alys," she continues. "Guide her into your mossy embrace. The forest welcomes her home. The earth beckons her feet onward. Continue to watch over us and show us your benevolence. As Wards we ask and command it. *Daudir, kemempru gi'emres.* Daudir, keep her. Daudir, preserve her."

Clem lifts her mug, her hand shaking. "Daudir preserve her."

"Daudir preserve her."

"Daudir preserve her."

"Daudir preserve her."

"Daudir preserve her."

Poppy sniffles, half asleep. "Daudir."

The forest is witness to their meal, another rule followed, another tradition honored.

When they're done, they migrate back to Granny Alys's room like a fledgling flock of geese.

On padded feet, they climb into bed beside Granny Alys and fall asleep.

# 18

***September 2024***

Back in the house, Juniper has prepared a meal. Candles flicker low on the table—lit directly on the wood, their wax bleeding slow tears onto the grain. The sight makes my inner antiques dealer twitch. Juniper herself looks eerie and alarming, cavern-eyed, thin as dusk. The shadows hollow out her eyes in the same way they used to do to Granny Alys. She looks skeletal, otherworldly. Deranged.

I pass a disposable wipe to Ivy without a word. She takes it with a glance of quiet gratitude and scrubs down her chair with the kind of precision usually reserved for surgery. Hazel catches my eye and mouths, "Me too?" A petty instinct to pretend I didn't see it is quickly quashed by years of distance. I slip a wipe into her hand as Juniper turns to the woodstove. She's plating dinner.

These are the same plates.

"Just like old times," Hazel says, her smile tight as a wire.

An imaginary clock chimes in my bones. I glance down at my watch. Seven o'clock. Of course.

I wonder how Juniper keeps time with the grandfather clock broken. Maybe there's still a battery ticking somewhere in this house of rot. Or maybe she just feels it—like a tide, a ritual etched into her marrow.

She spoons out lumpy stew—gray, green, and grave-dirt brown. A little cloud of steam rises from each bowl, thick with a smell that clings to the back of the throat. We wait, spoons idle, as she lowers herself into the chair at the head of the table. Her eyes close.

She exhales.

"Forgotten Daudir," she intones quietly, sending a ripple of unease through us. "Your daughters have returned, just as I promised. Just as I swore. We give thanks for your bounty. We honor your glory. Bless us with your mercy, Harbinger of Death."

The words slither across the table like a snake. Hazel scoffs under her breath. Ivy shifts. I sit very still, waiting for this to be over.

The first bite tastes like damp soil and secrets. Mushrooms. Moss. Rain pooled in stone. It's the flavor of the woods we once ran through barefoot, the taste of leaf rot and stories whispered under blankets. I chew, slow and aching. No wonder Juniper is vanishing.

"You need to come with us," I say, grit of fleshy mushroom and soil in my teeth.

Ivy and Hazel glance at me. For one flickering, hallucinatory instant, they look like hares frozen in moonlight—silent, alert, fragile. Two giant white rabbits in jeans and shirts, forks paused halfway to harelips. My heart stumbles. But no. Just my sisters. Tired women waiting for someone to lead.

Juniper lifts another spoonful of stew, steam coiling like incense, a puff of moss and mold rising into the air, invisible.

"Everything is as it should be," she says.

I release a quick breath, exhaling contamination. "June, enough. You're clearly suffering here, so we're leaving tomorrow and you're coming too."

She slams down her spoon, flicks of food laughing into the air. "I'm thriving!"

"You're emaciated!" I match her volume. "Tell me exactly how your Forgotten God is taking care of you when your body is eating itself alive?"

The tendons in her neck distend, thick as tree roots, and her lips go thin. "Daudir provides."

I point, sharp. "Does he provide the needle you've been using to scar yourself?"

Juniper runs a hand over her tattoos, crude images of mushrooms, plants, spiders, antlers. "They're tributes. Sacrifices. Offerings."

*"Mutilations."*

"Clem—" Ivy's hand finds the table, reaching gently for mine.

Juniper cuts her off. "Granny Alys—"

"Granny Alys taught us to respect the forest using a fairy tale!" I shout, standing so fast my chair shrieks against the floor. "Allegories. *Children's* stories. Something we'd understand. That's all. She didn't even know Daudir's name! The name *we* gave it!"

Juniper's eyes catch mine, dull and bottomless, long gone from any sense of reason. It's like looking at someone who is brain dead. Like someone halfway between prayer and madness.

"He is Forgotten," Juniper says, soft as dust.

"Daudir isn't real!" I scream, and my voice echoes back tenfold.

"Clem, please," Ivy begs, standing now too. Her hand catches my forearm. "Stop. Beltane has her. She's not ready."

Juniper sits rigid, breath sharp through her teeth, ribs flaring like a xylophone in distress.

The silence thickens.

Hazel clears her throat. "We should . . . eat. She went to all this trouble."

She gives me a look. Something close to pleading. I want to rage, to crack this table in two. To force them to stop indulging in this fantasy. But Ivy's hand stays on my arm, anchoring me.

So, bitterly, I sit.

We eat. Slowly. Grimly. One spoonful at a time. Even Juniper, eventually, picks up her spoon, smiling in that awful beatific way that makes me want to run screaming into the sea.

The plates empty. Miraculously.

We clean them together in silence, scrubbing chipped crockery under the faucet, the sink filled with well water Juniper pumped in herself. She doesn't complain. Doesn't speak.

After an awkward good night, I head up to my old room, not relishing the prospect of climbing into the damp bed, sliding into those mildewy covers. Again, I wonder what madness made me get on that plane in London. Twelve hours in a cramped seat, and for what? Next time, I want silk sheets, a claw-foot tub, and chocolates left on the pillow.

The house groans as we climb the stairs—like it's remembering how to fall apart. The whole thing could collapse on our heads while we sleep.

Behind me, the corridor stretches long and dark. I shut and lock my door.

An hour later, a tentative knock. The door creaks open like a groan, and Ivy pops her head in.

"Can I?"

I lift the blanket. She slides in beside me, teeth already chattering.

"Yours is wet too?"

"'Fraid so. But it'll warm up faster with two of us."

We lie together in silence, warmth spreading between us like a slow miracle.

After a beat, she speaks again. "You shouldn't have attacked her."

"I know," I mutter. "This place makes me feel like I'm unraveling. I lose myself in it a bit. And she needs to face reality," I add.

"It won't help to beat her over the head with what she won't see. She's been here for twenty-five years, Clem. *Twenty-five* years. Alone. She didn't get a dose of the world outside of Beltane like we have. She never got a normal life. She needs care. Gentle care."

I'm shaking my head before she's finished, even though I know she's right. I don't have the patience for tact the way I used to. I've lost my once-great skill for peacemaking, for meekness, for silence, and for obeyance.

"She's too far gone, Ives."

But Ivy hasn't lost her rosy glasses yet. "Maybe not."

I want to believe her. But the woman out there is no one I recognize.

Ivy settles against me, and we fall into silence, broken when the door creaks open again. Hazel hurries inside, and Ivy opens the blanket in welcome. The three of us huddle close, shivering in the moldy sheets like the orphans we are. Just like old times.

"This fucking sucks balls," Hazel whispers, her teeth chattering, and it's so perfectly her that hysterical laughter bubbles up my throat, punctuating the air like a rifle.

Ivy begins giggling as well, until the room is full of melancholy amusement.

"God, your toes are ice," I mutter, still laughing as I kick Hazel's feet away.

"No shit, Sherlock. I need your heat—come back!"

She hooks her feet around mine and yanks them closer.

A noise outside the door makes us stop, and we listen. When it opens, Juniper enters, a silhouette. A shade.

"Just like it was always meant to be," she murmurs, her dead-eyed smile so creepy I want to crawl out of my skin.

"Juni," I say, tentative. "I was thinking that, if you want, we could go off island. Find offerings for Daudir. Toys for the Forgotten God. Supplies?"

Juniper just stands there. She smiles her eerie smile, shadows pooling in the hollows of her face.

"You can try," she says.

She turns, still smiling, and leaves us alone, shutting the door firmly behind her instead of climbing in with us, no doubt off to haunt some other rotten part of the house.

"She agreed," Ivy breathes.

"Not exactly," I say.

Hazel snuggles back down into the damp sheets. "It's as close as we're going to get."

"So, we'll leave in the morning, then?" Ivy asks.

I nod. "Agreed."

"Agreed," Hazel intones, yawning.

Well, thank Daudir for that.

# 19

***November 1999***

Granny Alys has become a sacred thing.

It is Clementine who lays the beetles on her eyes—one shimmering green as polished candy glass, the other brown and cracked like aged bark. She almost mourns their presence, how they cover those feather-thin veins. Veins that are empty. Veins that are dead roots—just for show.

Poppy's fingers worry the pocket of her dress and draw out a dry, shriveled mushroom, placing it solemnly at the center of Granny's brow. A tiny black insect races across her head like a secret, and none of them move to brush it away.

"What's that for, poppet?" Juniper's voice is silk, her hands needling gently into Poppy's hair.

Poppy moves away from Juniper, away from the bed. "Her other eye."

Her other eye. Clem contemplates Granny's forehead and thinks, yes, that seems right.

Hazel runs Granny Alys's old phonograph in the corner, slowly turning the handle, and a tinny record plays the voice of someone from long ago. A woman singing about her lost love and the ocean that divides them. It makes Clem want to cry, but she doesn't. Instead, she lifts Poppy and together they sit in Granny Alys's chair. It feels like it's hers now. She and Poppy have been the only ones to use it since.

Beneath her beetles, Granny looks like she's listening to the song. Like she might cock her head and smile at any moment.

"She looks like an angel," Ivy says, brushing the back of the corpse's hand. On the other side, Holly mimics her. They always sit on the bed, one on either side of Granny, two little guardians.

Holly smiles. "A forest angel."

They have spent time tucking moss around her body. Putting patches of lichen on her arms. Acorns in her hair. Pine cones around her feet. She is a dead mural, a puzzle of human and forest. Ward and Wood.

Willow went looking for more flowers earlier in the day—just to the edge of the boundary. It didn't feel safe, she said, to step beyond it—even during the day. Not yet. Not quite yet. She had wanted to put flower petals between Granny Alys's lips like nectar, in case she wanted something sweet on the other side, but they have all died away now, buried beneath a thin crust of snow that is already climbing higher.

By the fire, Juniper crouches like a watchful crow, feeding the flame to keep the chill at bay. Two days have passed this way—silent, hushed. They only leave Granny's side to eat in the dining room at seven, and even then, Clem feels Daudir's gaze on them, as if they've overlooked some sacred rite.

But who is left to say what is proper?

Who is left to teach them ceremony?

Willow sits near the vanity as if listening for an answer, lips pinched white. Clem would reach out to comfort her, but Poppy is heavy and warm in her lap, and Clem can't make promises she doesn't believe.

By morning, Clem wakes to find Willow at the window, her breath fogging the glass, eyes fixed on the lightless forest. Clem rises and slips her fingers into Willow's cold hand. Willow neither flinches nor returns the touch.

"Are you okay?" Clem whispers.

The shake of Willow's head is almost imperceptible.

Clem swallows. "You feel it too?"

The look Willow gives is raw and trembling. "Something's wrong," she breathes.

"I know."

And as morning drags into afternoon, the house seems to shrink around them. They rise only to kiss Granny Alys's cold cheek in ritual greeting, soft lips to dead skin—a promise of love continued.

They eat dried plums and apples in the room and drink water pumped into the bathroom sink. They only leave to relieve their bladders but come right back after that is done.

But Willow cannot be still. She paces the floorboards like a restless ghost, leaning into the window as if hunting some distant shape. The twins murmur, a trembling litany, their voices like sharp needles stitching up the silence, the energy as palpable as two galaxies colliding. Tension twists between them, a gathering storm, until Willow is overcome.

"Something's wrong," Willow bursts at last, when the sun is sinking lower, back to pacing the room, her bare feet thumping on the floorboards, little drums. "Something's wrong."

The twins rise as one. "I think so too," Holly says, and Ivy repeats it. "I think so too."

Juniper unfurls. She lay on Granny Alys's right side in the night. Now as she stands, she dislodges some of the acorns from her hair. They roll onto the floor, more discordant drums, and Clem's skin feels like it has pinched too tight and will soon claw itself right off.

"There's something we've missed," Willow insists, eyes bright with a strange light. "Something we haven't done."

Juniper comes to Willow's side, stilling her with a hand to the shoulder. "We need to offer a sacrifice."

Juniper is so calm, so sure, and her purple dress is so regal and soothing that Clem's skin relaxes back into place again. Her ears strain for the answer, which will surely come in Juniper's voice, carrying the cadence of relief.

When Juniper looks up at them, her gaze is fathomless. "The forest requires tribute," she says. "A balance must be restored."

And they believe her.

Juniper goes to Granny Alys's vanity, opens the top drawer, and removes a small silver object. Clem can't tell what it is until Juniper sits beside Granny Alys and begins to clip her fingernails, collecting the little shards in the palm of her hand. When she's done, she smiles at them with a calmness that spreads through them like water.

They rise as one, like dancers pulled into a hypnotic rhythm. They scatter into the thin snow, barefoot, white as ghosts, a hush so deep it feels like prayer.

They kindle a flame at the clearing's heart. It is slow to take, but fire is hungry, no matter how cold, and soon the logs are dying.

Juniper scatters Granny's nails into the flames; they wink like fireflies before vanishing into black embers.

Caught up in the moment, Clem is unsure who makes the suggestion—or if anyone makes it at all. Perhaps it is simply understood, collectively, as the thing that must be done. The thing that was missing.

Juniper is the first to make the cut, however. Locks of silver-blond hair fall in ethereal whips to the ground until she has a jagged short haircut all around. She gathers her offering and throws it into the fire, watching as it sparks, glistens for a fraction of a second, and then curls into black threads of coiled char. Clem holds Poppy while Juniper cuts the fine blond hair away—this feels more like a sacrifice than anything else has. Poppy sucks on her thumb and watches the silk threads fall with wide, wondering eyes. Hazel, last, her hands steady as she lets go of what little softness she has left.

They all know the price is right, and the feeling that rises between them is Daudir.

Daudir's approval.

Daudir's blessing.

Daudir's unending love.

And then they dance.

Long into the deep, blue dusk they dance, feeding hair, and then dresses, into the hungry flames, dancing before the boundary of wood and bone, feet melting fragile snow, howling their grief at the moon.

For Granny Alys.

For their parents.

For themselves.

The flames never lick beyond the boundary, and Clem knows—can feel in her bones:

They have answered some call.

And they have been heard.

Clem stirs before the morning light, roused by a ghost of movement at the forest's edge. She blinks against the dark, sees only five shapes curled close to the dying fire—her sisters, pale and dusted with the scattered ash of their secret rite.

Hazel is not among them.

Without thought, Clem rises, feet soundless on the forest floor. Something draws her after a faint trail of sound, a sylvan whisper through the trees. Hazel's slender form glimmers just ahead, a forest nymph, and Clem keeps to the deeper shadows, waiting to see if Hazel needs help. She doesn't want to intrude if Hazel wants to grieve alone.

Down, down they go, until the trees part and the lake gleams, a polished mirror. Hazel hurries to the oldest hemlock, its hollow knot high and dark like an empty eye. Clem watches as her sister tucks a tiny tuft of white-gold hair inside—a fragile offering, or a wicked secret—before stepping into the water to wash ash from her skin.

And Clem's heart aches.

Her hair. Hazel kept some back, a small treasure, hidden and sacred, kept separate from the fire—and the rest of them.

Clem melts farther into the shadows, unnerved that Hazel is keeping secrets from the others. From her. She closes her eyes and waits, feeling the forest around her, waiting to see if Daudir is angry.

She listens, feeling the dark woods draw close, feeling Daudir in every hush and quiver of branch and wind.

She feels nothing.

Nothing but the breath of water and forest, gentle and untroubled.

Perhaps Daudir knows. Perhaps Daudir understands.

Perhaps Daudir, too, was once a child with something small and precious He could not let burn.

# 20

***September 2024***

By late morning, my bags are packed.

I'm ready to get out of here. I could barely sleep, no longer used to the noises of Beltane. The wind whispering to the leaves outside, the hoots of unseen owls, and the screeches of skittering creatures in the undergrowth. Beneath that, the creak of the house itself, settling into slumber, harmonizing with frogs in the distance. In London, the sound was always people and cars. People and cars. That's all. Predictable. Safe. Known.

I head down early, my roller case bumping against my leg like a tired dog. From the kitchen drifts the tang of iron and fire and something wilder: meat. Juniper stands before the stove, red chunks of meat sizzling in a battered skillet, quickly turning brown. She doesn't see me and bends down to feed a split log into the firebox, hair loose around her face, and for an aching instant I see Granny Alys resurrected. Granny Alys, whom, before today, had faded like an old photograph in my memory. A flat impression more than anything truly real. But here, it's like she's alive again. In the smells, in the walls—in Juniper.

"You have meat?" I manage, careful as a deer stepping into a clearing.

She looks up, cheeks flushed by heat, and smiles like someone who knows a secret. "Rabbit. Found it in my snare this morning."

My stomach knots. Rabbit—that old hunger, that old nausea. I know I won't eat so much as a mouthful. Already, I feel my skin tightening with the desperation to get away. Juniper won't waste any of it, I know, and visions of wide leporid eyeballs floating in my soup solidifies my intention to abstain.

"Daudir provides," she murmurs, and I roll grit between my teeth at her back.

"Is Ivy up yet?"

"Not yet."

"Hazel?"

"Outside."

I head out, leaving my case just inside the doorway in case of fickle rain. I still remember how it was: brilliantly sunny days turned stormy in moments, smell of petrichor in the air.

I need to find Henry. Need to feel someone rooted in the present. Need to plan an escape. And I need to *not* think about what we did in that shack out in the forest.

I just have to figure out how to bring Juniper with us. Yesterday, she had smiled that smile—the one that tells me she expects the forest itself to fight on her behalf. To rise up and hold on to her, as though Daudir will knot the trails and twist the tides just to keep her. And when that doesn't happen, when she's on the boat, staring back at Beltane growing smaller, and Daudir has done so much *nothing* to keep her, I have to be ready for her world to break. And her to break with it.

I'll need to catch the pieces.

By the time I reach the forest's edge, Hazel is already there, gazing into green shadows. Beyond the low bones of the old fence, the forest has crept back in, claiming its own. Bracken as high as my ribs. A patch where the firepit once glowed and we spun like moths in the dark.

I still remember the day I discovered that there were bones hammered into the earth between some of the wooden posts. The crazy way Granny Alys smiled and said, "Our ancestors. They keep the boundary safe." Like it was some necromantic kind of witchcraft—a perimeter built from corpses.

Hazel looks up as I approach, face painted too carefully, like waxwork. "Juniper hasn't been keeping up," she murmurs.

She looks like a clown doll, but I don't say that. We all have our masks.

I kick at a fern. "Juniper hasn't been maintaining anything." I look back at the house. "I don't think she can. It's too much to do for one person. And she's—well, look at her. She's starving."

"You think she'll come with us?"

"Leave Beltane?" I shake my head. "I don't know. Maybe. She sounded weird last night. Off."

"Maybe if we stayed a few more days, we could convince her. Maybe she just needs a bit more time with us, for normality to seep past her barriers."

I look back at the house, dark windows like the eyes of a spider, and I shiver.

"Look, do what you want. But I'm going to Henry. Ivy's still asleep. If you're coming with us, then wake her and get packed up. Be ready. And maybe . . . maybe pack Juniper a few things too."

Hazel stares into the trees for a long time. "You think we made it all up?" she says at last.

"Daudir?"

"Everything."

That stops me. Of all of us, Hazel was the last to believe. The last to give herself to the Wood. Yet here she is, voice trembling like an unsure prayer. She's asking *me*, convert Clem, who dove into all that hysteria with eyes wide open and ruined our family . . .

I feel the danger.

"Yes," I say firmly. "We were scared children who needed a myth to fill the dark. We lost everything for a warped fairy tale."

Hazel nods, too slowly. "I know. It's just . . . being back." She laughs, shakes her head. Like she can't believe she's saying it. "Last night I thought I heard something. Out there."

"You're not used to wild places," I say, forcing lightness. "It's creepy when you've been in a city for so long."

"Maine is very different," she admits. "Portland is loud, bustling, energetic. You can't be lonely there."

I hadn't known she was in Portland. But I suppose it makes sense. Just like Ivy moving to Illinois, Maine is far enough away from Washington state to try to forget. Not quite as far as London, but then, I had more to atone for.

Each of us carries a shard of Beltane like some cursed heirloom.

It occurs to me that I've barely asked Hazel a single question. Maybe that's on purpose. Getting to know her again feels . . . dangerous. Life has an equilibrium now that works for me. Hazel is, and always was, a spanner in the works. Someone I loved who wanted to hurt me.

She watches me a long time. "Want me to come with you to find Henry?"

"No," I say, too fast. "You stay. Pack. Look after Juniper." My heart thuds as I turn, my cheeks flaming to match. "I think I'll just wake Ivy myself before I go. Give her a chance to get ready."

Inside, Ivy's room is a blank stage, but her bag is here, already packed and ready to go. No Ivy, though.

I head back downstairs, seeking out Juniper. She's still cooking the rabbit, the meat now hidden in a huge pot of watery broth, spongy clumps of green bubbling on top.

"Still haven't seen Ivy?" I ask. "She wasn't in her room."

She looks up with sleepy eyes. "Oh. No, I haven't seen her. But don't worry. Daudir is watching over us."

Her smile is serene. Gross.

Achingly like Granny Alys.

I call Ivy's name into the house, into the garden, into the forest's edge—into Beltane—my voice sinking into the dark-green hush.

Nothing.

I bump into Hazel coming in, arms crossed against her ribs. She reads my face. "No sign?"

"No. She must have gone to Henry already. She was determined to leave."

"Would she have gone alone, though?"

"I don't know. Maybe."

I'm not convinced, but what other option is there?

"You sure you don't want me to come?" Hazel asks again.

I step around her. "Just get your things together, like I told you. Be ready to move when we get back." I pause at the threshold. "And like I said . . . grab some stuff for Juni as well."

She nods, still rubbing at her arms. "Be back before dark."

I clench my jaw and hurry outside.

I don't want to be back at this godforsaken cabin.

It's telling that Ernest chose to build it on this side of the island, the farthest place from civilization without actually being in the ocean.

"Henry?" I call, not wanting to intrude, hoping that I won't need to actually knock, feeling him between my legs, thick, hot, warm.

I shudder and clench my teeth, jaw beginning to ache with all the tension I'm biting back.

Henry comes to the window, peers out with a frown, and then his face brightens when he sees me.

I see his lips shape my name through the glass. "Clem."

Ernest comes around the side of the house, chewing tobacco and looking mean. *"Quoi?"* he spits.

Henry exits the shack, takes my arm, and pulls me away. "Come on. Let's talk in private."

For a moment, I think he's taking me back to the shed, and I don't fight it. But he stops short, in a small clearing in the forest where the trees are sparse and a glorious view of the Pacific stretching outward opens up my lungs.

This side of Beltane is more coastal. Unfamiliar and open. I prefer the cool shelter of sparse, salt-licked trees, the dance of sea air on my skin, of the fragile peace of Henry's hands as they draw me close.

His lips find mine in a deep and urgent kiss, and for a dizzying second, I forget why I'm here.

"You okay?" he asks when I pull away.

I don't have time for preamble, so I launch right in. "Did you take Ivy off the island?"

"Ivy? No. Why?"

I swear under my breath. "We can't find her. Hazel and I want to leave, but not until we find her."

Henry stretches his neck, staring back at the cabin. "The boat hasn't left the dock since Ernest brought you in. But, listen—I'm leaving tonight. For about a week. So, if you want off, you'd better come now."

A chill fingernail under my skin again, now edged in urgency. "I can't leave without Ivy."

"You've got till four," Henry says. "Latest. After that, I'm gone. And I don't want to be out on that water after dark—there's a storm coming."

The wind is already changing, carrying the smell of rain and warning. I stare back the way I came, swallowing. "Okay. Thanks, Henry."

I turn to go, but he catches the crook of my arm in his grip and pulls me back. I collide with him harder than I think he intended. He searches my face for a long moment, then he leans in and presses his lips to mine again. Tender now. Like a promise.

"I hope you'll come, Clem."

I blink up at him as he lets me go, then force myself to move, my feet carrying me back toward Beltane house. Every second counts. A few short hours to find Ivy—and then, maybe, the strength to leave this cursed place for good.

# 21

***December 1999***

The howl of silence is punctuated by the crunch of bare feet breaking through thin layers of near-frozen snow. The girls, wild and resolute, run when they can, but mostly, they walk.

Here and there they pass the effigies Clem built with her own hands—with occasional help from the twins—twig-boned figures scattered among the trees, as if the forest itself had sprouted fragile gods from root and marrow. They pay no mind to their aching soles; pain is merely a thread in the fabric of their devotion. Sometimes they stop to warm their feet with their hands and breath, tucking their toes into scraps of cloth, their cheeks red as berries against the cold.

The effigies are Clem's proud achievement, her anchoring purpose. Bent shapes blessed for Daudir, like an offering, like treasure.

"Watchers," Juniper had whispered one day, eyes bright as moons. "Protectors," she named them. Spirits of the forest. Little gods of their making. They will stand sentinel at the edge of their world. Keep them safe.

It is good to see them appearing all over the island, well enough away from Ernest's cabin that he will never encounter them. Indeed, they hope the Watchers will do their part in keeping him away. Wards made by Wards.

Clem grows more daring with their construction, using wood and vines and, now, crowning them with moss, ribbon, buttons, and even clumps of bracken that die over time, browning into something beautiful. Willow has climbed some of the trees to tie the lighter of the effigies into the branches so they dangle like woodland sprites.

Now the older effigies sleep, buried beneath a quilt of fragile, glacial white. They're strange snow folk, huddled together like an enchanted village—a village created by Clem, where only they and Daudir may walk. The newer ones, sharper and unyielding, still stand proud, but the snow will come for them too. Their decomposition has been frozen in time. Entropy in suspended animation.

Daudir provides.

A small deer with budding antlers, no more than little pointed horns, tiny forks diverging in each one, thrashes in one of Juniper's snares. The deer blinks, jerks its head, cries with pitiful little bleats. Tries to get away, like it must have for hours already—but can't. Juniper's snare is strong. Granny Alys taught her well.

Juniper regards it with solemn grace, then unslings her knapsack and draws out a carving knife, one that is imprinted with the grasp of Granny Alys's palm.

Clem feels a strange stirring in her belly as Juniper wrestles the deer into the crook of her arm. A tangle of sympathy and hunger.

Poppy and Willow come running up, their voices too loud in the hush of subtle falling snow. Poppy's face brightens for a heartbeat before her gaze makes the journey from rope, to knife, to Juniper's hand. Dimples dent her forehead.

"Juni, don't," Poppy whimpers.

Juniper presses a finger to her lips, hushing the world, then tightens her grip, both on the deer and the knife. She draws the blade across the deer's throat in a single sure stroke.

Crimson spreads across the snow. A gruesome Popsicle. A bed of blooming roses.

Poppy screams and tries to run. But Willow holds her back.

Clem warms her feet in the pooling heat before it fades.

She understands the need for this death, even if she feels it could have been done differently, somehow. The next delivery is not for another two weeks. And the canned and bottled supplies are rapidly dwindling. So are what remains of the autumn harvest.

There are seven Wards, and they have to eat.

And maybe . . . maybe this sacrifice had to be seen. Felt. By all of them. By Daudir. The Spectacular Seven don't hide. They share the hard parts. They don't shy away when things get ugly.

They are daughters of Daudir, and Daudir has provided.

Clem nods, proud, when Juniper glances her way.

Back at Beltane, the house breathes a blood-tinged scent of change. The girls haul the deer onto the dining table, the sacred heart of their home, the tablecloth soaking scarlet as they work. It paints their hands, their legs, the floor beneath them. It dries sticky in Clem's lifeline, her heart line, her destiny line. She clenches her hand and opens it again, hating the feeling of it all tacky. The way it's beginning to cake.

Willow leads Poppy from the room. "Let's have a bath," she says, but Poppy is still hiccuping little cries and doesn't answer. The twins stare at the deer with a singular focus, like they see the gift that it is. Beside them, Hazel tries not to gag, her throat working overtime to keep bile down.

Juniper wipes her hands on the legs of her jeans, staining them. "Clem, help me."

Clem's chest warms; she is proud to be needed. "Okay. Um. What do we do?"

Juniper thinks for a moment. "The head first."

Hazel retches and coughs. Retches again.

"Get out of here," Juniper growls at her. "Go do something useful. Find something in the cellar to go with this. Old potatoes we missed, carrots—anything."

Hazel doesn't need telling twice. She heads for the kitchen and down into the cellar faster than is necessary.

"Go help her," Juniper tells the twins when Hazel's retching echoes up the cellar stairs. "And close the door behind you."

They do what she says, but they look back several times with a soft sort of reverence. As if Clem and Juniper are somehow sacred, somehow chosen, somehow holy. Clem sees Holly dip a finger into the blood on the table before hurrying away. What game are they playing now?

Alone, Clem and Juniper set to their task like priestesses in a rite, carving and sawing through stubborn sinew and bone. But making a body into meat is a grisly, messy operation. It takes far longer than either Juniper or Clem anticipates. The neck bones end up requiring a saw, after the bread knife and other lesser implements fail to sever. Clem's hands, slick with sweat, fail to complete the task, so Juniper takes over, wrapping the handle of the saw in a washcloth they will now use only for this purpose.

Even cleaning the skull is laborious. Clem will use it, a grim crown that will top her next effigy, one she hopes will sing to Daudir Himself. If the effigy is good enough, Daudir will come. Show Himself at last.

This effigy will be something new altogether. Bone and wood, just like the boundary wall.

And so, the days pass, chilly with secrets and heavy with scent.

Another small thing changes in their world when, on a surprisingly mild day in December, Willow brings home a baby hare from one of the smaller snares. Clem finds her playing with it in her room, nudging it across the quilt in a game it cannot win.

"It chose me," she tells Clem, eyes shining, cradling it like a Raggedy Ann even as its tiny body grows limp. "It's my friend."

"Where did you find it?"

"In the woods," Willow says, her voice small.

The string from the snare is still wrapped tightly around one of the back paws, cut deep into the flesh.

"When?"

"This afternoon."

Clem doesn't scold. Doesn't pull away. Let Willow keep her treasure. Let it rot slowly in her hands, for what is rot but the forest's own magic?

Clem strokes the dead fur, feeling the fragile bones beneath skin. "Beautiful."

Willow's smile is like the sun.

A week later, Willow is quite openly carrying her dead toy around. None of the sisters intervene. It is a gift, after all. A gift from Daudir.

Weeks later Willow's friend has been reduced to bone. And when sickness steals into Willow's blood, they do as they have been taught. As one, after a supper of deer and mushrooms, they carry her to the edge of the woods and lay her, bundled in blankets, in the snow. Daudir's effigy, topped with the deer's proud skull, stands at her side, a vigilant god.

They call to Him with their songs, asking Him to draw out the sickness and leave behind only strength.

And by morning, Willow sits up.

She stands and turns to face the forest. The other sisters do the same, scrutinizing the trees, wondering what to look for.

Is this Clem's doing, she wonders? Or Daudir's?

Juniper notices first, that Willow has an uncanny glint in her eye. She stares into the endless trees as though seeing something they can't.

Daudir has saved her; this they know. And maybe given her something more.

When they walk back to the house, they're a little rawer, a little wilder, than before. They are daughters of the forest, because the forest is an infection and all of them have the fever.

Still, when they eat, they eat at the table.

That never changes.

When the December supplies come, it is Juniper who greets Ernest at the dock. He has already dumped most of the supplies at the end of the pier. A large Ward pile, a smaller d'Aboville one. He works silently under plumbeous clouds, never making eye contact.

Juniper is the one who takes the reins. "Granny Alys is unwell. We'll be hauling in the supplies from now on so she can rest."

Ernest eyes them for a long moment, eyes narrowing even as his lips curl sideways. He takes her in, his deeply recessed eyes trailing up and down her thin frame, assessing. For a moment, Clem worries that he'll argue, because he looks like he wants to pick a fight, but then he shrugs like he couldn't care about anything less, and walks off, grabbing a box of supplies and loading his own cart.

"Can you help us load the boxes?" Juniper calls to his back.

"You've got 'ands," Ernest throws behind his back. "You've got feet."

Clem watches the little muscles in Juniper's jaw work. "Get the others. But leave Willow behind to watch Poppy."

Ernest finishes loading his meager supplies into his cart, then heads off without another glance. So be it. Ernest is a ghost at their threshold.

Clem does as she's told, hiking back to the house, clearing a little more of the leaves and branches out of her way as she goes. She wishes Henry were here.

It takes the five eldest Wards and two exhausting journeys to haul and push the loaded cart up the five-hundred-yard incline to the house, a task made more miserable by the rain and the irregularity of the terrain. Henry made this chore much more fun back in June, and September's delivery had seemed very different with Granny Alys here to give the girls advice about what to do.

But everything is up to them now.

And so they wheel their harvest home together, a solemn procession that winds up the hill and into Beltane, into the house that hums with forest breath and wild secrets.

Each sister has her part now. A vital role in the life of Beltane, every one as integral as the next.

Clem, their Effigist, who builds the statues and creatures that they put into the forest. Juniper, their Hierophant, who translates the twins' dreams and communes with the Wood. Hazel, Alchemist, who cooks their meals; decorates their festivities; and brews mushrooms, moss, beetles, and worms into tea. The twins, yet unnamed, know that they, too, will receive their purpose; and Willow, their Seer, who perceives Daudir as much as anyone can, their barometer in the storm. And Poppy, their jewel, has become a kind of watcher, pointing to things that may be important, if only the others are open enough to see.

And beyond them all, Daudir listens.

# 22

***September 2024***

"She's gone."

The words tear free, ragged and breathless. My heart is a wild thing now, thrashing against my throat, trying to bang its way out, eager to be rid of me. I lurch into the kitchen, pacing, pacing . . . like Willow that night, when we fed our hair to the flames and pretended the smoke could carry our grief away.

Juniper moves like she's underwater, cleaning her plate at the deep sink, rinsing her mug. Her long sinewy arm pumps water. There is a deep, sluggish moan, a metallic clang of pipes, and then the water flows, thick as blood, into the sink, one torturous pump at a time. Agonizing spurts. Sweat beads at her temple, washing away any pitiful calories she just consumed.

But I can't think about that now. Can't focus on Juniper when Ivy is gone.

"She's gone," I say again, tasting it now. The loss. The fear.

Juniper doesn't face me. Just keeps pumping water. "Who?"

"Ivy. I can't find her anywhere."

"Did you check her room, or—"

"I've checked everywhere, June. *Everywhere.*" My voice cracks on the last word.

That gets her. She stops her pumping, then faces me, pale and drawn. "You're sure?"

I glare. "No one's seen her. I even went down to Henry and Ernest's place. They haven't seen her either."

Hazel drifts in, sleep mussed. She groans. "Is there coffee?"

I wrap my arms tight around myself, trying to contain the panic clawing at my insides like climbing ivy. "Ivy's gone."

Hazel's yawn dies. "What?"

"Ivy. Is. Gone."

She blinks at me. "Is . . . is the boat still here?"

"Yes. I checked."

Juniper blanches. Wipes trembling hands on her skirt. "It's Daudir," she whispers. "He's come to claim His due."

Hazel scoffs, like it's a joke, but I don't have time for this.

"She might have gone for a walk and got lost or something. Lost track of time. We need to look for her."

"I thought you said you looked everywhere?" Juniper says.

"Clearly I haven't. We'll search the whole island. Together. Now."

Hazel nods, shaken. "Okay, uh, yeah. Let me get my boots."

We scatter, me to the entrance hall, where I pace, trying to keep from bursting out of my skin.

"This is Daudir," Juniper says, following me. "It's for the years of neglect. For your abandonment!"

I round on her. "Shut up! Just—*shut up*, Juniper. Ivy could be hurt, and you're rambling about your damn delusion!"

"You can't ignore a wild god for twenty-five years and expect Him to be lenient—"

My fury detonates, white hot. I feel it in the sinews of my cells like red ants pinching. "We gave Daudir everything! And what did it buy us? Misery. Rot. Death without reason. Don't you see it? There was no plan. Just cruelty. A game we played because we were scared children." I can't help my sneer. "Wake up, Juniper. I won't keep coddling you or this story anymore. It was a lie. A fantasy! A game we played because we were scared."

Juniper shakes her head. "You don't believe that."

"I do. What kind of god lets children run around playing with a corpse like it were some—some *doll*?"

"Granny Alys was an oracle, and we were happy!"

"You're not remembering the truth!" My voice rings in the glass of the broken grandfather clock, but I can't hold back anymore. I can't keep pandering to her insanity. "You're seeing things through rose-tinted glasses," I say gently, "but that's not the reality. You need to *wake up*. Granny Alys wasn't an oracle. She was a corpse. You need to remember the way her skin went green in less than a week, and later, totally black. How mold bloomed on her belly before it burst, how her skin liquefied!" My voice rises again, fury blooming over indignation, petal upon petal, looking for something to strangle. "You're not remembering how the smell was so potent we tasted it for *years*. You're forgetting the flies that came in spring and the maggots that came after that. You're forgetting *eating* those maggots because there was *no food*."

Juniper holds out a hand to stop me, but I am a tidal wave.

"You're forgetting the way her bed rotted beneath her from the liquids in her body, and how they seeped all the way through and into the floorboards, the stench infecting our bones. I bet the stain is still there, isn't it?" I laugh, near hysterical, but I want to vomit. "We left her there because we had some messed-up idea that she was part of Beltane, that she wanted to be preserved. We were too shell shocked to do anything but make up a fairy tale. Don't tell me a benevolent god would want that."

She stares at me, lips trembling. "Daudir *is* benevolent," she says at last. "When He's respected. He is a wild thing that you made promises to—and then you left Him behind."

Hazel barrels back in, boots laced, eyes sharp. "We ready?"

I meet Juniper's gaze, my breath ragged. "Yeah. Let's go."

We spill out into the night, but Juniper's voice chases us. "You can't ignore Him forever, Clementine!"

And for the first time in my life, I want to strike my sister. But Hazel beats me to it. Not with a slap, but with a scathing look. "I don't owe Daudir anything," she says, and there's more venom in her tone than I've heard in decades. "And I don't believe in him."

Juniper recoils like she's been struck, her face a mask of shattered glass. "Don't . . ." She barely speaks, her words so fragile, so soft, that they break on their way out. "Don't . . ."

"I don't care about the Forgotten God of the Wood," Hazel says, then turns to the forest and yells, "*I don't care about Daudir!*"

Juniper almost collapses as she rears back. Her legs give out, but she catches herself at the last moment, staggering backward, her mouth frozen in a rictus of horror. With shaking hands, she covers us from her sight and backs away into the house.

Hazel stares after her, teeth bared, her cheek twitching like a fuse.

I'm angry. As angry as anyone. But beneath my own rage, something gnawing at the edge of my shoulder makes a suggestion I don't like.

*She seems a little* too *angry, don't you think?*

"Let's go," I mutter, and head into the toxic green tangle that is Beltane.

I scream Ivy's name until my voice frays to a threadbare croak, rasping beneath the tangle of branches that stitch the canopy tight above me. The sun is high and indifferent, too hot for September. I consider turning back for some water, but what if Ivy's just beyond the next bend, broken and waiting? What if she's fallen into some ravine the island kept hidden from us all these years, bleeding into the moss?

So, I go on.

My hands swell and itch from some unheeded plant pushed aside, and my feet pulse, swollen with my heartbeat—and still I push on. The island isn't large, but large enough. Large enough for the green to be something to drown in, for the woods to feel endless. Large enough for predators we have forgotten to fear. Large enough to vanish in.

Juniper's words ring in my head. *Daudir* is *benevolent. He is a wild thing that you made promises to—and then you left Him behind.* Hazel's words too. *I don't believe in him.*

Well, I don't believe in him either. We were children. Sick, alone, abandoned, and desperate to cling onto anything. And yet . . . his name scrapes at my skin like burs.

I pass the Guardian rock, that moss-scabbed boulder shaped like a giant's skull. I glare at it as I go. *Fantasy.* Pure fantasy. How we kept it going for so long is beyond me. And Juniper . . . Juniper was *nineteen* years old by the end. How did she allow it?

A sound stills me. Leaves shiver. Something moves—close. Coming toward me. My breath knots in my throat. Hide? Or stand? We never saw bears here. But what do I really know about this place anymore?

Then—Hazel's voice, breaking through the hush.

*"Help!"*

I run, thorns catching at my sleeves. "Hazel! Hazel!"

*"Clem!"* She sounds spent, breathless with fear or weariness I can't tell. *"Hurry!"*

"Keep calling! I'm coming!"

But she doesn't call. She sings. High, thin, frayed at the edges, with long, aching silences between the words that turn the sweat cold on my back.

*One too many two-eyed rabbits,*
*three or four of good clean habits,*
*five little sixes bound by bone,*
*seven little girls safe at home.*

I push through into a clearing I don't know, a patch of earth gone bare in the sea of green, ringed by hollow-root trees whose limbs bow under the weight of age. Moss drapes their arms like shrouds.

Hazel sags against one of them, holding on to a root.

But the root writhes. And Hazel gasps, "I can't hold on much longer."

I lunge forward. "Are you hurt?"

Her voice trembles, and she sags farther. "Take her."

It's not a root. It's an arm. A woman's arm, pale as bone, clawing from a root hole, straining, not to grab Hazel, but to flee.

"What—" I begin.

"She's been here," Hazel breathes, her voice splintering. Tears carve slow paths down her dirt-smeared cheeks. She shakes her head, as if trying to rattle the horror loose, and lets the arm slip from her grasp into mine. "She's been here all along."

I frown, squinting into the hollow's dark mouth, where roots hang like strands of hair.

A face emerges from the gloom, grimy, gaunt, piercing blue eyes lost in their depths. It isn't Ivy.

It's another sister altogether. Our beloved Seer, who vanished in Beltane more than two decades ago without a trace.

I'm holding on to Willow.

# 23

***February 2000***

In late February, as early-spring buds are beginning to show their optimistic faces, Clem presents the twins with a gift: a matched pair of deer leg bones, one from the left, one from the right. She has perfected the art now—the whitening, the careful scraping and polishing—until the bones gleam with the pale beauty of moths. They are flawless, humming faintly in her hands with the life they once belonged to.

The twins' eyes shine when they see them, and they waste no time adorning their new treasures. Ivy paints hers in soft sage, the shade of young leaves after rain; Holly chooses a darker green, the deep hush of pine. Both coats glimmer with the last of their glitter nail polish, the shimmer of something magical, nearly gone. At first, Clem's heart sinks at the sight. It feels like desecration, a defacing of the sacred gift. But when the bones catch the light and glint like dawn water, she feels it: This is right. Daudir guided her hands.

Three days later, the bones are gone.

Beltane house becomes a storm of searching. The twins pull apart cushions, empty drawers, scour the woodshed. Clem joins them, but the bones do not reappear.

"I think I saw Willow with something green," Hazel murmurs on the second day, almost absently. "She's been sleepwalking, you know."

It's true that Willow's night wanderings have begun again, for the first time in years, but to imagine her a thief?

Clem rolls her eyes. "That could have been anything. This house is made of green."

And Hazel's small smug smile as the quarrel grows . . . that smile troubles Clem most.

But the twins latch on to the idea like two wolves with a bone, jaws locked, immovable. When they confront Willow in her bedroom, she denies it with a vagueness that leaves them no peace. Since nothing can be proved, the twins are forced to retreat, but a grudge takes root between them, thin and dark, like the first cracks in ice. Clem remembers the twins' strange chant on the boat:

*Ripples in the fabric*
*Frays in the yarn.*

In particular, Clem doesn't like the self-satisfied smirk on Hazel's face when she sees the girls arguing. On instinct, Clem slips away, following the pull of the woods. The trees close around her as she makes for the lake, to the tallest hemlock and its hollow knot—Hazel's secret place. Something in this doesn't sit right. Hazel's hand is in this whole mess, she knows.

And there, hidden in the dark embrace of the tree, she finds the bones.

Clem presses them to her chest, glancing about as if the forest might be watching. She slips them inside her dress and hurries back to the house. She doesn't know what to do. Return the bones to the twins? Confront Hazel?

Any decision she makes, and any ensuing discord, will be her fault. She can't bear the idea that she may start something she can't take back.

In the end, she leaves it to Daudir. *Your choice,* she whispers, and lays them on Beltane's doorstep, a silent offering.

She can't—*won't*—intentionally worsen any disharmony between her sisters. She can't take their choices into her hands.

Poppy finds them in the early evening, and squeals with delight, rushing straight to Juniper in the informal living room, where they are all gathered in front of the fire. Juniper takes them, looking dismayed, and Hazel stiffens beside her, color draining from her cheeks.

"I knew you took them," Holly hisses at Willow.

"I didn't!" Willow's voice trembles with outrage.

"Where did you find them, Pops?" Juniper asks.

"Doorstep."

Juniper's mouth twists. "Daudir gave them back."

Clem hesitates. "Isn't . . . isn't that a blessing?"

Juniper meets her gaze, solemn. "It means He took them first."

Juniper sniffs and gets to her feet, clutching the bones like a gavel. "We need a sigil. One of protection and of devotion. You remember what Granny Alys said. The Forgotten God of the Wood is nature itself. Both light and dark. Benevolent and malevolent, shelter and snare. We need to remind Him of our devotion."

"What's a smidge?" Poppy asks, taking one of the bones and trying to spin it like a baton.

"A *sigil*. Here, I'll teach you."

Juniper shows them a way to draw out the first letters of all their names, one on top of each other, and to eliminate common shapes. To create a sort of symbol out of the letters until one is formed that feels right. They try and try, commenting on what should stay and what should go, until in one beautiful moment, they all feel it.

This is the one.

"I'll paint it on the doorstep," Juniper says. "There's some leftover white lime paint in the cellar."

Clem follows her out of the living room and out into the hall. "Shouldn't you wait until morning?"

Juniper's pace increases. "It needs to be now. We must be safe. We must show Him we believe."

Juniper finds the paint herself, insisting that as Hierophant, it is her duty. They watch her work, Poppy slit-eyed and yawning. Juniper burns herself in the process, but by moonrise, the house has a white sigil blazoned on the front step. The mark gleams like frost. The house feels held.

"We believe," Juniper whispers, eyes closed, when it is done.

Then, she shuts the door firmly on the ever-watchful woods.

Clem can't help but worry that the burn is a sign that Daudir is displeased.

When she hears the twins and Willow bickering upstairs at bedtime, she knows that she has done nothing to solve any problem at all. She may only have made things worse.

***March 2000***

Clem watches the battle play out in silence. She lingers in shadows, where the air hums with secrets. She watches, unseen, as this quiet war unfolds.

Each dawn brings a new shrine. The twins, their fingers deft as weavers, lift Granny Alys from her bed and set her in some chosen place—at the hearth's edge, beneath the window's pale gaze, once even at the door to the cellar. A movable doll.

They crown her anew each time: a braid of acorns, a collar of buttons, a circlet of lichen. The next day, the tokens change—snakeskin drapes where lichen lay, a broken shell where the buttons were. Their hands shape her like clay, like wax, as if trying to summon back the life that left her eyes long ago.

And each day, Willow goes looking, moving Granny Alys back to her sagging bed on her own.

It is a silent battle of wills.

One morning, the light spills strangely through the stairwell. Clem pauses. There, on the steps, Granny Alys waits, propped like an offering, arms outstretched, wrists lashed with twine to the balustrade. The angles of her limbs, the tilt of her head, speak of crucifixion, or perhaps of surrender.

Without thinking, Clem's fingers find the little trinkets hidden in her skirt pocket. Scraps of costume jewelry, old beads, a chipped brooch. She presses them into Granny's near-hollow sockets, one by one, until the light catches, and they sparkle with something like life. For a breath, Clem sees her. Not the husk, but the woman she was: fierce, laughing, strange as the Wood itself. Alive. Joyful. Otherworldly.

She is a haunting of beads and bone. An angel. A wraith.

Night falls. The house creaks and sighs. By the dying firelight, Poppy sits on the stairs and curls close to the still form, her small hand finding Granny's pinky finger, their skins cool against one another. Her voice rises, soft as moth wings:

*In the wood where no crows fly,*
*stands a tree that breathes a sigh.*
*Knots for eyes and mouth of bark,*
*god of light and god of dark.*

*Old Maude sleeps inside the trunk,*
*skin in moss and bones all shrunk.*
*Wrap her up in birch-bark skin,*
*leave no trace and don't go in.*

*If you knock once, she'll not wake;*
*knock there twice, her branches break.*
*Knock there thrice, beware the sound;*
*Hear her voice and you'll be bound.*

*Sleep now, child; the moss is thick,*

*The candle's out, the clock won't tick.*
*When you dream, don't call her name;*
*Old Maude's dreaming just the same.*

Poppy kisses Granny Alys on the cheek, and when Clem follows to do the same, she wonders where they will find Granny Alys in the morning.

Morning comes slowly, dragging a pale, watery light across the floorboards. The house holds its breath, as if waiting. But Granny Alys remains where she was, untouched, unmoved, her besparkled gaze fixed on nothing at all.

The twins are hunched at the dining room table, wrapped in one large duvet, pressed so close they might be one creature with two heads. Their hands clutch steaming mugs, fingers white at the knuckles, as though warmth alone might tether them to the world.

"What's going on?" Clem asks, bleary, her breath fogging in the chilly air.

Willow follows close behind, both in rumpled pajamas, hair tangled, feet bare. The cold of the floor creeps up their legs. Clem pauses, sensing the crackle in the air.

The twins turn haunted eyes on her just as Juniper rounds the kitchen corner, hot iron skillet in covered hand.

"The twins have been given a message," she says, as if delivering the weather.

Clem glances instinctively at the large window, then lowers herself into the chair beside them, wood creaking. The room feels smaller somehow, drawn in tight around them. "A message?"

Willow crosses to sit opposite Holly, gaze wary, arms folded as if to brace herself. The mugs clink softly against the table.

"A dream. A message from Daudir. I've translated it."

Willow's brow furrows. "What dream?"

Holly's voice is soft, distant, as though she speaks from somewhere far away. "A great tree . . ."

Ivy's words come on its heels, a twin echo. "A falling mountain . . ."

Their voices weave together, threads of the same dark cloth.

"Turmoil."

"Turbulence."

Juniper sets the skillet down with a clatter, breaking the spell. She scrapes charred mushrooms onto a plate, the scent sharp and bitter. "Calamity is coming. We'll need to offer a sacrifice."

The word hangs heavy in the room, and the air thickens.

"They're lying," Willow says darkly. "They're just trying to get back at me."

Juniper softens, but the steel remains beneath. "You are the Seer, Willow. That can't be taken. You hear the Guardian stone, you see the threads. The twins . . . they're Oracles. Prophets. They glimpse what lies ahead. We knew Daudir would reveal their titles, in time. That's all."

She shrugs, like it's a small thing, but Clem can see the storm building beneath Willow's skin. The tremor in her jaw, the tight coil of her hands. She's trying to contain it, but it hums there, waiting.

Not for the first time lately, Clem doesn't know how to mend this tear in the fabric of their family.

Days slip by, heavy with heat and tension. And then— the storm. An unusual spring tempest that splits the sky, lightning tearing the night like cloth. When morning comes, the tallest hemlock at the lake—Hazel's hidden refuge—lies shattered, its great body sprawled in ruin.

And Clem knows then. The message was true. The twins are what they claimed to be.

Daudir does not abide secrets.

# 24

***September 2024***

We drag Willow, kicking and biting, back to Beltane house.

She flails on the floorboards like a deer in a trap, and for one awful, flickering second, my instinct is to knock her on the back of her skull or take a knife to her throat.

I shut my eyes. Force my mind to another place. My little flat above the shop in London. Safe, small, civilized. The faded vintage wallpaper I put up myself, the apple green trim I painted, slowly and carefully, on the chair rails. The Louis XV chair with its spindly legs, the medieval chest at the foot of my bed, solid as a promise. Pieces lovingly chosen by a woman who lives a civilized life.

My world. Mine. Not this.

A sharp shock of her teeth as Willow bites my arm, crunch of my skin, blood welling hot and fast. I cry out and whack her across the face. She sprawls, hits the floor hard, spits out a mouthful of my blood.

"Fuck!" The word rips from my throat, ragged. "Fuck, Willow—Jesus Christ!"

Juniper's feet pound, heavy on the stairs. Quick. "What's happening? What's—"

She freezes mid-step. The sight of Willow, blood smeared, wild-eyed, stops her cold. There's fear in her face. Real fear.

I know instantly.

"You knew she was alive." My voice is low, shaking. "You knew."

Juniper's lips shiver. "Why did you bring her inside?"

I lurch for Juniper, but Hazel holds me back. "You let us think she was dead!"

Juniper blinks, coming out of her shock. "She *was* dead," she says thickly. "Until she went to Daudir, she was dead."

"You fucking lunatic—"

Hazel's voice is small but steady, her hand still locked on to my arm. "She's been out there this whole time? Out in the woods like . . . like a stray dog?"

Juniper's mouth twists into something like a smile. Wide, cracked at the edges. "She's with Daudir. Can't you see? She's more than she was. More than a Seer now. She's blessed. *Chosen.*"

I tear free of Hazel, moving away from Juniper. I have to put space between me and that smile. That smile that says it was always a game to her. And now the game's swallowed her whole. There is no hope of breaking her free now.

"Okay," I mutter. My pulse is pounding in my ears. "Okay. We need help. Ivy's still missing, and now Willow's appeared out of the blue for the first time in more than two decades, looking half dead. We . . . we need to call the police."

I lick my lips, trying to sort one chaotic thought from another.

Hazel edges closer to me, eyes never leaving Juniper, who's crouched beside Willow now, stroking her hair, crooning nonsense like a mother to a fevered child.

"Fine," Hazel says. "Go. Get Henry. I'll keep them from . . . I don't know, setting themselves on fire."

I almost smile. But then I remember . . . Henry's gone. He told me he was leaving. And I did nothing.

"Goddamn it," I hiss. "He's gone. I should've stopped him, but I got caught up with—" I gesture to the mess around us. "This. He won't be back for a week."

"Shit. And what about cell service?"

"Nothing. Not since I got here."

"Me neither."

Hazel glances toward the window, as if the woods might have changed. As if help might be coming. "And we still haven't found Ivy."

"I know."

She turns her back on Juniper and Willow, whispering close to my ear. "You don't think Juniper did something to her?"

I stare at her. "You mean like lock her up?"

She gives me a meaningful look. "Yeah. Exactly like that."

I look past her to what's left of Willow. She's little more than skin and bone now, eyes too large in her face, hands curled like claws. Juniper looks positively radiant beside her. "I don't know anymore. I don't know a damn thing."

And then Juniper's voice cuts through, sharp and clear. "You can't take her from Beltane."

Her voice echoes through the room, startling me.

Hazel is the one to stand up to her. For once. "What the hell are you going to do to stop us?"

I cross my arms, look down at Willow. Ragged, ruined—but alive. "You've been feeding her. She didn't survive this long out there on her own."

Juniper makes as if to caress Willow's tangled hair. "In winter, she sleeps in the cellar. She's working. You don't see it, but she's doing Daudir's work. She remembers. Even if you don't."

"She's insane," I snap, before I can catch myself. "Just like you."

I turn to Hazel. "Watch them. I'm checking the boat. Maybe Henry hasn't left yet."

Hazel nods. "Don't be long."

When I leave, Juniper's smile is crawling after me, worming under my skin. But I won't let her in. Not this time. Not ever again.

# 25

***March–April 2000***

Their little dollhouse is warping at the edges.

Clem finds the curling wallpaper charming; the hum of unreliable electricity is a continual background song. Mold and mushrooms bloom up the walls like forest diamonds, eating the bad things left behind. The hunger that lives with them is no longer a foe. They have befriended it, learned its name, invited it to join their games.

When they howl at the moon, it hums low in their throats, thrumming songs that carry them into sweet, strange trances that last hours.

This is the best game Clem has ever played.

Her sisters have never felt this close, the forest has never felt so safe, the world has never been this beautiful. And all the concerns of the past—the missed TV shows, the forgotten friends, the lost school lessons—none of it matters.

Clem can *feel* Him.

She felt Him after they burned several tablecloths, a sacrifice to ask for warmth, begged for in the coldest, most brutal winter days, and the bluebells burst into bloom. She felt Him when she sacrificed three mushrooms from her dinner plate and found seven growing on her bedroom windowsill a week later.

Daudir is in her veins.

She and her sisters are drunk on Him. His love imbues their bodies like sugar wine, like golden nectar. They sprawl in sunbeams or shadows, giggling at nothing and everything, at the sheer splendor of His divinity, His terrible, beautiful grace.

They fell another deer, and another. Poppy helps Clem dissect the body into parts, a raw bone clutched in her fist like a prize. Willow points to the woods through the dining room window, Daudir's window, and all the sisters laugh hysterically. Sunbeams and shadow flirt between branches like lovers. All is as it should be, and somehow, more.

Then, in the soft breath of early March, as the island grows ever warmer, Granny Alys starts to change. There is music in the house now, and the mushrooms, their beloved mushrooms, stretch across floorboards and up walls in enchanting patterns. Clem watches them sprout—soft green, ashen gray, velvet black—and feels only wonder.

Poppy is first to eat them, small fists full of soft mushroom caps, her mouth teeming with the forest's sacred bread. She sits at Granny Alys's bedside, where the old woman's body has sagged and split, like a shell returning to earth, like a flower in bloom. Poppy's cheeks are rosy with joy as she eats, as though receiving a blessing.

Juniper is slow to understand, pulling Poppy's little face away, trying to scoop out the soft remains of the mushrooms, but Poppy clings, bites, wails, and kicks, possessed by her deep knowing that this is meant to be. Uncertain at first, Clem joins, holding Poppy's arms, and Willow grips her feet. Juniper's tears are ones of frustration as she pries the last of the forest's gift from Poppy's mouth.

"They'll make you sick!" she cries, though her voice is uncertain, for who can say what harm Daudir's gifts can do?

And the mushrooms *are* gifts. Daudir's offering. The girls pluck them from the walls as though the house itself were a candied garden, a secret delight straight out of a storybook. Sacred, sweet, and strange. Clem imagines Granny Alys smiling, her voice a honey-thick murmur: *Pick them, my loves. They'll do you good. Let them nourish you.*

In the doorway, the twins stand still as stones, their wide eyes not on Poppy, nor the chaos, but on Granny Alys herself. Clem sees in their gaze the glimmer of that wild knowing, the sense that Granny, even now, is feeding them. Nourishing them. *Let poppet eat,* Clem thinks she hears, the ghost of Granny's voice wrapping around them like a shawl. *Won't do her no harm.*

"Granny Alys is taking care of us," Willow murmurs, releasing Poppy's feet.

Clem lets go of Poppy's arms and steps back. "She's right. This is a gift."

Juniper shakes her head. "How do you know?"

"Can't you tell?" Holly says, her breath a sigh.

"One too many two-eyed rabbits," Juniper says softly. Her voice is thready, warbling with questions.

Willow picks up the refrain. "Three or four of good, clean habits."

"Five little sixes, bound by bone," Clem sings.

Poppy grins, her cheeks ruddy with life. "Seven little girls safe at home."

Ivy picks a mushroom from the wall and places it reverently between her lips. Her eyes drift closed as she chews.

"Daudir is with us," Willow says, her eyes glittering with joyful tears.

"And Granny Alys is with Him," Clem confirms, and reaches for the spores.

***June 2000***

The supplies continue to arrive every three months, as if sent by some distant spell, and with them, in the warm breath of summer, comes Henry. In the days before his arrival, Clem bathes in the lake, letting the water cleanse her like a baptism, so that when he sees her, it feels as though the world itself has been made new. With Henry by her side, it is easy to believe life could never be more perfect.

But as the island softens beneath the sun's return, a strange itch takes root in Hazel's feet. She scratches and scratches, the sound of her nails against toughened skin a cruel music that frays Clem's nerves. The days stretch long, filled with the rasp of Hazel's misery.

"You're going to grow fungus between your toes," Holly teases one afternoon, eyes bright as a magpie's. "You'll be sprouting mushrooms in no time!"

Hazel lets out a horrified yell, scrabbling at her toes like she wants to rip them from her feet, peering between them as though expecting to see tiny silver-capped mushrooms unfurling there.

Ivy giggles in that eerie way the twins share, smile wide as a Cheshire cat, pupils dilating. "Daudir is calling you home."

"Or punishing you," Holly adds, smile sharp as thorns. Clem almost laughs, thinking what perfect little dolls they would make, these twins, if only she could stitch their wicked grins in place.

Holly's grin is infectious. "Scratch, scratch, little beetle!"

Hazel sobs, wild and desperate. "He's not punishing me! I've made sacrifices! Same as all of you!" She tugs at her hair, now growing long again, brushing her shoulders like a white veil.

"Maybe He wants your face next," Holly says, and her grin is as cruel as the forest.

Juniper stands between them, a dead hare clutched in her fist. "It's only athlete's foot. Soak your feet in some apple cider vinegar. There's some left over in the cellar."

Hazel rushes away, and the twins snicker, heads together like cackling crows.

"Daudir doesn't speak to you for your tricks," Juniper tells them, and at last their laughter fades, their faces softening.

"We just wanted to have a bit of fun."

"Then go skin this hare." Juniper hands them the week's gift, and their faces light with glee.

"Daudir gave us a big one this week," Ivy murmurs, stroking the soft fur like a charm. Clem hopes this creature will be food, not a plaything. She wonders, not for the first time, where Willow hid the bones of her dead rabbit friend. Perhaps she'll ask for them one day . . . for charms, for safety.

When Henry arrives with the summer run, he hugs Clem tighter than she can remember ever being held before in her life. Clem feels his arms around her and thinks she could stay there forever.

"You cut your hair," he says, his fingers brushing the ends that fall just below her chin, eyes full of warmth.

It has been eight months since she and her sisters cut off their hair to honor Granny Alys and restore the balance. It's grown more than four inches since then, long enough that when she turned fourteen in January, she could put two tiny bows in. Now she can even braid it.

"We needed a change," Clem says softly, and feels the beautiful weight of all they have experienced.

"I like it. Very modern."

Together they haul the supplies, and Henry chatters about his world: hockey tryouts, botched school science projects, his mother's triumph at finally becoming a nurse. Clem listens, heart aching and full. She tells him of simple things: light snowfalls, chopped wood, the crackle of the hearth. She keeps the other truths—the rites, the sacred mushrooms, the forest's playful beauty—tucked safe inside.

"School isn't all it's cracked up to be, though," Henry says. "I think I want to go into the trades. Do something with my hands. Like building, maybe. Or carpentry."

Later, by the lake, they sit with their feet in the water, the hemlock tree's absence a hollow she feels in her bones.

"I wish I could send you letters," Henry says, voice soft as the ripples lapping at their toes.

"Letters?"

"Yeah. I write them anyway. I just can't send them anywhere."

The thought of his words, floating out there for her like little paper boats, makes her throat tight.

Clem hasn't before thought about the fact that they don't get mail. It has always been given that the supplies come in every three months and that's all. With Granny Alys's having gone forestward, the topic of school hasn't even been brought up. The idea that any of them would ever leave is laughable.

But getting a letter from Henry would be lovely, during the long cold months especially.

"Henry . . ." She almost confides in him, about Granny going forestward, and about the hard cold months, when Daudir tests them the most. The truth flutters at her lips like a moth against glass. But the moment catches, slips.

He blinks at her through the sunlight.

"Did you see we lost the hemlock tree?" she asks instead.

"I did. Storm?"

She nods. "We've been cutting it for firewood."

"I saw the marks."

"That's not what I was going to say."

"I know." He takes her hand, so warm it burns. "What is it?"

"I can't tell you."

"You can tell me anything."

"I can't."

"You don't trust me?"

"It's not that. It's not just mine to tell."

Henry looks out at the water, his grip gentle, patient. "I understand. It belongs to all of you."

"Yeah."

"Then ask them. If they say no, I won't ask again. If they say yes, I'll listen. No judgment."

"But you'd tell."

He laughs softly. "Tell who? Ernest? I don't know if you've noticed, Clem, but it's you I come for."

It is true that he spent nearly every day last summer in her and her sisters' company. And it looks like this summer will be the same. She knows it, and the knowledge is as sweet and terrifying as Daudir's gifts.

"I'll ask them tonight," she says, and squeezes his hand like a promise.

# 26

***June 2000***

Clem brings Henry to the clearing well before sundown, when the light still clings to the leaves like honey, and the air smells of damp moss and woodsmoke. Willow and Hazel move about like sprites, hanging laundry on a long line strung between the house and the trees. Dresses, tops, and little white underthings billow in the breeze, like flags from some secret country. But Henry doesn't seem to notice.

"We need a family meeting," Clem says, though the words feel heavy on her tongue.

Hazel's eyes travel down, clocking their locked hands. Clem drops Henry's fingers as if burned, folds her arms, and sinks onto a log near the firepit—the same pit where they burned their hair in memory, in magic, in promise.

Henry sits beside her.

Willow's smile is gentle. "I'll fetch the others," she says, and disappears among the trees, as light and quick as a deer.

It's a tense wait. It wraps around Clem, tight as a cord. Hazel hums to herself, checks her reflection in a small cracked mirror she pulls from her pocket, and wrings the last drops from the wet fabric of a dress on the line. Clem moves to help, hoping the work will steady her, will fill the space until the others arrive. But the knot in her stomach only grows.

When the rest of them come, they gather in a loose circle around the firepit. Clem is taut with nerves.

"What's going on?" Juniper asks, arms crossed, the only one still standing. The shadows of the trees paint stripes across her face. Her expression is carved from stone.

"Ask Clementine," Hazel says, her voice sweet as syrup. She tosses Clem a glance that cuts.

Juniper's brows lift, sharp and accusing. "Well?"

"I—" Clem's throat is dry. "I've come to ask if we can . . . well, Henry was wondering if—"

She glances at him, pleading silently for rescue.

"I asked Clem to tell me what's been happening here, since I was last on the island," Henry says, his voice calm, as if this is all simple.

The clearing shifts, the reaction instant. The twins rise at once, as if pulled by the same string. Hazel throws her head back and roars with laughter, startling the crows from the trees. Willow shrinks smaller, folding in on herself. Juniper's eyes flash like summer lightning. Only Poppy is unbothered.

"I been chopping wabbit!" Poppy yells, her voice slicing through the tension like a blade. The woods fall silent at her cry.

Henry laughs, warm and genuine. "Have you? That's no easy task. How do you manage it?"

Poppy nods, proud. "Wif a knife! Chop wabbits good."

"I thought," Clem says softly, "that it might be better to have an ally."

Juniper paces, slow and thoughtful, watching Henry through narrowed eyes. "Ward business is Ward business," she says at last. "You understand that?"

Henry nods. "I understand."

"And this island protects the Wards."

Henry does not flinch. "I understand."

Juniper stops, draws a breath deep as the lake. "Nothing changes if we let you in. Except, you can come as you like. And you'll have a key, of sorts. To the door."

"I don't want to make anyone feel uncomfortable—"

"Granny Alys is dead."

Her words drop like stones into the hush.

Henry blinks, caught off guard. Looks at Clem. Back at Juniper.

"Daudir!" Poppy shouts into the quiet, and the air seems to hold its breath.

"Daughter?" Henry asks, gentle.

"Granny Alys is dead," Juniper says again, voice sharp as flint. She reaches over and picks Poppy up. "That's all you need to know."

"When?" Henry asks.

Juniper looks to Clem, bouncing Poppy on her hip.

"November," Clem answers, her voice a thread. "It was in November."

"You buried her?"

"We honored her," Juniper says. "And we continue to honor her."

Clem takes Henry's hand, slow and sure, and feels Juniper's gaze. There's something new in Juniper's eyes. Pleasure, or pride, or maybe a fierce sort of relief.

"If you tell . . ." Clem whispers.

Henry nods, finally getting it. "You'll be taken."

"From the island," Juniper confirms. "From us. From you."

Henry swallows, staring up at Juniper. The moment is one Clem can see like threads in the air. Their purposes are realigning, mirroring each other, coming together in a neat and tidy understanding.

Henry's fingers tighten around Clem's. The moment hangs between them, fragile as a spider's web, glinting in the last light.

"No one needs to know," he says softly. "You're doing just fine."

The night they choose for Henry's initiation is bright, the sky blanketed with stars, as if the heavens themselves lean close in order to witness what is about to unfold. The air carries the scent of fire and moonlight.

Clem leads Henry by the hand, silent, her eyes bright with purpose, proud that he came all this way in the dark to be initiated.

A fire burns low in the pit, the coals breathing red. Around it, the sisters have gathered. Juniper tall and solemn, Willow with her hair unbound, Hazel with her hands stained from the herbs she has crushed into a paste. Poppy hums a tune that has no words, only the shape of something ancient. The twins sway to music only they can hear.

The clearing feels different tonight. The sisters have strung bones and feathers and strands of woven fraying ribbons from the branches above. Bowls of mushroom water glisten on stones, each one reflecting the firelight like a dark eye. The air hums with a quiet power, as if the island itself is listening.

Clem brings Henry to the center, her whole chest humming with anticipation.

Juniper steps forward, her gaze steady. "Do you come of your own will?"

Henry nods. "I do."

"And do you vow to keep what you see and hear tonight, and what you have already seen and heard, safe within your heart?"

"I do," Henry says again, though his voice trembles, and Clem knows he feels the weight of this moment too.

Juniper nods, satisfied. She gestures for him to kneel beside the fire.

Juniper moves first, dipping a cloth into one of the bowls of mushroom water. It drips, dark and fragrant, as she lifts it and begins to wash Henry's hands. The liquid is cool, almost silken, and it leaves a faint shimmer on his skin. As she works, she murmurs under her breath in their secret language. A prayer, a blessing. Words that Henry can't understand but can feel.

Willow follows, pouring a thin stream of the water over Henry's hair, letting it run down his neck, his shoulders. The scent of the mushroom brew rises, earthy and strange, like the forest after rain. She smooths his hair back gently, as if he were her own brother, and whispers a prayer under her breath.

The twins place each of their bowls on the floor and tell him to bathe his feet. He removes his boots and his socks without arguing and places a foot in each. The twins grin and Henry returns it.

Then Hazel comes, carrying a small bowl filled with ash from the fire in which they burned their locks and Granny Alys's nails—ash they saved and stored in little glass bottles. She dips her fingers into the gray, and pauses, watching Clem. Clem's back bristles a little, but Hazel's scrutiny isn't enough to dampen this sacred moment. She meets Hazel's eyes and waits. Hazel marks Henry's brow, his chest, his palms with dark, sacred smudges, mutters a quick, "*Wenemklobu'aumonem.*"

*Welcome.*

Clem brings her own bowl to Henry's lips. "Drink," she says, her eyes glittering with fever.

His eyes never leave hers, and he drinks the mushroom water down with perfect trust.

Poppy offers Henry her bowl, but drops it before he can take it. Clem's mind reels, worried that this is a sign somehow of Henry not passing some divine test. She holds her breath, mind reeling.

But Juniper only smiles. "The earth should be anointed as well. Good thinking, Pops."

Poppy grins, like she meant it all along.

"These are the signs of belonging," Juniper continues. "You are of us now. What touches you, touches us. What harms you, harms us. What you protect, we protect. Do you accept this bond?"

"I do," Henry whispers, and his eyes sink closed.

Clem holds out a key carved from bone, small enough to fit in Henry's palm. It is a small thing, and crude, too, one she worked on in secret. "For the door," she says softly. "So you can always come back."

It doesn't actually unlock anything. They never lock out the forest. But the symbol is potent, and when Henry takes it, his fingers curl around the shaft as if it is the most precious thing he has ever been given.

Henry pauses, then quietly slips his button bracelet from his wrist and onto Clem's. She places her other palm over it, and blinks back sudden tears.

The sisters join hands, forming a circle around him. The fire crackles low, the shadows dance high. Together, they begin to hum . . . a sound that is not a song but a memory, a promise, a spell woven from blood and earth and love. The air thickens, charged with the weight of this promise. The forest leans closer, and even the night holds its breath.

When the hum fades, Henry rises, different now, marked by them, claimed by them, part of their secret tapestry.

Clem takes his hand last, their fingers fitting together like they always have, like they always will.

And above them, an owl screams its blessing.

Henry and Clem kiss for the first time by the lake, an hour before she'll need to be home to eat at the table. It happens in a quiet moment, not one that either of them had planned. The water is as still as glass, and the air hums with the songs of frogs and cicadas.

Clem has imagined this, in passing, but never truly believed it would happen. Not until Henry. Not until that almost kiss the night Juniper let him into their inner world, when he had leaned in, hesitated, pulled back. So shy, so awkward it melted her from the outside in.

It is everything, and nothing that Clem might have expected.

His hands fumble on her dress, hers at his jeans, and it should be difficult, and it should feel wrong, and maybe she should have asked Daudir first, but . . . she feels Daudir watching. She feels His presence in the woods; feels eyes on her as Henry lowers his body on her own.

They touch and they kiss and they lie in the grass together, and when Henry takes her hand in his again, it is moist as morning dew, but she doesn't mind. One day, she will give herself to him in every way that a person can. She knows it. But that moment isn't now.

After he kisses her a second time, her heart beats as it did the first time she took a deer . . . wild, fast, full of something ancient. She kisses him with a fever she worries will infect him. Maybe it already has.

"Do you like me being here in summer?" Henry asks, fiddling with the button bracelet on her wrist, almost as if he fears he doesn't belong.

He asks it, she thinks, as though he feels he is intruding. But he is the furthest thing from an intruder. He is the missing piece, can't he see?

Clem watches the sky, the slow drift of clouds. "I *love* you being here in summer."

How long these summer days are.

He watches her for a while. "I'm glad you came to live here," he says, and turns to look up at the sky with her.

"I am too. I don't regret anything."

And mostly that is true.

And Clem means almost all of it. She doesn't regret coming here. She doesn't regret honoring Granny Alys. She doesn't regret cutting off her hair or killing the deer or bleaching bones for effigies. She doesn't regret Daudir, and most of all, she doesn't regret Henry.

There's something sacred here, in this moment, something that these stolen kisses have almost touched—but not quite. Henry's skin is as warm and as comforting as a fire in winter, as soft as lake water in spring.

A raw and wild *something* is waking within her, a part of her that she has left sleeping for most of her life. A part that she wants to open, explore, and live in. So, when she rolls over and reaches for Henry's fly, she is the one in control this time.

# 27

***September 2024***

It seems obvious that Juniper did something to Ivy. Locked her away, maybe. I can't stop my brain from thinking: *Or worse.*

Juniper was always our protector. Our shield. A mother, even while our real one was still alive. She kept Granny Alys's rules with almost religious devotion, made Daudir a place where we could lay down our fears like burdens at a shrine. But I also have to reckon with the rest of it: that she kept us away from the world, that she let us rot among bones and grief and silence. That she let us live with a corpse.

That she taught us how to kill.

That's not protection. That's a curse disguised as a lullaby.

No thirteen-year-old should know how to sever a spinal cord. No child of four should suck maggots from the folds of her grandmother's jaw and think it's a kindness.

No.

Juniper failed us. Yes, she was a child herself. But she was almost nineteen when the worst came, old enough to choose differently. She chose Daudir. She chose the dark. And it damaged us in ways she can't—won't—understand.

And I am a big part of that. I was so quick to reinforce her lie with one of my own, to cement the choices she made, all because I didn't want to lose my family. But I can't risk following Juniper down into her delusion and lose Ivy like I lost the others. I won't make the same mistake twice.

And I can't just assume Juniper hasn't hurt Ivy. Not now. Not after discovering she knew about Willow all this time, kept it hidden, never sought help. I must assume she's done something drastic again. Maybe in Daudir's name. Maybe in her own. Either way, I think Ivy's in danger. Or starving. Or worse.

I wait until long after the house settles. The hour where time breathes slow, where things move behind walls. The floorboards stop creaking beneath invisible feet. The walls no longer tick with cooling heat. The roof groans one last time, sighing as it presses down over our heads, and falls silent with a last *tick, tick, tick*. When all I can hear is the blood in my ears and the wind licking the glass, I slip from my bed.

Beltane is different at night. She exhales rot. Every nail and hinge feels sentient. Like little spies, watching. The hallway stretches longer than I remember, the air chalky with dust and mildew and breath.

The stairs moan beneath me as I descend. I tiptoe across the entrance hall and into the dining room, through to the kitchen, which smells like copper pennies and black soil, the perfume of something buried too long. I stand before the cellar door, my hand hovering over the knob—an old familiar friend turned stranger.

It isn't locked.

That fact makes something in my chest tighten. If Ivy were down there, wouldn't Juniper lock the door? Wouldn't she secure it like everything else she's ever hidden?

But maybe she's chained. Maybe she's gagged. Maybe she's—

I push the thought away and head down.

At six feet tall, Juniper is barely ninety pounds. Ivy could knock her over with a feather. But I have to check. I have to try.

The light from my phone flickers over slick stone and wooden beams swollen with damp. The air is thick. Chewy. It presses against my skin like a wet cloth. And there, where once were boxes and preserves and the forgotten clutter of generations, are bones.

Piles of them. Neatly, obsessively stacked. Skulls with empty sockets facing one another like they're mid-conversation. Pelts curled in on themselves, shrunken and mummified, like scabs peeled from Daudir himself.

I hate how they make me feel at home, how welcoming and familiar the signs of death are. So intimate that it's like walking through my childhood bedroom.

I run my fingers over a pelt. The membrane's been left intact. It's crusted now, puckered like something trying to curl into itself. Badly done. What a waste.

And that's when it happens.

The buzzing.

It starts low, just behind my ears, like a swarm of flies pressing through the walls of my skull. My breath catches. I freeze.

From the far corner of the cellar, something shifts.

A shadow, maybe nothing, but it *moves*, and I know with the certainty of cell-deep instinct that something is watching me. I feel it between my ribs. A stillness like a scream I can't let out.

I try to lift my phone light, but my limbs won't answer. My body is stone, and in that stone, the dark moves. And also . . . doesn't. It *deepens*. Like an optical trick, like looking at a tunnel that's growing wider and longer and hungrier—and not changing at all.

The buzzing intensifies. It's in my teeth now, in the marrow of my bones.

And still, I can't look away.

There's a *presence* in the black. Not a person. Not a beast. Something old. Watching me the way the pit watches the falling stone.

I don't know how long I'm frozen. Minutes. Hours. The dark bends around me, expanding. Clenching. Breathing.

Finally, logic claws its way through the fog. This is just a fear response. Imagination. Pareidolia. I force myself to move. My fingers jerk up. The light flares.

And there, in the beam—

Piles of sticks and rocks. More bones. Pelts. Tangled twine. Nothing but objects.

Dead things.

I exhale, ragged, jagged, mildew on my breath.

"What are you doing down here?"

The voice, Juniper's, cuts through the dark like a blade. I shriek, spinning, light shaking in my grip.

She's sitting in the shadows beside one of the malformed effigies—dark wood bound in crude knots, its limbs misshapen, barely more than a bundle of sticks stitched together with obsession.

I shine the light at her. Her eyes shrink back, pupils huge and mirror black.

"I was never as good an Effigist as you," she says softly. Her fingers are cracked and raw as she winds twine around a gnarled branch. "I've been trying to make new ones. Yours rotted years ago."

She studies the branch, her voice dreamlike. "I think it's the intention that counts more than the shape."

"Whatever passes the time," I murmur, though I'm transfixed by her hands as they wind, wind, and wind the twine.

"I made a mess of the skins," she says, nodding toward the curled pelts. "Couldn't figure it out."

"You left the membrane layer. You have to scrape it clean. The veins. The fascia. Everything."

Juniper looks up at me, her busy hands stilling. "How did you know that?"

I shrug. "I suppose it seemed obvious."

"You see? You were always a natural."

"None of this was natural, June."

She exhales, and the sound scrapes the walls like claws, passing between us, ghostlike. "Why did you stop believing?"

I regard her, wondering if I should be honest. "Not sure I ever really did believe."

"You did," she says, voice quiet. "You believed more than any of us."

A laugh slips out of me, bitter as bile. "Maybe. And what good did it do me? What good did it do you?"

"I'm happy," she says. "I'm safe. I'm loved. I'm protected." She pauses for a long moment, and then gets back to her twigs. "I never left Beltane. That means something."

"It means nothing."

Juniper smiles. It's an old, hollow thing.

"Are you happy?" she asks. "Are you loved? Are you safe? Or do you feel like a beetle under a boot?"

"What did you do with Ivy, Juniper?" I snap, turning my flashlight on her full force.

She shies away from the light again, but I don't relent. I want her to see me, really see me.

"Where is she?" I demand again.

"If she's not here," Juniper says slowly, "then she's with Daudir."

The cold that washes over me is so sharp it feels like a cut.

"What does that mean?"

Juniper stands. Her shadow warps against the stone. "It means I don't know what Daudir wants. For her. For you. For any of us." She meets my eyes. "I would never hurt you. Any of you."

I want to believe her.

She steps closer. "Come on. Let's have some tea."

I hesitate. "What, no bug elixir?"

She chuckles, and something of the old Juniper shines through. "Not today."

Hazel comes down, ruffled in a silk nightgown, her hair wrapped in a heatless-curl headband. Gold silicone patches still sit under her eyes like she's a beauty blogger on vacation.

"You're up early," she rasps, taking a seat next to me at the dining room table.

I blink bleary eyes. "Is it morning already?"

Hazel gives me a sideways look, then glances at Juniper across the table. "Have you guys been awake all night?"

"I couldn't sleep."

"I don't sleep much anymore," Juniper adds, back to being fucking weird again.

For a few hours, it was almost like she was herself again. We talked, trying to bridge the gap of decades, but mostly we sat and listened to the rain while I tried to ignore the creepy feeling of eyes on my back beyond Daudir's window.

With Hazel's dawn arrival, I realize that it's all been a performance. Juniper's theater. Her invitation. She's trying to reel me back in. Into the belly of Daudir.

Stupid.

"Did you leave Willow sleeping?" I ask Hazel.

She frowns. "No? I thought you were with her."

My stomach flips. "I left her tied to my bedpost so she wouldn't run off into the woods again and get hurt."

"Yeah, I know. I thought you moved her."

We stare at each other. Chairs scrape back violently. We run through the house calling Willow's name. Stupid. So fucking *stupid.* I let Juniper distract me. Let her get in my head again. Let her try to burrow in there like a mouse on a mission.

We search the house. The attic. Every room. My room.

Nothing.

"Not there," Hazel says, meeting me in the kitchen on my way to the cellar, which we check together.

By the time we're all back in the dining room, we accept that Willow has well and truly gone.

I rub my eyes, trying to keep my temper in check.

"She probably went back to Daudir," Juniper says dreamily. "She's safe. She's home."

"I tied those knots myself," I say, my jaw aching with tension. "If she got out, it's because someone *let* her out."

I force myself to take a breath. Now Ivy *and* Willow are gone. I thought this was Juniper's doing, that she was messing with us. Except I was in her company *all night*.

The only one I wasn't watching . . . was Hazel.

# 28

***The approach of autumn, 2000***

Summer hangs heavy over Beltane that year, thick with warmth and the droning hum of bees. The days drip by like honey. Slow, golden, endless. And in those days, Clem carries Henry's touch like a secret flame, hidden beneath her skin. They meet at the lake, beneath the sun's greedy gaze. They kiss in the hush of the pines.

At night, the air is syrupy and sweet, the sky the deep indigo of sleep, freckled with stars. Clem lies awake, the sheets tangled around her ankles, the open window breathing the scent of clover and sun-warmed earth into her room. The curtains rise and fall on languid tides, and she watches, adrift in the hush between waking and dream, her whole body burning with new sensation.

Soft as a deer's tread, the trellis creaks beneath her window. The scrape of boots on bark. She sits up, heart fluttering. Henry's face appears, pale and boyish in the moonlight, eyes shining with mischief and longing.

"Clem," he whispers, voice low, as if the night itself might overhear.

She moves to the window, pulls him inside, the room suddenly charged with something electric, ancient, inevitable. His hands are warm, rough from work and sun, and they tangle in her hair as she pulls him through the window, pulls him close. The curtains billow around them, veiling them in gauzy white, the room lit only by moon silver.

*I'm dreaming,* she thinks. This must be a dream.

But he is here, hot and real in her arms, like some kind of fairy tale.

They lie together on her bed, limbs braided, the warm night air caressing their flushed skin. His breath is warmer against her neck, his heartbeat a steady thrum against her ribs as he presses into her. Outside, the world is still—the crickets, the sighing pines, the distant call of an owl—and inside, it feels as though they are the only two souls that have ever existed.

Kiss of lips in the hollow of her throat, along her sweat-dampened hairline, muffled groans and sighs.

"I'll never forget this," he whispers, sleep and sated desire thick in his throat.

They fall into sleep, tangled in each other, the summer night folding around them like a secret story.

But summer, like all beautiful things, begins to fade. The days grow shorter, the nights cooler, the air tasting faintly of wild figs and smoke. When Henry is gone, Clem misses him like a limb. She spends her days at the window, chasing the warmth of those nights in memory, imagining the letters he would write if he could, the promises he would send on paper thin as moth wings.

Then, autumn. A Wednesday in October, a raging storm arrives, not gentle, but wild—a hairy deluge that traps them in the house, walls pressing close, the air sharp with cold. Confined to Beltane house, the sisters play their games. Silly invented ones where stones are thrown into the air and sticks have to be picked up in various quantities before the stones clatter to the floor. Or ones where one sister hides but makes a noise every so often until she is found. They invent rules and punishments, make trades and offer deals.

They keep the fires lit as much as they can, hoarding the warmth, but the wood won't last forever. The generator broke in July, and somehow it didn't seem very important. They use the gas Ernest brings to soak the wood, helping it take in the fire grates. The rest, they store away. Mostly, it's useless.

"It would be so much more fun if Henry was here," Ivy sighs, the weariness plain in her voice.

Clem can feel it, too—the way the twins are fraying at the edges, boredom blooming into something sharper, hungrier.

They have played one too many rounds of the same old games.

"How about we play again, but Holly goes this time?"

She's so busy thinking of ways of keeping them tame, locked in step with a low-grade claustrophobic panic that's infecting the walls, that she fails to predict Hazel.

"I don't know," Hazel says, gathering up the sticks. "I'm not sure *I'd* want to be sloppy seconds."

She meets Clem's eyes as she says it, and Clem's stomach drops into her feet. There is a knowing on Hazel's face, in the cruel curve of her mouth. *Sloppy seconds.* What does she mean? *I'm not sure* I'd *want to be sloppy seconds . . .*

The words echo and fracture in her mind. Sloppy. Seconds. Of course she knows what it means, but does *Hazel* mean what it means? Does she mean . . . that Henry was with Hazel before her? That Clem was not his first, not his only? That Hazel was?

A cruel curve to Hazel's mouth seems to confirm her fear.

No.

Her heart buffets like a blizzard in her chest, unchecked, like a bird battering itself against glass.

"What do you mean?" Holly asks, her sharp little ears pricking at the tension.

Clem's vision swims. Sloppy seconds. Sloppy seconds.

"Spill," Ivy says, grinning, sensing blood.

Clem steadies herself with a hand to the floor.

Hazel only smirks, gray-eyed and dangerous. "Boys pretend to like you to get something. Then they move on to the next gullible idiot."

The room is suddenly too small, the air thick as wool. Clem's body goes cold with horror. Henry . . . and Hazel? Could it be true? She remembers them talking by the lake a few times over the summer, but that means nothing . . . doesn't it? He also spent time with Willow and Poppy and Juniper and the twins. Hazel isn't anything special.

She forces her hands to keep picking up the sticks, forces herself to look away from Hazel's smirk, from the glint of satisfaction in her gaze.

"She's just pretending she knows something," Holly says, breaking the moment by snapping a twig and then throwing it into the grate where the fire takes it. "I'm bored."

"I'm hungry," Ivy adds.

Without another word they scatter toward the kitchen, where Juniper is teaching Willow and Poppy to make flatbread with the flimsy remnants of the flour.

"Lying about what?" Hazel asks, face innocent as an abyss. "Not all of us keep secrets."

And with that, she's gone, leaving Clem alone with her churning thoughts, the ghosts of summer nights, and the cold, creeping doubt that maybe, just maybe, Hazel is right.

When Yuletide comes around again, it rushes forward in a flurry of muggy snow.

The storm arrived at dawn, carried in on a breath of air colder than the sea had known in months. All night, the island had listened to the wind whistling low, rattling cedar boughs and bending moss-dripped alders, but the rain never came. Instead, the first flakes drifted down in silence, clinging to the fir needles and the sodden ground like they were reluctant travelers deciding to stay.

By midmorning, the snow is steady. Thick, wet clumps that plaster the roof and muffle the soft forest floor. It sticks, improbably, even as the ground steams faintly from its warmth. The air smells sharp, almost metallic, as if the ocean itself has turned brittle in the cold.

For a few hours, the whole island transforms. The mossy logs wear white caps, the spongy soil hides under a thin crust, and the usual *drip*

*drip drip* of rain is replaced by the hush of falling snow. Even the gulls seem bewildered, wheeling low and calling against the pale sky.

By late afternoon, the snow sags from branches in great sodden clumps, sliding off the roof in sheets, running into rivulets down the narrow paths. By the next morning, the island has returned to its frigid green self, only the memory of whiteness lingering in the hollows and the chill of it still hanging in the air.

The wild sweetness of summer has long since leached from the world. The warmth that once gilded Clem's skin now feels like a memory she can't quite hold. The cold is deeper this year, biting, bitter, and she wonders if its only winter's doing, or if Hazel's poisoned words still linger, chilling her from within.

She ruminates on Hazel's hint, that cruel, barbed thing tossed so carelessly, and feels it coil inside her like a secret she can't forget. It gnaws at the edges of her heart, mingling with a strange, unsettling sense that she has forgotten something vital. Some ritual, some offering, something that should have kept them safe. She misses Henry fiercely, as if he were a lost part of herself, but even that longing is now shadowed by doubt. What if he was never truly hers? What if Hazel was right?

The tension runs through the house like a seam of unease, a grain of sand in flour. Beltane house groans beneath winter's weight, as if it, too, shares the burden of unspoken things. The walls feel too tight; the air too thin. They need to get out, to hunt, to spill fresh blood on the frozen ground.

The twins, once buoyed by their visions, have fallen into an uneasy stillness. All summer and fall, Holly and Ivy whispered of Daudir's messages: the hemlock's maiming, the dream of fire and ash, retold so often it became legend. But as November waned, and Granny Alys's ascension day passed, the dreams stopped. Clem sees the relief in their faces, the quiet ease of children no longer kept sleepless by gods. And yet, that peace feels false, as if it's only waiting for the next storm.

Still, something is wrong. Clem feels it in her bones, in the way the wind claws at the windows. Again, obsessively, she wonders if this is all because of Hazel's insinuation. Maybe it's the secret of the stolen bones, heavy and unspoken? Or is it guilt—guilt that she's let the strife between Holly, Ivy, and Willow fester, that she's stood by in silence? She justifies her noninvolvement by telling herself that were she to say anything now, it would only breed more discord . . . so she remains silent.

Or is it Willow herself? The way Clem finds her bed cold some mornings, empty, as if she's vanished into the night. No footprints in the frost. No explanation.

Meanwhile, the twins play their macabre games, turning Granny Alys into a kind of totem, a ghastly elf on the shelf. Once again, each morning reveals her in some new tableau, posed with the casual mischief of childhood layered over deep, unsettling devotion.

They've become bolder now that Granny Alys is so light, her skin leathery and stiff, her bones familiar and malleable.

Monday: Granny reclines in the bath, a chunk of stale, moldy bread clenched in her clawed hand, crumbs stuck to her withered jaw.

Tuesday: She kneels in the pantry, head bowed against a shelf, fingers crooked around a jar of cloves, caught mid-theft.

Wednesday: She lounges by the hearth, one brittle arm propped behind her skull with twine where bone has splintered, as if resting from a long day.

Thursday: She lies in Willow's bed, a grotesque stand-in, a mockery of comfort in the place where Clem found only emptiness hours before.

Poppy shrieks with delight each time Granny Alys is found, clapping her hands, her voice bright with wonder.

"Silly Nana!" she cries, while Holly and Ivy exchange sly glances, pleased with their handiwork.

And now, new rites are born: Morning prayers, *Gi'emhares joposhe*, whispered with breath steaming in the frigid air; midday baptisms in the half-frozen lake, their limbs blue and trembling as they wade in; supper at seven sharp; and after, the nonsense songs chanted to the forest through Daudir's windows left bare so He can witness them.

They curtsy at the end, barefoot and wild-eyed, draped in tatters and pelts, shadows of the city girls they once were.

Clem watches it all, feeling the weight of bare feet on icy floors, the sting of cold in her blood. She hasn't worn shoes in nearly two years. She wonders if she remembers how.

Granny Alys is delicate now, her skin paper thin and yellowed like old lace, her sinews and cartilage shrunken to jerky.

So, it's no surprise that one cold morning, when Holly and Ivy get into an argument over where Granny should go next, disaster looms. Their bickering rises through the house like an off-key carol, the tune wild and unpredictable. Little Poppy, delighted by any excuse for a song, hums "Jingle Bells" over the top of it all, adding a cheerful harmony entirely at odds with the scene.

"The cellar," Holly declares, her voice sharp as the frost on the window, clutching Granny's fragile arm like it's a prized doll. "Daudir wants her close to the roots. That's where the messages come clearest. You *know* that."

"The attic!" Ivy snaps, tugging the other arm with righteous fury. "Closer to the stars. He's sending signs from the sky lately. You just don't pay attention!"

Their voices overlap in a discordant duet, root versus sky, screeching like two magpies fighting over a bit of string. The cobwebs in the corners tremble with the force of it. In the kitchen, a pot boils over, sending out a hiss of steam, mingling with Poppy's ever-louder, caterwauled song. Ignored by all.

Juniper appears, summoned by the noise, with Hazel hot on her heels, a look of glee sparking in her eye. Drama, at last. Clem watches from her spot in the corner, where she's assembling the beginnings of an effigy out of brittle twigs, thinking: *Every house has its holiday traditions, I suppose.*

"Cellar!" Holly yells, digging her heels into the moth-eaten rug like a mule.

"Attic!" Ivy roars, yanking harder.

And then—*rip*. A sound like old paper tearing, followed by a sharp *crack*. Both of Granny Alys's arms pop out of joint and tear from the skin that barely held them, sending each twin sprawling backward onto her backside, both clutching a complete arm bone. What's left of Granny Alys collapses in a heap, like a forgotten marionette.

Dead skin cells float like glitter in the air between them, catching the light.

The room is quiet for half a heartbeat.

"You broke Granny Alys," Holly whispers, mouth gaping.

Ivy's lower lip wobbles. "*You* broke Granny Alys."

Poppy pauses her singing just long enough to burst into giggles, clapping as if it's the best magic trick she's ever seen. Poppy has adapted to this strange new world as if she's stepped into a fairy tale and decided to stay. Every day is a wonder: Granny's brittle bones, the endless rain, the strange new rituals. To her, the house is alive, enchanted, a playground of oddities. Poppy has started speaking to the frost patterns on the windows as if they're old friends, and she sleeps curled in animal pelts as if she's always been a cub at heart.

Juniper pinches the bridge of her nose and sighs like she's aged a decade.

"She started it," the twins say in chorus, each brandishing the stolen arms at one another. As if they might duel.

Juniper surveys the scene, deadpan. "Well. Might as well save the bones for something useful. Clem?"

Clem groans but rises, brushing bits of bark from her skirt. The twins hand over the limbs, sheepish now that the excitement has dulled. Clem gathers what's left of Granny Alys into her arms, careful not to lose any more pieces, and heads for the cellar.

She has no idea what she'll use them for, but they are good bones. It would be a waste not to put them to work.

There will be a purpose for them. There's *always* a purpose.

Granny Alys, as always, doesn't complain.

***March 2001***

On the second anniversary of their arrival, Ernest brings supplies, but neglects to bring Granny Alys's newspapers. Juniper says nothing. Ernest says nothing.

And so, the days continue.

# 29

***September 2024***

I wake sometime after midnight, groggy with lack of sleep.

The room feels too quiet, too still. My breath catches, ears straining for a sound I can't name, something that must have pulled me from sleep. The air feels heavy, as if the night itself has seeped through the cracks in the walls, pressing cold fingers against my skin.

I sit up and push the blanket back, trying to hear over the thudding of my heart. The floorboards groan beneath my feet as I cross to the window. Outside, the world is draped in darkness, the trees are nothing but a sea of formless shapes, the boundary between clearing and forest lost to shadow.

Something holds me there, staring. Looking. Searching.

And then: movement. A flicker, swift and sure, between the trunks. A shadow darker than the dark. My pulse skips. I press my palm to the glass, leaning closer, eyes straining. There. Again. A shape, darker than shadow, sliding between the trees, where no one should be.

*Daudir.*

The thought comes unbidden, sharp, and I don't know if it's hope or fear that clenches my stomach tight. Ridiculous. Insane.

But I have to know.

I turn from the window, breath quickening, and reach for my jeans. I could wake Hazel, or Juniper. I could tell them I saw something in the night. But no. Juniper will only feel confirmed in her beliefs. Hazel will only warn me to stay inside until morning.

But I have to know, one way or another. Because I did see something. I'm sure of it. Quickly, I dress, and grab my cell, hesitating. The battery is low, but holding up, and I need the light.

I need to see for myself.

I move quietly, as quietly as I can. The floorboards are complicit in their unusual silence as I creep down the stairs, across the hall, and to the door. Only when I reach for the handle does the floor creak, traitorous. I pause, hand outstretched, ears tuned to the noises of the house, to the movement of my sisters inside it. There is nothing but stillness.

I backtrack to the dining room, where I left my boots, and slip them on with trembling hands, realizing I was about to rush into the woods on bare feet that have grown soft and delicate.

Then I head back to the front door and turn the handle. The latch clicks louder than it should, and I freeze, half expecting a voice to call out from the dark. But Beltane stays silent. I open the door just wide enough to slip through and close it like a whisper behind me.

The night air hits me hard, sharp, biting, carrying with it the damp rot of leaves and the faintest smell of smoke. I hesitate, heart beating fast, gaze fixed on the tree line. The shape is gone now, swallowed by the blackness beneath the boughs. But I know where it went. I saw the path it took.

I cross the yard quickly, boots crunching over earth. I pause at the boundary, thinking. Deciding. Justifying. The old warnings come, unbidden, Granny Alys's voice a memory I can't quite grasp: *Be back at Beltane before sundown. Don't go past the boundary after dark.*

I try to picture her face, but it's faded, smudged by time. Just a voice now, and words that sound foolish in the cold night air. Just a skeleton. Just bones. Anyway, why should I listen? Why let old fears keep me from the truth when I can't even remember the why of the rules?

I swallow my fear and step over the boundary, heart hammering so hard I feel it in my throat. The forest swallows me whole. I pull out my phone and put on the flashlight, scanning the trees around me. I feel better with the light than I did in the dark, but that lasts only a moment.

The trees crowd close, bare branches scratching at the sky. I move quickly at first, my breath loud, too loud. Every crack of a twig beneath my boots makes me flinch. The deeper I go, the more the dark presses in, thick and heavy.

Something snaps to my left. I freeze, head and phone whipping toward the sound. Nothing but trees, silent and still. But I can feel it. I can feel *something* watching. The stories come back, suddenly too real. Daudir moving between the trees. Daudir watching. Daudir in control.

I shake the thoughts away. Focus. I came for answers.

The ground dips suddenly, and I stumble, sliding down a slick slope hidden by dead leaves. A branch catches me, sharp as a knife, and I cry out as it rips through my sleeve, into my arm. The pain is immediate, hot. I clutch at the wound, fingers coming away sticky with blood.

I used to know these woods so well, but only in daylight. We never strayed after dark. I force myself to calm down, to remember that the path to the house is only just behind me, but I'm shaking now, breath coming too fast. The woods are too quiet. The air too still.

And then, a sound. A definite, deliberate *step*. Heavy. Close.

"Willow?" My voice cracks, thin and small in the dark. "Willow, stop it. It's not funny."

But even as I say it, I know. Willow would be lighter, quicker, a flicker between the trees. This is . . . bigger. Heavier. Wrong.

*Not human,* my mind screams.

The night seems to deepen around me, fighting the light in my hand, and the branches press in close. I can't see it, but I can feel it. The weight of a gaze. The low, steady sound of something breathing where nothing should be.

Panic seizes me. I turn, slipping on the wet leaves, and run. The forest tears at me as I go, branches grabbing at my coat, thorns scratching my skin. I don't look back. I can't. The thing behind me is close. Too close.

For a terrible moment I think I'm lost. Shouldn't I be at the boundary by now? Then it appears like salvation through the trees, low and overgrown, but *there.* I throw myself at it, racing over, tripping on the other side. I don't stop. I scramble to my feet and cross the yard, boots pounding the earth, and through the door, slamming it shut behind me.

I lean against the wood, gasping, blood dripping from my arm, heart beating so loud I can't hear anything else. If it comes, will the door be enough to keep it out? I gasp in my air, and wait, ears straining, and as time passes with nothing but my own panic for company, my logic centers kick slowly back into place.

Elk.

Fox.

Coyote.

Deer.

Logical explanations. I remember something else Granny Alys told us. *This is an old growth forest.* Plenty of animals to choose from. Any of which could have made that stepping sound.

"Seriously?" I breathe, pressing a fist to my stupid-ass head. "You coward. Scared by a deer."

I listen again, but there is nothing. Just the silence of the house and the dark pressing at the windows.

I turn and face Beltane house, feeling stupider than ever. Here I am, off chasing shadows, when the enemy might be in these very walls.

# 30

***August 2001***

A month before Poppy turns six, the summer storms hit the island in full force, turning everything muggy.

The well floods three times, turning the inner boundary into a quagmire and keeping the sisters occupied with buckets, spades, and mops for endless days. But Clem barely notices the filth or the toil. Her heart is too heavy.

Henry didn't come with the supplies in June.

There has been no word. No letter. No message passed through his father. Just his absence, so total it feels like a hole torn in the world. Over two months now, and Clem has tried to fill that hole with work, with repairs, with building effigy upon effigy, with keeping the water out of the cellar and the house upright. But none of it kept her mind from circling back, again and again, to Hazel's smirk. That awful, knowing smirk.

She doesn't believe the implication. She trusts Henry implicitly, except . . . the thought won't leave her alone.

The questions gnaw at her as surely as the storms gnaw at their home.

And then, on a rare morning when the sun dares to break through, Poppy wakes with a fever.

It is an accident that Clem is the one to find her. Heading out of her room and down the hall for breakfast, she almost trips over a small stick-and-bone doll, the one with little sparrow feathers around the neck like a high collar, and yellow button eyes.

Tutting, she picks it up, smoothing down a crooked feather.

"What are you doing here, Mara?" she murmurs. "I didn't make you to end up killing me, you know."

She turns to Poppy's room and knocks on the half-shut door. No answer. Sighing, she pushes it open and finds Poppy still tangled in her thin, fraying quilt. She reaches to rouse her little ruffian of a sister, but as her fingers graze Poppy's skin, she recoils.

Too hot.

Not the muggy warmth of a child in sleep, but a scorching, damp heat that speaks of nightmares and midnight groans. She is *burning.*

"Poppy," Clem whispers, heart thudding, brushing sweat-soaked hair from a flushed brow. Poppy moans, limp and listless. Her beloved rabbit stuffed animal, the one Clem gifted her more than two years ago now, and which is normally clenched tight in sleep, lies discarded, as though flung away during a fever dream.

Pale hair clings, damp, to her forehead and temples, and when Clem shakes her gently, she flings an arm above her head, whimpering.

Poppy moans, small and lost, her pale hair stuck to her brow. The rabbit toy lies abandoned, forgotten. Clem lifts her, startled by how solid, how heavy she's become, and carries her downstairs, quilt trailing behind like a ghost.

"Something's wrong," she shouts as she races down the stairs, stopping now and again to hoist Poppy back up into her arms. "Juniper! Something's wrong!"

The twins are sitting in the doorway, door flung wide to try to coax in a nonexistent breeze, and when Clem yells again, they jump to their feet and come hurrying.

"Where's Juni?" Clem pants, rushing past them and into the informal living room. She's going to lose her grip on Poppy any moment, and wants a soft landing.

"I don't know," Holly says, voice hitched in rising panic. "What's wrong with her?"

"Find Juniper and tell her Poppy's sick." When they stand and stare, unmoving, she snaps, "Now!"

Clem rushes into the kitchen, pumping water into the sink, thankful that the flooded well hasn't caused a shortage of water. She dunks a cloth inside and then hurries back to Poppy with the dripping clump and presses it to Poppy's head. The child groans, flinching away, scrabbling weakly at the source of the discomfort.

The others trickle in, and finally so does Juniper. "What's happened?"

"I don't know. She's hot. Really, really hot."

Juniper takes Clem's place, kneeling beside the sofa. Clem watches her eyes dart this way and that over Poppy's face, the wheels turning in her head.

"The bath—the copper bath upstairs in Granny Alys's bathroom. Let's get her up there. We need to get her covered in water. Bring the temperature down."

They comply without thinking, Clem and the twins hauling Poppy up between them, Willow and Hazel rushing ahead to prepare the tub.

"Stop!" Hazel yells when they've reached the landing. "The water's not pumping up here!"

She hurries out, shaking her head. Willow looks pale and terrified.

Juniper's lips purse, and Clem feels a jolt of fear that Juniper will panic too. But she doesn't. Of course she doesn't.

"The lake," Juniper says. "Let's get her to the lake."

It's the longest walk to the lake that Clem can remember. The sky is churning above them, the clouds low and hostile. The yellow-tinged purple of bruises.

Another storm is coming.

Poppy is barely conscious when they carry her out. Her pitiful little moans stopped along the way. Her limbs dangle, loose and hot, her breaths flittering like a moth. Beneath half-closed lids, tinged the delicate purple of lilacs, her eyes roll and roll and roll.

She groans again, fighting weakly, and says nonsense things. Names none of them know. Songs no one taught her.

The Wards move in silence, the kind that sits in the mouth like a prayer, bare feet soft in the mud, carrying Poppy two by two like something fragile. Something sacred.

Clem's mind is reeling. Why is this happening?

What have they done wrong?

Juniper leads the way, jaw clenched, eyes forward. The lake lies ahead, just past the tree line, expanding dark and wide under the turbulent sky, the promise of cool, chilled water only feet away.

Behind Clem, Holly and Ivy whisper to each other in anxious fragments, fingers white-knuckled where they clutch Poppy's legs. Willow follows behind, head buried in Granny Alys's old herbal almanac.

"She's scorching," Holly whispers, adjusting her grip so that Poppy jolts a little in Clem's hands.

"I know," Ivy says, and her lip trembles. "I have a bad feeling."

"Me too," says Hazel, and Clem feels a spike of anger like a thorn in her side.

"Ssh!" Juniper commands, and Clem is glad. She doesn't want them to voice her terrible thoughts aloud for fear of making them real.

"*She's going to die,*" Holly whispers, and Clem's head screams with a high-pitched frequency that's so sharp, so sudden, that she almost loses her grip on Poppy altogether.

"Don't say that," she grits out.

"What? I just said she's going to be fine."

The trees open at last, spilling them onto the soft moss of the lakeshore. Faint lines of mist rise off the water, pale as a stolen breath. The lake reflects the angry clouds, roiling with indigestion.

"Careful," Juniper says as they wade in.

Their nightgowns float out around them, silk thin with age and damp. The water creeps up Clem's legs like a warning. Cold. Still. Waiting.

They lower Poppy slowly, gently. Her skin is burning against Clem's hands, even as the water laps at her ankles, her knees, her ribs.

"Is she shaking?" whispers Clem.

"No, she's not," Juniper says, voice hollow.

The shock of cold brings no shiver. No jolt. No gasp. Only a slight hitch in her chest—and then nothing.

"Further," Juniper says, her voice cracking. "Deeper."

They sink her in to the neck, five pairs of hands holding her afloat.

"How's it going?" Willow calls from the bank.

"Don't know," Clem yells back, her voice feeling too loud, too brazen in this sacred moment.

Poppy's hair fans around her body like pale pond weed. Her eyes remain shut. The lake licks at her fever, greedy and cold, but she still feels warm.

Juniper, supporting Poppy's head, presses a wet palm to her forehead. "Still warm. We need to put her under completely. She needs to get cold."

Clem isn't sure about that, but the others are already dunking her, so she follows suit. They put her under for only a moment, but she comes up groaning. More lively than she was before, at least, Clem thinks.

"Again," Juniper says.

And they dunk her under.

"Again."

And they do.

She whimpers, sputtering water, and something passes between the sisters like a wind, or a sigh, or a thread pulled tighter.

"She's waking up," Clem says, breathless. "It's working."

When they lift Poppy out of the lake, she feels heavier. Cooler. Her eyes don't open very far, or for very long, but she's shivering now, teeth chattering and skin broken into gooseflesh.

Clem is exhausted, and so are the twins. So Juniper carries Poppy home. Inside, they put her back onto the sofa and cover her lightly with the throw.

Nothing to do now but wait.

By six o'clock, she's worse than ever.

Outside, the sky has opened, new torrents of late-summer rain pelting the island full force.

"We have to take her outside," Juniper says. She is pacing the living room rug, biting on her thumbnail. "The lake helped, but I think we didn't keep her cold enough, and now the fever is worse."

"The rain?" Hazel asks.

"Yeah. I think it's the best option."

They hoist her up again, carrying her out and then laying her down just inside the boundary so that if she's to open her eyes, she'll see right into the trees. Clem suspects Juniper is trying to make sure that *Daudir* sees *her*.

Juniper stands for a moment, peering from Poppy to the trees beyond, before turning abruptly and heading back inside.

"Juni?" Hazel calls, but she is already gone.

When Juniper returns, she is holding the huge elk skull and antlers, the one from the lounge—the one they used to celebrate Poppy's fourth birthday. She puts it on her head, securing it using the hanging strap, faces the trees, and raises her arms.

"Chant," she commands, voice muffled by bone.

Hazel looks strangely unsure in the rain, hair flattened against her head. Just as unsure as Juniper had looked before she hid her face behind bone. But Juniper is going to be nineteen in less than a week. She's older than they are—she's grown. Still, Clem worries Juniper might be out of her depth. The way she herself is.

"Daudir, be with us," Willow whispers.

"Daudir, hear us," the twins call, louder.

Clem finds herself screaming. "Daudir save us!"

Her voice rings into the trees like a siren, and even the rain pauses for a moment to listen before clattering to earth again.

"Daudir save her!" Juniper screams, bone muffled but strong.

Awe rises like a wave in Clem's chest as she watches Juniper. She is otherworldly, eerie and powerful, the antlers spreading toward the sky like angels' wings.

"*Daudir save her!*" they all scream.

They scream it so loudly their throats grind and tear. They don't care. On and on they scream it. *"Daudir save her! Daudir save her! Daudir save her!"*

They scream, and they chant, and they dance in the rain, driving the mud up their feet, their legs, smattering it over Poppy so she looks flecked in blood, quickly washed away by the rain.

The sky rumbles and Clem feels a surge of raw terror. This isn't right. Something isn't right.

Juniper senses it, too, the crackling of electricity in the air. "You *will* save her!" she shrieks.

When lightning strikes in the distance, Juniper bends low, an unbalanced half human, half thing, and hauls Poppy up. "Help me!"

Clem and Hazel pull the skull from Juniper's head, buckling under its weight. It's a monster of a thing, and Clem wonders fleetingly if Granny Alys shot it herself. But no. She said it was Ernest, didn't she? Long ago. The memory is a whisp, fragile and ghostly.

The others help carry Poppy back inside, putting her down on the sopping sofa. Poppy is shivering now, but she's still hot. Still way too hot.

Again, there's nothing else to do but wait.

"I found this," Willow says, taking Juniper and Clem aside after endless stormy minutes.

Hazel and the twins sit at Poppy's side, biting their nails, trying to keep the palatable sense of doom at bay.

Willow hands Juniper the herbalist's almanac, and Clem is so grateful that Willow thought of this. Juniper pages to the lengthy section at the back for remedies.

Clem reads over Juniper's shoulder.

"Cold baths," Juniper murmurs, her finger running over the list. "Did that. Alcohol rubs. No alcohol. Camphor oil, no, eucalyptus oil, no, high garlic diet—don't have enough." Her finger stops. "Does yarrow grow on the island?"

There's a picture of it on the page. Clem thinks she's seen it before.

"Yes!" Willow cries. "Yes, I've seen it! By the lake—we just passed some!"

Juniper looks up at them. "Get it. And hurry."

Clem and Willow don't need telling twice. They're out the door before Hazel or the twins can even ask what's happening. Storm be damned. Lightning be damned.

"You sure you saw it?" Clem asks, panting as they run, swallowing mouthfuls of torrential rain. She can barely make out the track, let alone specific plants.

Willow nods furiously. "It was right there. The book said they would be umbels. Look for clusters of little white flowers."

Willow is right. The yarrow is easy to find, even in the downpour. Clem's heart soars when she sees it, endless clusters of white flowers with feathery leaves.

She looks up at Willow in wonder. "Daudir provides."

Willow's eyes glitter with moisture that has nothing to do with the rain. "Daudir provides."

They grab handfuls of the precious plants, flowers, leaves, stems, and even roots, since they don't know which parts will be needed, ripping them free without a moment's hesitation, and hurry back to the house.

Inside, Hazel has already been working to get water boiling, the woodstove raging. The pot on the stove is slowly heating. Clem wishes it didn't take so long for water to boil.

Clem reads from the almanac, instructing Willow, who cuts the plant into tiny pieces, using the leaves, flowers, and stems. They tip the mess into the pot and let it steep for five minutes. Juniper comes in to ask them how long three different times.

"We have to wait for it to cool," Willow says, when the infusion is ready. It steams, a warm honey color, on the counter.

"Add a bit of cold water," Hazel suggests.

"Won't that dilute the effects?" Clem asks.

Willow bites her lip. "I think so. Better to wait."

When the liquid is cool enough to drink, they bring it to Poppy in her favorite mug. Juniper helps her to sit, but she groans and her head flops to the side, away from the liquid.

"Come on now, poppet," Juniper coaxes. "A little drink and then you can go back to sleep."

Poppy groans again, pushing the cup away with a weak hand. "Hmmnnnnn . . ."

"One little sip, baba," Juniper says again, pressing the cup to Poppy's lips.

Then, surprising them all, Poppy opens her mouth and drinks more than half, as though she's dying of thirst.

"Good girl," Juniper murmurs. "Good girl. This will make you feel so much better."

When the mug is empty, Juniper sets it aside.

Wind claws at the rafters, and rain lashes the windows in sharp sheets, turning the world outside into a smear of shadow and sound. The trees are thrashing so violently, Clem worries they'll come crashing down around their heads.

The six of them sit and watch Poppy, her cracked lips the color of clay, her red cheeks, her moist brow. Each of them praying for the yarrow to do its work.

In a few minutes, or an hour, or a day, or a week, Poppy stirs.

"Weird," she slurs, her eyes rolling to us and back into her skull again. "Tongue . . ." She pokes out her tongue, pale and grotesque.

Her eyes roll toward them again, and her pupils are blown black, a sight that strikes terror so deep into Clem that she whimpers.

"Something isn't—"

Poppy begins to laugh, her eyes wide now, those black pupils yawning like voids. "There's maggots in your hair," she slurs, high, strange, like discordant bells. She giggles. "Wormies!"

Juniper touches Poppy's face.

Hazel checks her hair. "There's nothing in my hair."

"I told you no," Poppy demands over Juniper's shoulder. "Go away. I said no!" She groans, and tries to get away, arms flailing. "Daudir, no!"

They all still. Then Juniper turns to look behind her, slowly. Cautiously.

But there's nothing there. Just the empty room, the old fireplace and peeling wallpaper.

Poppy begins to pant, then bursts into tears, shivering, before cackling like a mad thing. "Bunnies! There are bunny rabbits in the sky!"

Juniper licks her lips. "She's . . . she's connected to Daudir. It's working. We just . . . just need to wait."

Clem closes her eyes, gratitude filling her to the brim. *Thank you, Daudir. Thank you.* She has never been more thankful, nor more filled with love, as she is in this moment. For all that Daudir is. For all that Daudir brings.

On and on, Poppy cycles between agitation and stupor, breath quickening and then falling shallow.

And then all at once, Clem feels as though she *is* Poppy.

The ceiling is the sky, and the sky is too close.

It presses down like a blanket soaked in boiling water, and a white buzzing, squishing noise fills her ears. Like flies. Like maggots.

Poppy cries out again, but surely her mouth is full of cotton, with ash, with something that tastes of dead flowers. Clem spits, and Poppy spits, but the rotten petals don't fall. They float, hover . . . sink.

"Are we outside?" Poppy whispers, eyes staring at the ceiling, and Clem can almost see what she sees. The forest. An endless sky. Rabbits flying in the clouds above, their ears flapping like giant white wings.

"No, darling," Juniper says. "We're in Beltane. Beltane is keeping you safe."

Poppy takes a gasp of breath. "Falling . . . up."

Clem puts a hand on Poppy's chest. Her heart is hammering right through her rib cage.

"Juni," she begins, but then Poppy laughs weakly, and her eyes roll up into her head again, and her body arcs, stiffening toward the ceiling. Her hands curl into claws, and she convulses in violent twitches.

The sound coming out of her is grotesque, horrifying. A terrible gargling of air forced from little lungs.

*"What's happening?"* Ivy cries, and Holly grabs her, pulling her away.

Poppy's body is jerking now, mouth frothing, teeth gnashing air.

The seizing stops in a terrible quiet, punctuated by Poppy's little gasps. She is so red in the face now it looks like she might burst.

Her eyes move in little steps over to Juniper, and then she goes still.

Nobody moves. Nobody breathes.

For a long, agonizing time.

"Poppy?" Juniper's voice is barely there. "P-Poppy."

Clem can barely think around the deep knowing that six Ward hearts beat in this room, and no more.

A breath. A scream. *"POPPY!"*

The storm howls on, rattling the bones of the house, and the bones of their hearts.

# 31

***August 2001***

"We should put her in the woods."

Clem isn't sure who says it. The only thing she's sure of is the yawning emptiness inside her. A vast sea, swallowing sound, swallowing breath.

Time drifts. Heavy. Endless. None of them move. None of them dare.

It hurts to breathe.

"We should . . . put her in the woods." The voice again. "She liked that spot with the big-leaf maple. She said . . . the leaves looked like stars."

The voice is watery. That alone makes Clem lift her head.

It's Hazel. Hazel's lip is quivering, her cheek damp. Juniper sits folded in on herself, a fallen curtain. The twins, cross-legged on the floor, silent as stones. Willow isn't even in the room anymore.

Clem swallows. Licks the sorrow from her lips, taste of death.

Ivy's voice is a whisper. "We can't just . . . leave her there."

"If only we could trade," Holly says softly. "Give Daudir a different life so he'll give her back."

"A life for a life," Ivy murmurs, eyes glassy.

Clem's voice is a wraith. "We should plant her."

Juniper looks up. Blue eyes find gray, storm clouds meeting stone.

Clem repeats herself. "Plant her outside."

"Like rose clippings?" Holly asks. "Like Granny Alys taught us?"

Clem nods, and something ancient stirs inside her. "And . . . and I have an effigy. A special one. I didn't know what it was for, but . . ."

Long nights in the cellar . . . she had built it without knowing why. Her hands working as though guided by another's will, driven with a purpose she didn't understand.

Now she does. And a terrible purpose it was.

Juniper shifts, her voice a broken thing. "Like roses."

They bring everything they need to the big-leaf maple, laying out bowls and blankets, twine and bone like a solemn offering.

They bathe Poppy in mushroom water and drape her in moss, gifts for the soil.

The effigy is erected first. Clem gives her sisters detailed instructions about which pieces fit together, which branches twist and connect, which vines interweave, and which ones loop and tie. Where the rocks should be placed, and where the bones belong. It is her most intricate project, a canopy statue woven of the Wood itself.

They plant Poppy shallow, so her roots might take hold. They weave her small arms into the waiting limbs of the effigy. She fits, perfectly, terribly. A few nails through her little palms and forearms ensure she won't lose her grip. The vines slink around her neck in a fibrous choker, and her hair falls in pale rivulets into the shadowed spaces left between wood and stone.

And Granny Alys's bones? The ones Clem knew were for a greater purpose? Here is that purpose, at last. Rib bones make up the core of the wings, fleshed out by parts of the fallen hemlock tree, twisted vine maple, cascara, and black cottonwood. The twigs feather out like fingers. Like feathers. Thigh bones and scapulae, sternum, spinal column and ulnae—all of Granny Alys's precious bones find their place, woven together to become Clem's finest work. She doesn't even feel as if *she* is the one creating: It feels more like her hands are being divinely guided.

Guided by Daudir.

They bury Granny Alys's skull in the soil beneath, so that Poppy will grow from wisdom.

And the crowning glory . . . the sacred elk skull, placed over Poppy's head, antlers reaching for the heavens.

When it is done, when she is planted up to her mid-calf and the effigy rises behind her, Clem and the others step back, back, and back.

The silence of the Wood is proof enough.

She is a thing of magnificence. Her presence is so tangible, so powerful, so *other*, that she's hard to look at. As if staring into the Mandelbrot fractal, or the eye of a nebula, knowing the nebula looks back.

Juniper falls to her knees, staring wide-eyed and slack jawed. Clem feels it too. She is ravished with a thrumming awe, riven before the majesty of the god before her. Poppy and the effigy have become one . . . a whole new being entirely.

"Daudir," Juniper whispers. *"Daudir."*

Clem's skin breaks into gooseflesh, and her hand trembles as she reaches up, and up, and up.

"Daudir."

Willow doesn't say another word.

And she doesn't sit at the table with the others at seven.

Five of seven seats occupied. It feels like none.

"Willow has joined Daudir," Juniper informs them, solemn. Serene. "She is more than Seer now. She is Companion."

And so, it is done.

Ernest does not come in September.

Clem, Holly, Ivy, and Hazel wait by the dock, day after day. By the twelfth day, it is clear that there won't be an autumn delivery.

Juniper says that Daudir is testing them. Testing their faith. Testing their resolve. They are a part of Beltane, and Beltane will provide, so long as they remain faithful and strong. So long as their devotion does not waver. Clem is filled with zeal, a desperate willingness to do anything, *anything at all*, to prove that she is faithful. That they are all faithful. That they deserve to be saved.

Daily, they pray at Poppy's effigy—Daudir's place—watching as the maple leaves fall around them like jewels. The air is sacred here, and Clem rarely wishes to leave. Now and then, she catches sight of Willow, but never for long. The Companion is as fleeting as the shadows.

They pray.

Worship.

Leave offerings.

Make sacrifices.

The forest follows them home. It whispers inside the walls of Beltane now, chattering in a language none of them understand. Still, it feeds them. Mushrooms grow on almost all the walls, beetles and bugs make their way inside. Juniper and Clem find hares, deer mice, voles, squirrels, and even a crow trapped in the snares. There is always a little bit of meat and a lot of fungus. They work together skinning and storing, preserving and canning, while Hazel and the twins work to repair the windows, the walls; clear the chimneys and keep the house in firewood.

The house seems alive with the spirit of the Wood.

On a day that the sisters have forgotten to keep track of, they make their daily visit to Daudir beneath the maple, a basket of offerings on Hazel's arm. Today they have brought the last of Clem's button collection, some black tea steeped in lake water, Poppy's flat rabbit stuffed animal, and a quilt from Granny Alys's blanket chest.

But when they arrive, the clearing is empty.

The soil has been churned up, as though something or someone has dug out the effigy and Daudir along with it.

Juniper's breath leaves her in a whoosh. "Daudir's gone . . ."

"He's been *moved*," Hazel says, dropping the basket. The offerings go rolling over the dirt.

Clem's heart is pounding in her chest. She would give almost anything not to be here. For this not to be happening.

Ivy searches their faces, looking terrified. "Someone took Him?"

Holly is crouching down beside Hazel now, the two of them examining the soil. "Spade marks."

Hazel's eyes meet Clem's. "You did this."

Clem steps back, but Hazel is already advancing, teeth bared in a feral hiss. She looks terrifying. "You moved Him!"

Clem stammers. "I-I didn't—"

Hazel grabs her by the ruffs of her grimy dress, yanking hard. It is the first time since they were small children that Hazel has laid hands on her in anger. She shakes Clem so that Clem's teeth clank together.

*"Admit it!"*

With a yell, Holly tackles Hazel so they roll in the freshly churned earth. "Stop it!" Ivy screams.

Panting, Clem scrambles away, turning pleading eyes on Juniper.

But Juniper has turned her back on the whole scene. Hazel and Holly continue to fight, calling each other names they have never used, throwing insults and accusations. Clem barely takes it in. Far more horrifying to her is Juniper's slumped shoulders, her lowered head, her complete and total air of defeat. Slowly, she removes the purple ribbon in her hair and lets it fall.

"It's the end of the world," Juniper says, before she collapses entirely.

# 32

***September 2024***

I keep an eye on Hazel all day.

When we search the woods, I insist on staying together. She says nothing, but I know she realizes this isn't for safety. We walk, and we look, but we don't talk.

Back at the house, the three of us eat a silent meal at the table, and afterward I wash my hands. The water comes away a murky green. I feel infected by this place. Hazel, too, seems discomfited, and when we settle in the living room in front of the fire, she pulls out baby wipes and a manicure set, getting to work on her nails.

Juniper makes us a mug of gross mushroom tea each, but it's warm and I drink it. Hazel also seems resigned to there being no better fare. I am haunted by memories. Memories I don't want. Memories I had put away and forgotten. They rear up at all moments, triggered by every corner of this cursed place.

Mostly, though, I am full of anger. I am so pissed off by the whole mess of my life, with nowhere to put it. Eventually, it spills out.

"You know we killed her, right?"

Hazel stills, the endless scratching of her nail file finally falling silent. "Don't."

Juniper is quiet.

I am gnashing on my rage now. "We gave her something else. It wasn't yarrow."

"Clem."

"Water hemlock. Or poison hemlock, probably. They look the same."

Hazel slides her nail file into the pocket of her manicure set and zips it shut with an aggression that satisfies a tiny part of my anger.

I push harder. "We *killed* her." I can't say her name. None of us have.

"Shut the fuck up, will you?" Hazel snaps, and I want to laugh. "What's the point of bringing it up now?"

"Oh, I don't know. Maybe I want to imitate you and become a master shit stirrer."

Hazel bites her lip but doesn't engage, which irritates me.

Juniper's reply is predictably serene. "Daudir will provide. Daudir will take care of Ivy and Willow, wherever they are. We are Wards. We are safe."

"I was the one who moved Daudir," I say, wielding my secret like a fully loaded gun.

It hits the mark.

Hazel's eyes grow cold, her voice low. Dangerous. "What did you say?"

"I said," I say carefully, "that it was *me*."

Hazel is shivering with suppressed rage now. "I knew it. I fucking knew it."

I raise my chin, defiance and recklessness waging war. "I wanted to bury her." Some of the fight leaves me. "It felt wrong seeing her like that, rotting out in the open. I didn't want her to become like Granny Alys. Her body liquefying like that . . . the bugs, those goddamn worms and flies. I just . . . I couldn't bear to see her like that. So, I moved her to another part of the forest."

Hazel smiles like someone who's just been handed permission to burn it all down, of someone proved right, and ready to make it hurt.

"It was *my* effigy," I say, trying to reclaim some of the fading defiance. "*I* built it."

"And that gave you the right to just steal her?"

"*I* put the nails in her hands. *I* sawed her fucking feet off!"

The memory is a burst blister. After all these careful years forcing myself to lock the details away, here they spew like so much pus. Foul. Vivid. Inescapable.

*We need to clip the stem so she grows tall.* This was my reasoning. My logic. My words.

I remember thinking that it was a beautiful thing, cutting off her feet. Diagonal, like Granny Alys taught us. Like the rose stems.

I was very good with the saw by then, and the bone hardly splintered at all. I did the work carefully, one leg at a time, and when I was done, two perfect, beautiful little feet sat side by side, beneath the arching maple.

Other memories come, equally unwelcome, equally inevitable. Vivid. No longer tinged by the fairy-tale cloud that made everything feel better, prettier.

That terrible, early morning in the year 2000. March, it was. Or April.

Hazel was shrieking from Granny Alys's bedroom, and we all came running. Through the near-impenetrable haze of blowflies and bugs, we all saw the little shape sitting on the bed, hunched over the corpse.

Poppy sat in the mess of liquid from Granny's open belly, which had begun to sag and leak the previous evening, and which was now sunken and splayed like it had exploded from the inside out. Poppy was putting fistfuls of wriggling, pale maggots into her mouth. Here and there a fly made its way inside too.

Juniper was the one to rush forward and grip Poppy's jaw, scooping out as many of the half-masticated maggots as she could, but it was obvious Poppy had been at it for a while.

I remember how she shrieked and writhed, a skeleton child, as Juniper worked, and how I had to hurry forward and hold her little arms back.

Poppy bit down on Juniper's hand, and she cried out and slapped Poppy so hard that silence rang through the room for a full second before Poppy gave an almighty wail. Juniper used the opportunity to scoop out the rest of the mess.

"They'll make you sick!" she yelled over Poppy's screams—screams I can still hear. *"You'll die!"*

The twins were watching from the doorway, but they weren't watching Poppy, or the unfolding commotion. They were watching Granny Alys with an otherworldly attentiveness.

By the end, Poppy was wailing the roof down, and Juniper had to pinch her hard on the arm to get her to release her grip on Granny Alys's sopping nightgown. Once detached, Juniper hauled her up and hurried from the room, calling, "Lock that door behind you!"

It was Hazel that ushered us all out, closing the door firmly. Holly and Ivy were both so eerie, so still, that I worried they'd gone full-on catatonic. Until I saw the look in their eyes. That feral look of desire. They wanted in that room.

I ran down the stairs after Juniper and Poppy, across the entrance hall, through the dining room, and into the kitchen.

"Hold her," Juniper ordered, and I did it without thinking.

"Willow, hold her feet—don't let go!"

Willow, looking every bit as stunned as I felt, did as she was told. We watched as Juniper forced her fingers down Poppy's throat, so far down that Poppy screamed, gargled, retched—and vomited. All over Juni's hands and mine. Over and over Juniper forced Poppy to expunge the dead maggots from her stomach until she was beet red and exhausted, voice raw with retching, a long line of snot running from her nose into the sink.

And where was Hazel? Where was Hazel when we had to force our baby sister to puke up corpse mushrooms and maggots? Where was Hazel when I cut off her beautiful feet?

I come back to myself like a car crash. "I was the one doing it all, the ugly work none of you would touch. Butchering the deer that kept us *alive*, bleaching the bones for effigies we thought kept us safe. So, yes. I moved Daudir's effigy. It was my *right* to move it. *My right!*"

The shock of my yell rings a frequency through the room.

Hazel's anger is so scorching, it satisfies. "How fucking dare you. You call *me* a shit stirrer?" Her scoff is the smoke of a dying fire, curled with disdain.

I plow on anyway, some of the energy leaving my body. "Only, when I went back to bury her the next morning . . . she was gone." I take a sip of tea I forgot I was holding. "I suppose being taken off and eaten by coyotes is better than rotting nailed to a kid's art project."

"Daudir moved Himself," Juniper says, nodding.

I shake my head. "Nothing will convince you of anything else, will it? You'll stubbornly go on believing in this child's play forever."

"Daudir moved Himself," Juniper repeats, a stubborn tilt to her chin, but . . . are there cracks forming? Is that a sliver of doubt I see in the twitch of her cheek?

My laugh is scornful. "Head stuck in a bell jar. She was dragged off by some animal."

"I don't believe you," Juniper says, voice shaking.

It gets my attention. "Yes, you do."

"Leave her alone," Hazel cuts in quietly.

"And what did you do with Willow?" I ask, turning on her. "You were the only one who could have let her go. What were you hoping for, huh? That she continues to starve out there?"

"I would never hurt Willow, Clem! And I wouldn't hurt Ivy, either, if that's what you're implying?"

"I'm not implying it; I'm *saying* it. Who the hell else?"

Hazel's eyes flash. "I don't know—*you*?"

"You'd love that!" I yell, and I can feel myself losing my grip, the hysteria creeping in like old times. "You'd love me to be the one to blame, like always. You tried to take Henry, and now you're trying to hurt me by taking Ivy!"

"How could I take Ivy anywhere, you idiot?! There's literally nowhere to go!"

"Shut up!" The words crack out of Juniper's throat, not loud: violent. Her face is red, twisted with emotion she hadn't meant to show.

Her voice doesn't just rise. It breaks.

It is grief sharpened to a point, rage scraped bare.

She looks at me, all wide eyes and bent mouth, as if I am a stranger. As if I have just ripped open her chest and laughed at what I found.

"Shut up," she says again, smaller this time, shaking now. She chokes on a sob. "You've . . . you've taken everything from me. You . . . you really moved Daudir that day?"

My cheeks burn, shame creeping over me like a virus. But I can't lie anymore. I can't hide. I wanted to believe too. For almost all our Beltane years, and in secret for far longer. I wanted to . . . but this fantasy cost us everything. At some point, every child needs to grow up. It's Juniper's turn.

"Yes," I whisper. "I'm sorry. Yes."

Juniper's face crumples, but she doesn't look away, doesn't hide from the truth.

"But . . . when you went back to the place you put Him . . . he was gone."

"There are animals on the island, June. You know this."

"But . . . the signs I've been seeing," she says, her voice so small, so breakable, it sounds like it belongs to someone half her age. "The reason I sent for you all . . ."

It twists something in my chest. But someone has to be strong enough to tear the veil.

"I didn't see any signs. I still don't. And . . . and neither did Ivy. She told me so."

Juniper nods, tears streaming down her cheeks, barely cutting through ancient grime. "Sometimes, at night . . . when it was dark . . . in secret . . . I wondered if it was Willow. Leaving the signs, I mean. Little stick figures. Symbols cut into stone. I let those thoughts have a tiny life in me . . . just in those quiet moments. Tiny, treacherous thoughts. And now . . ." She shakes her head, covering her face to say what she needs to say, as if by hiding herself away she can face it more easily. "I wonder if Willow moved Daudir from the place you put him. And I wonder if Willow took Ivy too."

I nod. "She could have freed herself from the bindings," I reason, glancing at Hazel. A peace offering.

She seems as stunned by Juniper's broken faith as I am. "Could have, yeah."

I nod. "Okay. We need to get her back. We need to stop her delusion. She isn't well."

Hazel puts down her manicure set. "How do we do that? Finding her last time was an accident, and I barely held onto her before you got to me."

"We'll need a trap."

"Like a snare?"

As grim as it sounds, it might be the only way. "Yeah."

Hazel nods, and, after a moment, so does Juniper. "Okay," she says, and she looks smaller than even Granny Alys did at the end.

She looks like her heart is breaking, along with the sky, which has opened its tears upon the island once again.

# 33

***September 2024***

It's been more than two decades, but my fingers remember.

The twist of the fibers, the roughness of the twine, the way to bend and curl and loop over. How it becomes a meditation, losing yourself in the work.

Juniper and I are in the living room, making snares. They'll be just big enough to catch an ankle. If hidden well. And I'm going to follow Juniper and Hazel around to *make* sure they're hidden well.

Hazel never learned how to make them, so she's doing what she can to keep us fed.

I focus on the work, letting it calm my jagged nerves, letting it be a focus from the maelstrom inside. The loop is secured, noose knotted to slip easily but hold fast under tension. At the base of the loop, I tie a second length, this one to lead to a bent sapling that will provide the snap. The key is the trigger.

I've already carved a few rough toggles. Short, straight sticks with a notch, thin and sensitive. A bunch of trigger sticks, too, angled like rib bones. These will hold the bent sapling down, one balancing on the other like a riddle, tension resting on breath.

I'll need to find forked sticks to anchor the triggers at each snaring site.

Each snare is perfectly simple, perfectly invisible.

Just as Beltane taught me.

Hazel comes into the room with three mugs. No chance of it being hot chocolate or even a black coffee, I suppose. More moss-mushroom water, no doubt.

"We won't be setting snares until the storm passes," she says, handing one over to Juniper and putting mine on the side table.

She hasn't even looked at me since the argument, and I find that I don't care. She meanders over to the window, pulling aside the curtain to peer out into the black.

"I can't see a damn thing."

But we can all hear the wind, feel it shaking the bones of the house. It screams through the gap in the wall next door in the formal living room, the one that smells of animal fur, the one Juniper has turned into her own personal bone display cabinet. The rain is pelting the roof high above, now and then gusting the downpour against the window in fierce slaps that rattle the glass.

I know Hazel is right, but I keep making snares anyway.

She sighs. Takes a slow sip of her drink. "Remember when the well flooded when we were kids?"

She turns to look at me. Another peace offering.

I'm almost stubborn enough not to take it. "All that mud," I say, twisting more twine.

"We'd spend hours helping Granny Alys carry it all away, throwing it over the side of that dip."

"The void," Juniper says, smiling. "I forgot that part. The mud, though . . . clearing the mud is a constant. I've done it countless times, and I'll need to do it again in the morning."

She sighs, bony shoulders so thin it's hard to imagine her carrying anything.

Hazel and I exchange a look. A decision to do it for her when dawn comes. An agreement made in secret, a pact formed without words—the way we used to do when we were children.

Hazel puts her mug down and slumps on the sofa, wiping her hands on her pants. "It's sticky and wet here," she says. "Always was, even in the cold."

I can't help but smile, the whisper of a laugh breathing through my nostrils. "Even the thin snow was sticky."

Hazel's eyes warm, and her grin is a welcome sight. "Right?"

I reach for the mug she brought and take a small sip. To my surprise, it's sweet and not half bad.

I look up at Hazel, and she looks pleased and a little smug.

"Found some crystallized honey in the back of the cupboard."

I nod, and take another, much larger gulp. "Damn."

Hazel sighs sleepily and wiggles back into the flat, dank cushions.

"My employee, Matt, once remarked that I must have a real passion for my work," I murmur, sleep and a temporary sense of peace making my limbs and tongue loose. "He said nothing could distract me or draw me away. I asked what he meant, and he told me that more than once he'd seen me in the back room, inventorying, with a spider on my arm, crawling slowly up to the gap in my sleeve. Or in my hair, close to my ear. Once, a moth fluttered around my face and I didn't so much as flinch." I take another sip of Hazel's tea and get back to the snare in my hand. "I smiled, you know? Shrugged it off. I just smothered the discomfort and went on working." I look up at Juniper, feeling haunted. "It's because of the flies."

Juniper doesn't move, doesn't blink, doesn't react. She just listens.

"They swarmed her body for such a long time. So, so long. At first, we'd flicked them away, flinch out of their path, hold our noses. But, like with everything, we adapted."

Hazel wraps her arms around herself. "We invented stories and fairy tales," she says softly.

"We suppressed the horror." I close my eyes and think, *I deserved it.*

But did they deserve it?

Hazel lies down and lets her eyelids fall closed.

Juniper and I keep going. I figure we'll need at least twenty snares to have half a hope of catching Willow in one.

# 34

***October 31, 2001***

Maybe it happens because Clem dreams of Henry.

Almost every night now. Henry's hand—hot, dry, real—slips into hers in that quiet, weightless place between sleep and waking. His laugh hums in her ear, low and warm, the way it did when they lay in the shallows by the lake, sun drunk and tangled in reeds. His lips brush her hairline, and the world softens, just for a breath. And then she wakes. Empty handed. The room cold and hollow.

Juniper hasn't stirred from her fog. Ivy and Holly are shadows flitting through the house. No one speaks Daudir's name. No one dares. Clem should be terrified, but she's not. She's only tired. Only sad.

And Hazel . . . Hazel burns. She's the only one left with fire in her veins. She's off all day, a walking storm cloud. Pacing, pacing, the floorboards groaning beneath her feet. Clem feels her sister's gaze when she isn't looking—hungry, searching, dangerous.

It happens late in a day that feels like all the others—days that bleed together, soft edged and meaningless, tinged with the steady hue of Clem's rooted sense of guilt and shame. Hazel knocks but doesn't wait, just pushes into Clem's room.

Clem's fingers tremble as she hides the paper she's been writing on—a letter to Henry that will never be sent—and caps the old BIC pen.

"More secrets," Hazel says, voice bitter as wormwood, sharp as salt in a wound. "What is it now? A diary?"

"Nothing," Clem says, but too quickly.

Hazel scoffs. "Of course not."

She prowls the room, opens Clem's cupboard, lifts the secret, silent music box, winds it with aggression, scowls when no music plays. The air between them crackles, tight, waiting to break. She puts it down with unnecessary aggression.

Clem is oddly protective of it and wishes Hazel wouldn't be so rough. She almost says something, but a niggling in her gut holds her mute.

Hazel turns to stare out of the window. She's almost vibrating with that *thing* that Clem can't put her finger on now. Some kind of energy. She doesn't like it. It feels electric. Dangerous.

Deadly.

She has an urge to confess every terrible thought and deed she has ever had and done.

"You've been lying," Hazel says at last. She never turns away from the window.

Clem swallows hard. "Leave me alone."

Hazel finally looks at her. "You don't even deny it."

The silence is thick. Heavy.

"Deny what?"

A creak in the hall grabs her attention for a moment, before Hazel says something that steals her breath and zeroes her brain into a pinpoint of focus.

"I was there. That day. With you and Henry. By the lake."

The world tilts, and Clem's spine grows rigid, cemented in place. She knows the day Hazel means. There can be only one.

"I knew someone was watching," she breathes. "How long?"

"Long enough."

A spark of anger flickers to life. "You're disgusting. Watching. Spying."

Hazel scoffs, but it's flat.

"You're jealous," Clem spits, but there is no conviction there.

"Give me a break. I'm not the one who got us into this mess. The whole reason we're even here on Beltane." She waits for Clem to argue, or to fill in the blanks, but Clem is frozen. Rigid with horror. "To think, all this time you let us believe it was the rain to blame that night."

Their parents' faces flood her vision like oncoming headlights. She has been dreading the possibility of this day for years, dreading it like a slow storm she knew might be coming, unseen, over the horizon. She knows exactly what Hazel is talking about, of course, but she feigns ignorance.

"You're crazy." Clem folds her arms to keep herself whole.

"They didn't just die in a car accident."

Clem's vision jars, the edges of reality fracturing. This is terror, head on. She glances toward the hall and back.

"Stop," she breathes. "Shut up."

"Maybe you can explain it. In detail. Sit us down and walk us through it."

There had been a gnawing in her stomach all day, even at school. She couldn't focus on anything except the terrible feeling, like a lead ball of dread sitting in her gut. She was small. Desperate. She even went to confide in Penny about it after school but couldn't bring herself to say the words. Anyway—*what* words? She didn't know what this was.

All she knew was that she had to keep Mom and Dad inside that night. She had to make sure they stayed together at all costs. If she didn't, she knew something bad would happen.

Crushing the sleeping pills was a last-minute idea, and one she thought solved the problem. Mom had insomnia and took one every night. If she gave them a pill or two, they'd fall asleep before they left, and she could keep them safe. She used Penny's old mortar, the pestle grinding, grinding, until the pills were a white powder, soft as ash. She remembers her hands shaking as she tipped it into the whiskey decanter. Her parents' laughter, their glasses raised. Their toast to the night, to each other, to the road ahead. One drink, always one, before the road. But this time she would keep them home. This time, they'd stay safe.

Safe on the sofa, blankets up, heads nodding. Safe . . . until they left anyway. Too late, too drowsy. Until the storm and the dark and the crash.

It wasn't the rain. It was her.

And Hazel knows it. Somehow, she knows.

Voice wobbling, Clem reaches for her sister. "Hazel, please—"

"Don't!"

Holly's voice at the door. "What's going on?"

Clem wipes at her face. "Nothing. Just . . . just go to your room. We're talking."

"I think they should hear, don't you?" Hazel gestures for Holly to enter, and she does, Ivy close behind.

The room feels too small, the air too thin.

"Hazel, stop it. *Please!*"

The look on Hazel's face makes Clem hate her. She's enjoying this. She's getting perverse pleasure out of Clem's lowest moment, her deepest regret. She's trying to punish her, and she'll keep going until nothing but ash remains.

Without thinking, Clem lunges for her with a cry, but Hazel jumps out of the way, back toward the door. Reeling, Clem reaches for the music box, holding it like a brick, ready to throw.

"I'm warning you," she says, panting with desperation. This can't be happening. It can't. She's a cornered animal.

Hazel's voice is a blade. "Clem's the reason we're here. The reason Daudir hates us. She gave Mom and Dad sleeping pills the night they died. It wasn't the rain that killed them. It was her."

"*No*—no—I only wanted to keep them safe—"

"You killed them," Hazel says. And Clem can see in her eyes all the years of blame, all the weight of Daudir's wrath, all the grief she can't name. Damage done, Hazel turns to go.

Clem doesn't make a conscious decision to throw the music box. One moment it's in her hand; the next, it's arcing through the air and hitting Hazel on the head.

It lands with a dull but sickening thud, then falls to the floor and cracks into four jagged pieces.

Hazel stumbles, gripping the side of her head, and Clem rushes forward, grabbing her by the hair, yanking her back into the room. She falls over the broken pieces, and when Clem lunges, climbing onto her to pummel her with her angry fists, screaming nonsense cursed in their secret language, she doesn't realize that the tenor of Hazel's cries have changed. It's only when her fists come away bloody that she realizes something is wrong.

The twins are the ones to pull Clem off Hazel, who is sobbing hysterically on the floor, her hands shaking and covered with blood. When she gets to her knees and turns around, two large shards of the music box are sticking out of her face. One of them is lodged deeply beneath her eye. The other falls from her cheek, leaving a flap of skin hanging in its wake.

Hazel screams, *howls*, a sound no human should make.

Not in fear or pain. In rage.

"Run!" Ivy yells, pushing Clem toward the door.

Clem doesn't think. She scrambles from the room, along the corridor and down the stairs. Juniper is in the entrance hall, blocking her access to the door, so she runs through the dining room and into the kitchen, frantically seeking a solution. If she goes into the cellar, she'll be trapped. The storm doors are chained shut. Already, she can hear Hazel pounding down the stairs, yelling, "You're a killer! And I'll kill you first!"

With no other option, Clem rushes for the cellar door, but before she can open it, Hazel rounds the space and blocks her way, shoving her back toward the kitchen door. Clem turns to run, but Juniper and the twins have rushed in after them, and there is nowhere to go.

Hazel yanks open the kitchen drawers, searching for a knife, but Clem has taken most of them for building the effigies. At last, here, a vegetable knife, one that isn't so useful for carving bone. Not very long, but sharp. She spins to face Clem holding it up, point out. Clem doesn't know if Hazel is capable of using it. All the simmering resentments between them, a lifetime of microaggressions, is only the start. Clem's terrible secret is the straw that might break the camel's back.

Hazel looks feral standing there. Wild. Insane. Half her face is exposed, and the skin below her left eye is a bloody, gruesome mess, her eyelids swelling shut. The remnants of Clem's music box are nowhere to be seen.

"You," she pants, hunched, eye blazing, teeth bloodied and bared. "You killed our parents. It wasn't the *rain*."

Hearing it out loud again, now that she can process it fully, and out of the mouth of a beloved sister, is too much.

Juniper's voice is the only clear thing. Clear as a bell. "What's going on? What are you saying?"

"Tell her," Hazel spits, blood spraying between them. "Tell her how you killed Mom and Dad."

"I told you, it was an accident," Clem yells desperately, eyes darting between them all. "I just wanted them to stay in with us that night. They were always going away. I had a bad feeling—I thought something bad would happen unless I made them stay. I just wanted them to stay!"

Hazel spits to the side, blood and saliva. "She gave them sleeping pills."

They are all here to listen now, all except Willow, who still has not returned.

Juniper opens her mouth, but Hazel explodes.

"You're the reason any of this happened! You let us believe it was the rain when it was *you* the whole time!"

And she throws the knife.

Time slows, taut as a violin string, and Clem can't believe Hazel actually threw the knife.

It spins through the air, glinting silver, and soars right past Clem. There is a moment of shock, then relief, and then a sound that turns her insides watery.

"Ow!" Holly cries, and Clem turns just in time to see her pull the knife from high up on her right inner thigh.

"That hurt," she snaps.

Clem sees it. A circle of blood staining Holly's dress, spreading outward, down, stretching as though made of putty. Like a mishap. Like maybe she got her period.

Holly steps back, wiping her leg as if annoyed. But surprise is fast on its heels when her hand comes away dripping.

Ivy makes a little noise in her throat, then drops to her knees and presses her hands to Holly's leg. Blood is spurting between her hands now, and half of Holly's dress is sodden.

"Oh shit!" Hazel cries, hurrying toward them. Juniper lifts Holly and carries her, with more strength than Clem knew she had left, to the dining room table.

"Grab cloths!" she yells over her shoulder.

Clem grabs as many as she can find. Juniper snatches them and presses them into Holly's leg.

She looks wrong. Too pale. Too gray.

"I can't get my breath," Holly says, grabbing blindly for Ivy's hand.

"I'm here," Ivy says, finding and clutching her hand in her own. "It's okay."

Holly tries to get up, but Juniper pushes her down. "Stay still."

Something like panic in Holly's eyes, and she fights against Juniper's hand.

"Hold her down!" Juniper grunts.

Holly is fighting again.

"Hold her down!" Juniper screams. Outside, the storm screams with her.

"You hold her!" Clem cries at Hazel. "While I fix your mistake!"

She has the fleeting thought that she will run to grab her sewing needles and thread. That she can mend the wound herself.

"It was an accident," Hazel says, backing away. "It was an accident!"

"It's not stopping," Juniper mutters through clenched teeth, even though she is pressing her entire body weight on the wound.

Hazel, shivering, now hurries forward and tries to help, but accidentally knocks Juniper off the wound. It squirts out in a terrifying arch, and Holly begins to pant.

Not again. Not again.

Clem's mind is screaming.

Holly looks terrified. "I—I'm—dizzy—"

Her chest is rising and falling too fast, and she is too pale. "Keep pressing!" Clem yells, wiping Holly's forehead.

She's clammy and cold.

"Hello?"

A call from the entrance hall. Male.

Henry.

Clem is torn in half—half of her by the lake, a beautiful summer day, her secret finally unloaded onto understanding shoulders. Shoulders that were willing to carry it with her. The other half in the room upstairs, seeing Hazel's face contorted into ugly hate, and in the kitchen, throwing a knife meant to hurt—or kill—her, and instead finding Holly.

On the table, Holly's eyes roll, and she slumps.

"No," Juniper breathes, releasing the wadded and blood-soaked cloth to hold Holly's face and lift her eyelids.

The blood is no longer arcing out of the wound. It isn't pumping at all.

No . . .

Everything inside Clem breaks. Wide. A gulf she is losing herself to.

Holly . . .

"My dad's on the mainland, but he said I could take the boat—" Henry rounds the corner, his smile bright, until it freezes and falls. "Oh shit. What's happened?"

"Holly," Clem stammers. "It—she—"

Clem is becoming aware of something else. A shifting in the room. A darkening and a zeroing in. Several pairs of grief-stricken eyes are turning in his direction. Slow. Knowing. "R-run!" she yells, her voice hiccuping over itself. "G-get help!"

He stands there, staring at her.

"N-now!" she screams, throwing the towel at him to break his stillness.

He backs away quickly and then rushes from the room.

They need help more than ever, it's true. Things are completely out of hand. But that's not the only reason she sent him for help. She sent him for help because she can see the change in her sisters; the slow way their eyes slid over to him. She could—can still—see the singular thought reflected in all three of their eyes.

It was something Holly said when the seventh sister died.

*If only we could trade. Give Daudir a different life so he'll give her back. A life for a life.*

Before she can even blink, they are running.

Clem is helpless. She can only chase her sisters as they hunt Henry through the forest, hoping that he makes it out before they find him. Their screams are those of animals, not of girls, of creatures that are more teeth and nails and grief and raw hunger than flesh.

She only just makes it to the dock after them, crying with relief when she sees Henry out on the water in the boat, looking back at her with terror in his eyes.

At least he's safe. Even if he's the only one.

# 35

***September 2024***

It's the silence that wakes me.

It's eerie. Heavy, thick as wool. As if someone is watching, waiting, holding their breath.

For a moment I lie still, my heart tapping a nervous rhythm against my ribs. Then I understand: The rain has stopped.

Barely there ashen light seeps through the window, just enough to paint the shapes of the room in shades of ash and bone. Juniper lies curled into a catlike ball on the sheepskin rug in front of the fire, her small form barely rising with each breath. Hazel sprawls on the long sofa, mouth slack, snoring faintly, the sound somehow obscene in the hush.

I shift, the hard edges of the chair I fell asleep in biting into my spine. A crick stabs at the base of my skull. I wince, rolling my shoulders, feeling every year of my age in the stiff joints. Too old for nights like this. Too old for this place.

I slip my phone from my pocket, my thumb ghosting over the cracked screen: 5:47 a.m. Battery at 21 percent. No power, of course. The generator's long dead. Juniper never did repair it after it broke one summer. The thought of the signal flickers in my mind like a dying candle . . . there has to be signal *somewhere* on this damn island. I shut the phone off, cradling what little charge remains like a final ember.

Beltane groans softly as I rise, the floorboards sighing beneath my feet, air fuggy with spores. I move through it as if underwater, past the hearth where the fire's last glow has long since faded to cold cinders.

Outside, the world waits. I might as well see the damage done in the storm and get started on the mud.

The sky hangs low, clouds torn and bruised, but for now, they don't weep. Everything is still. Only the faint creak of the trees and the hush of my breath keep me company. Dew clings to my ankles as I walk through the tall bracken ferns.

To my surprise, the flooding isn't bad. Mostly just standing water from the rain itself. Puddles have formed between the bracken, and it feels like wading into a swamp that'll swallow me whole. But it's all surface level. Juniper's elk-skull-encircled candle tribute is unscathed; though a little drowned, everything is still in its place. I side-eye the bones and head for the well.

It stands like a stub of bone in a section Juniper has managed to keep clear of plants, the stones slick with moss, rope slack. It doesn't look like it's overflowed, but I should check the level in case it rains again today. Might be prudent to empty it a little.

I reach for the crank. The old habit guides my hand before my mind can catch up. But the handle won't move. It juts out rigid, stubborn against my effort. A fleeting flash of annoyance. It needs oiling.

Frowning, I try again. Nothing. The rope has gone tight.

I peer over the lip of the well, but it's so dark I can't see a thing. I fumble for my phone, fingers numb, and wait for it to boot up. The light flickers on, thin, feeble. I edge it over the lip, my heart pounding loud in my ears.

I've barely peered back over when a jolt runs through me, and my hand jerks in horror, and the phone slips from my grasp, tumbling into the well, the light spinning, spinning, past the obstruction and into black water only just below.

Hands shaking, I choke on a sob. Turn, and gag.

No.

No.

My mind is playing tricks on me. That's all. That's all.

My hands claw at the crank, useless, desperate. It won't turn, so I pull at the rope with everything I have. My breath catches. A raw sound tears from my throat—a sob, a choke, a prayer.

Please, no.

It couldn't have been what I think it was. What I thought I saw . . .

Pale hair, pale face, bloated neck swelling over the edge of a soft, familiar Scandinavian sweater. I did not see the flashlight strike wide, sightless eyes.

My breath makes a soft noise, half formed, and I shake my head, shake it, shake it, shake it . . .

I stumble back to the house, which looms like a broken tooth, somehow making it inside. My footsteps sound far away in my own ears, and I careen into walls and doors. Somehow, I make it to the informal living room, where Juni and Hazel still sleep.

"Sh-She . . ." The word splinters on my tongue. My leg gives way, knocks over a table; mugs scatter, ringing against the floor like bells.

Hazel startles awake with a yelp, and Juniper groans, rolling over.

The shivering won't stop, and my teeth clack against one another. "Sh-She . . ."

And now my hands are shaking harder than ever, the bones inside my skin clattering like dice.

"Clem?" Hazel's voice, still thick with sleep.

"W-went to ch-check the w-well—"

A cry breaks out of my chest like a howl, swallowing the rest, and I can't stop the noise now it's started.

They're by my side in a moment. Hands on my shoulders, voices urgent, lost in the storm of my shivering.

A panicked voice. "What's happened? Clem, tell me what's happened."

"She said the well, I think."

"We should look, maybe it's damaged—"

"No!" My hand shoots out, latching on to the first person it finds, clamps down hard. Iron tight.

"Ow, Clem. Let go."

Hazel is trying to get me to loosen my grip. I meet her gaze and force my brain to focus, my mouth to stop shivering.

"I-vy," I manage, my throat jerking the words free.

The color drains from her face. "No."

I say again: "I-vy. I-vy."

My whole body is shaking so badly I can no longer speak, only breathe and make choking sounds. Hazel wrenches herself free, and she and Juniper bolt for the door, their footsteps assaulting the quiet.

I hope I'm wrong.

I hope to all that is holy, and not, that I am wrong.

# 36

***November 1, 2001***

A purr of unfamiliar noise wakes Clem moments before Juniper hurries into her room, a white-faced Ivy and sweating Hazel on her heels.

Hazel doesn't look good. The wraps around her face are drenched dark, and she is breathing hard, her skin a clammy gray.

Before Clem can speak, Juniper clamps a hand over her mouth. "Quiet," she breathes. "Follow."

Clem does as she's told because the night is dark and stormy, but above that the thrumming noise is getting louder. The house creaks around them as they move, the noise outside swelling. Not wind, not rain, but a beating, mechanical heart.

A sudden click into place: It's a helicopter.

Juniper hurries them through the house and down into the cellar, closing the door and then locking it behind her. Clem didn't even know there was a key. Juniper pockets it in her nightgown and urges them on. The cellar smells of damp earth and old wood. Half-made figures stand in the corners, bone and branch, shapes with hollow eyes, watching, standing guard like malevolent shadow sentinels.

"Out," Juniper mouths pointing toward the storm doors.

"They're chained shut," Clem murmurs.

Juniper shakes her head. "I removed them. *Go.*"

The noise is so loud it feels like something pressing down on them, and when Juniper opens the storm doors into the night, Clem can see a chopper in the distant sky, getting closer.

"The forest," Juniper hisses. "Run!"

Lights flash in the direction of the dock, and they're so bright and unfamiliar that Clem flinches and runs with her sisters into the familiar dark. A dark beyond a boundary of wood and bone they aren't meant to cross after nightfall.

*Daudir forgive me,* she beseeches as she steps over the low barrier.

They run for the low-hanging yews north of Beltane house, the place the roots of trees are knotted, braided things. Hollow spaces that they've crawled into many times like ants in a colony, a place they call the Hollows.

They don't think; they just run, trying to outpace the chopping noise somewhere above.

Deep in the mossy roots, the girls hunker low.

The noise grows louder, an imminent threat.

Juniper checks behind, eyes sharp. "They've come. Scatter."

Hazel and Ivy vanish between the trunks, pale shapes swallowed by dark, but Clem doesn't want to separate.

"We should stay together," Clem whispers, panic rising.

"No. Easier to take us that way. Hide. Come back when it's safe."

Juniper cups Clem's face, briefly gentle. "Daudir will guard you. Have faith."

Then she is gone.

Clem hunches low in a root's hollow, heart hammering. The storm surges around her in a tempest. She's tempted to crawl farther into the roots and stay here . . . surely they won't find her then. But it's too close to the house, and she can hear voices—men calling Juniper's name. Her name. All their names.

The chopper is overhead, so she hunkers low and does as Juniper says: She runs deeper into the wood, praying that her sister is right. That Daudir will protect them.

She passes effigy after effigy, carefully placed by her own hand. She runs through the magical rainbow ribbon tree, which now only seems like cloth in tatters, past the Guardian rock, scuffing her legs on plants she can't make out in the dark. Branches whip her face, and the rain washes fresh blood away—and still she runs.

A voice booms from the sky, and lights roam the trees, searching like the eye of Daudir Himself.

Her heart screams in her chest.

*What have I done what have I done what have I done—*

When the light from the sky falls across her and then leaves, she thinks she's had a lucky escape. But then it finds her again and sticks like glue. She drops, crawls, but the beam clings, hunts.

Blinding.

Shouts. Heavy footfalls. Movement through the wood, and three large forms in black, heads giant and bulbous, are suddenly on her, grabbing her arms, grip like a vice, saying things she can't understand. They pick her clean up off her feet, and carry her back the way she came, ripping through the trees with no respect and no delicacy.

She screams. She screams and she bites, and it does nothing. Nothing at all.

"She bit me," one snarls. The blow comes quick, sharp.

The world reels.

Men. Men have come for them.

The house stands bleached in endless light, wrong and bare against the storm. Blue flashes split the dark. A megaphone cracks the air, shuddering the very rain.

They carry Clem into the dining room and put her onto a chair. Hazel is already there, her lip bleeding, her eye and face a swollen mess, the covering gone. She is swaying where she sits, the sickly gray color of her skin much worse. Beads of sweat collect on her forehead and on her top lip, and when Clem reaches out a hand, she flinches violently away, scowling with her uninjured eye.

Holly is still lying on the table, the cloth that failed to stem her bleeding huddled in a clump on the floor. She is uncovered, the expression of shock still etched on her face, eyes open. Turning cloudy.

"I want to see them!" a voice shouts from outside, before there's a minor commotion and Henry bursts in, two black-clad men on his heels.

Clem stumbles to him, wordless. The men look as though they want to protect Henry from her, which is absurd. He pulls her into his chest and presses the top of his lips to her head. His heart hammers wildly beneath her ear, a caged bird, terrified.

"Are you hurt?" he asks, holding on to her.

She only clings tighter. Nothing feels real. And everything feels real. She can't access any of it without losing her grip on the threads of her being.

Hazel scoffs and spits on the floor.

Henry stiffens, eyes sliding to Holly on the table, and away. "Shit," he breathes.

Ivy is dragged in, wet and wide-eyed, and finally—after a long time—Juniper. She lays a hand on each of their shoulders, and Holly's head, before standing in front of them, protecting her sisters from the outsiders.

The man who seems to be in charge speaks into the radio on his shoulder. The chopper veers off. Most of the men melt back into the storm. Three remain.

"I'm Detective Alan Ritcher. I need to speak to Alys Ward."

Juniper's stare is cold. She looks ferocious.

"Alys Ward," he says again, as if the girls are slow, as though they might not know human languages at all.

Clem licks her lips, but Juniper cuts in. *"Shehados ni'autaugijanid."*

*Say nothing.*

The detective looks between them, blinking, then says, for the third time, mouth bending slowly, "Alys. Ward. *Alys. Ward.*"

Juniper regards him through her scowl, then says, "She isn't here."

Detective Ritcher sighs, short and sharp. "Then I need to talk to the adult responsible for you."

"That would be me," Juniper says. "I'm nineteen."

"State your name for the record."

"No."

The man sighs, leaning down on the table. "Look. Clearly something terrible has happened here. You've got two options. You talk to me, or I haul you all in for questioning in separate cells. Which way are we gonna go?"

One word lingers in the air, and Clem knows he has her. *Separate.* It's the only thing he could have said to move her.

"Juniper Ward," she says, voice tight.

"What happened here?"

"An accident. Holly cut her leg. We couldn't stop it."

"And Alys Ward? Where is she?"

Juniper's lips thin. "She died a while back."

The other men exchange a look that Clem doesn't care for.

"Where is her body?"

Juniper is talking through her teeth now. "Buried, as our spiritual beliefs demand. I have everything under control."

"I don't believe that's the case, young lady."

"We do," Clem says, nodding vehemently. "We do."

He glances around the room, lip curling in a grimace of disgust. "Doesn't look like it to me."

"We have supplies," Clem says, "and we have the house and we take care of each other."

His eyes rest on Hazel, on the blood. "She needs help."

Hazel scowls weakly.

A man comes into the dining room and mutters into Detective Ritcher's ear. "Couldn't find anyone else. Island's clear."

The detective turns to Juniper. "Is there anyone else on the island?"

She shakes her head, and Clem frowns. Willow is. Willow is out there somewhere, alone in the storm. Unless . . . unless Juniper knows something that they don't.

The detective nods and pulls a notepad from his upper pocket. "I'll need your names and ages."

Juniper nods to her sisters, and so they hand over their information.

Hazel Ward, seventeen.

Clementine Ward, almost sixteen.

Ivy Ward, just fourteen.

Today. Fourteen *today.*

They forgot. In the chaos of Holly . . . in the blood and the shock and the fissure of their bond, they forgot. Ivy, fourteen. Holly, thirteen forever.

The first division between them. But not the last.

"What are you going to do with us?" Juniper asks, taking Ivy's hand, and maybe she remembers now too.

"With you, nothing. You're legally free to remain. But it'd be better if you come with us so we can clear up what happened. I suggest you remain available for questioning. It'll make everyone's life easier."

Juniper and Hazel exchange a look. "I can't leave the island," Juniper says, and a lie falls so easily from her lips. "I have crops, animals . . . I can't leave."

"Stay if you want. But you'll have to give a statement. The girls will come with us."

Juniper's armor is cracking. "Can't they stay too?"

"No. They're underage, and you're not fit to care for them."

Juniper's anger is palpable. "Of course I am."

"Not with a pending investigation."

Clem grips Henry's shirt tighter. "Don't let them take us."

"There's nothing I can do," he whispers.

She searches his face, looking for hope, looking for an anchor. But there is none. She lets him go and steps back. Steps closer to her sisters, even if they hate her. Because they are Wards; the forest is supposed to protect them.

And it doesn't. Not anymore.

Life as they know it is ending. The storm takes the rest.

# 37

***September 2024***

Ivy's last conversation is a haunting in my head. The lonely tone of her voice: a taunt. The lonely hush in her voice wasn't grief, exactly. It was the emptiness of a soul missing its other half.

*The holly and the ivy . . .*

Some may find it comforting, the idea that they might now be together somewhere, two roots tangled beneath the soil, braided together . . . but I can't. All I feel is the jagged tear of her absence, so much more vivid than the shock-hazed grief when Holly died. All I feel is robbed.

In the first days after they tore us from Beltane, I would close my eyes beneath stiff blankets that smelled of starch and strangers, and I would pretend. Pretend I was still in my bed in our spore-riddled house. That the hiss of pipes was rain on the roof. That the hum of the city beyond the window was just the murmuration of a Beltane storm.

Now, lying on my bed, I try the same.

It's 1999. Ivy is asleep next door. It is spring. We've just arrived on the island, and everything is new and good. The house is full of river light and newness. Granny Alys is padding down the hall, candlestick in hand, hair tumbling down her back like it always did. Like riverweed.

But it unravels. It always unravels.

I pull the quilt back and sit up. The cold of the floor shocks my feet when I rise, but it doesn't anchor me. All I can see is Ivy's body folded into the black mouth of the well, neck swollen past all reason, past all humanity. How long? How long had she been there, waiting in the dark while we searched the wrong places?

I feel like all my worst fears are right on my doorstep all over again.

If Daudir is real, then he hates me.

Morning gnaws at the house. Hazel paces the kitchen, a caged thing.

"We should pull harder," she says, voice thin with fury. "All of us this time. We can get her out."

"We'll only wedge her in harder," Juniper says. Like me, she looks broken. Tired beyond endurance.

"We'll rip her out," Hazel snarls, palms slamming the counter. "We won't leave her like that."

I can barely make myself blink, let alone answer her.

Juniper, looking gaunter than ever, heaves a sigh. "The rains will do it. Nothing to do but mourn and wait."

"Well, what happened to her?" Hazel snaps. "Did she fall?"

Juniper shakes her head. "Why would she have been out there in the first place? It makes no sense."

Their voices rattle through the house, loud and pointless. The silence behind their words swells like nausea. The mug of tea in my hands went cold hours ago, mushrooms congealed and slimy at the bottom like corpses.

I just can't feel much of anything.

Hazel and Juniper are at it again, their grief butting heads in a way I can't swallow. They circle, snapping like trapped wolves.

"Well, she didn't just *fall*, Juniper."

"I never said she did."

"Then what? She jumped?"

"I don't know what happened—"

"You apparently know *everything* that happens on Beltane, right? So take a guess."

Their grief splinters and ricochets, snapping against the cupboards, the counters, the sink. Something is knocked over—a cup, a bowl, a plate—shattering on tile. No one bothers to pick it up.

I don't look.

Their voices blur, like they're calling from underwater. Like I'm at the bottom of that black well too.

The sun limps across the sky, and somehow, I'm in the dining room now. The light stretches and fades with the hours. A crack in the old wooden dining table comes into focus. I follow it with my eyes as it wends its way through the fibers, stopping at a jagged point. Like lightning.

I can't track what they're saying anymore. Ivy is still down there, folded and waiting. And all they do is talk.

"We can't leave her—"

"Then you climb down and get her!"

Another silence. Sharper this time. Breathing, nothing else.

I blink, find a hot cup in my hand . . . When did that happen?

Someone is crying. One of them. Both.

The grandfather clock tolls. Wasn't it broken? Has it been chiming the whole time I've been back? Or is it in my head?

Can't remember. Seems unimportant.

I stay sitting. Hollow. Weightless, while the world ticks on without Ivy in it.

The storm returns, and we all know what it means. We taste it in the air and we wait.

At seven, we force old bread and cold oats down. We chew because we must.

Outside, the trees crowd close, watching us through Daudir's window.

"We should set the snares," Hazel says.

I force my jaw to unclench. Lick my lips. "In the dark?"

"If Willow's caught before morning, we could try to call someone."

I've lost track of the days. When did Henry say he'd be back? It's been an eternity already, and no time at all. Time is fraying, just like me.

I shake my head, trying to clear it.

"Someone clearly doesn't want us here," Hazel adds.

I blink at her, my frown sluggish. Does Hazel think this is Daudir? Is she starting to believe again? I watch her. The way her eyes keep darting to the ever-darkening window. The way her fingers run circles on the table, fidgety. I can't help but feel a niggling in my own mind.

The feeling that Daudir is here. Out there . . .

No matter how I try to ignore it, the old hysteria is looming as real as those storm clouds outside. It's the only feeling I have left.

"Okay," I manage, and Hazel nods.

We grab the snares from the living room and go outside, leaving the door gaping behind us. Juniper lags behind. She hesitates at the boundary.

"Come on," Hazel says, gentle now.

"I haven't crossed it after dark since that final night," Juniper says. She looks like a child again. Seeking reassurance.

Hazel holds out her hand. "We'll be with you."

And I can see it now, the way Juni's guilt mirrors my own. She carries it like a torch no one wants to see.

It's after dark now, so we use Hazel's phone light. She sees me looking and shrugs. "Brought a portable battery pack."

Hazel's light sweeps the trees, and we walk in a line, leaves crackling underfoot. She leads the way, scanning through the forest with the light, searching for a suitable sapling. I'm still struggling to *be* here. To focus. Even the cool air isn't enough to shake the fugue.

I'm in a daze as I set snares, some with twine, others with soft wire. A last resort.

And then . . . a strange feeling. A strange impulse. An urgency to move. I can't ignore it, so I follow. It leads me to a place I swore I'd never return to.

Daudir's place.

I turn to leave, but something stops me.

It makes no sense to leave a trap here. It's wide open. Willow will see it a mile away, but I'm here, and I have the materials. So, I set about it quickly. A torsion snare with guide loop. I secure it to the big-leaf maple, not really looking, and then I leave as quickly as I can.

We're already on our way back, circling around, when Hazel stops, and I walk into her back.

Somehow, I'm not surprised, though I'm still shocked.

Willow, sprawled in the dirt, half hidden in ferns, a leg twisted under her body. One side of her head caved in; blood sunk into the roots.

Seeing her washes away my stupor, and I scan the forest for signs of movement. I should have known something was wrong. The way the Wood was silent, even the bugs, owls, and nighthawks mute.

My brain distills into cool, calm clarity.

Someone did this. Did both. Ivy, and now Willow.

We are not alone.

"Get inside," I say.

Hazel and Juniper are loud. Too loud. They're bending over Willow, half screaming, half sobbing. But there's no time for that now.

"Inside!" I snap, louder this time.

They look up at me, and Hazel catches on faster. Her mouth falls open. I grab Juniper's arm and pull her away from Willow, harder than I meant to, but as hard as is needed. I practically have to drag her through the mud back to the house, a long and torturous walk that feels suddenly fraught.

When we're all inside, I shut the front door and secure the bolts. I force Juniper, still hysterical, to give me the key to the cellar.

I turn to Hazel, whose makeup is smudged, slipped sideways like a broken doll, but who looks clear-eyed and focused now she realizes what's at stake. "Check the windows, the doors. Any point of entry."

She nods, rushes off.

I take Juniper and shove her into the informal living room, closing and then locking the door. She'll be safe in there for now. She keens like a fox in a trap.

Next door, the hole in the formal living room's wall gapes like a taunt. I don't have the time or supplies to close it off. So I shut the door and slide the bolt across. For now, it'll have to do. I hear Hazel moving through the rooms upstairs, shutting the windows, closing the doors.

I rush around the first floor doing the same. Then I head down to the cellar, hairs standing on end, checking the shadows for movement, choking on the dark. I check each of the separate sections. They're empty. I hurry over to the storm doors and make sure they're locked. They are.

Then I do something I've wanted to do since I first got to this house but never dared. I take one of the large unused tablecloths from the kitchen drawer—and I cover the dining room window, blocking Daudir's view.

Hazel calls my name from the entrance hall.

I join her, jaw tight and heavy. "Secured down here."

"Up there too," she confirms, wiping her mouth. Smudging away the last of her lipstick. Her scars shine through the skin just above her lips, and a twinge of terrible guilt pings at my lungs like cholera.

"I locked Juniper in the informal living room. We should hunker down in there until Henry gets back."

She nods, wiping more makeup off her face with an unthinking swipe. "I'll grab some water and dried food."

"Get what you can find in the kitchen. Don't go down to the cellar. I've locked the door, and I have the key."

"Okay. Back soon."

When I unlock the informal living room, Juniper is curled into herself in the corner, rocking back and forth. She's so skinny that her arms wrap almost entirely around her body, hands overlapping behind her like two white flaps.

"Juni?" I murmur, coming closer.

She shakes her head. "Daudir . . . Daudir let her die. His Companion . . . his Seer." She gulps in a breath, wet and desperate. "He heard me . . . Heard my doubt. My confession."

"This isn't your fault."

"He heard me say that I sometimes questioned the signs . . . that I sometimes questioned if Willow was leaving them instead of him. He knew I was doubting. He *knew*."

Paranoia bubbles in me like a virus.

I bite my lips together. I don't know what is going on anymore except that there is a *real* threat outside. Whether it is Daudir or something else: It's here.

"We have to keep safe now, okay? Something outside—it *hurt* Willow. And Ivy. We have to make sure it doesn't hurt us."

It. Not he. Not she.

It.

I hear myself saying it.

Granny Alys's voice is so warm in my memory. *Beltane will always protect Ward blood.*

But she was wrong. She was so, so very wrong.

A flare of anger rises in me before it's smothered by a blanket of guilt. A niggle of doubt.

*What if you didn't do things right?*

I push the unwelcome thought away. It's just a compulsion. It's just old trauma worming its way back into my mind now that I'm here, now that new traumas have been added to my collection.

*This is your fault.*

I clench my jaw and shake my head, refusing to give in. Except . . .

What if Juniper is right?

That niggling thought again, toxic, infectious, so powerful because it is woven into the fabric of me, into the fabric of everything I have tried so hard to forget.

Two terrible words, backed by fearful and tentative belief:

What. If.

What if Daudir is real?

What if we merely named a thing that was already here?

What if the Forgotten God of the Wood was not Granny Alys's fancy?

And what if Daudir is coming to punish us for all the years of neglect? All the years I turned my face away. I was his Effigist, wasn't I? Builder of wards, watchers, and tributes. And I turned my back.

Those words. That niggle. That blooming, sudden question . . .

What if I was wrong?

And: What is there to lose?

I drop to my knees in a moment of violent contrition, pressing my palms together.

"Daudir," I whisper, and Juniper goes still. "Daudir, blessed protector of Beltane and of those with Ward blood. I see now. I was blind . . . I turned away from the forest. Forgive me. I beseech you. Forgive me for my blindness. For my neglect. For turning away when things got difficult. Daudir, Forgotten God of the Wood, forgive me, your weak Effigist, for her blindness. Forgive your Alchemist, Hazel, for losing her way. Forgive Juniper, your Hierophant, who faltered. We hold steadfast in your presence now and call upon you to protect us." I shut my eyes, warm tears dripping from my chin. "But tell me now, what can we give? What can I give to be let go? What would it cost, to earn our freedom?"

# 38

***December 2001***

The boat that takes Clem, Hazel, and Ivy from the island is a stranger. Clem stands at the stern, watching the silhouette of Beltane shrink against the horizon, and knows with a bitter finality that she will never see Henry again.

The authorities come with their notebooks and their quiet, prying eyes. They question the Ward sisters about Poppy, about Willow, again, and again, and again, until their voices seem to echo off the very walls of each new group home. Until the questions feel like rain on stone: steady, endless, carving something hollow beneath the skin.

But no Ward gives an answer.

Not Hazel, who keeps her silence like a blade clenched between her teeth.

Not Clem, who simply looks down at her hands and waits for it to be over. And not Ivy, whose gaze remains fixed on some invisible point in the distance.

And so, in time, the authorities stop asking.

Poppy and Willow are presumed dead.

Later, before the foster hearing, Juniper writes a letter. Four words—old words, worn smooth with use—and a single sigil that no one outside the siblings can understand. And slipped into the fold: a single juniper berry, dark and shriveled like a dead eye.

*Ni'au shejadni auji Wenjaklo'auwen,* the message reads.

*No sign of Willow.*

And still, the sisters are pressed for answers that they will never give.

Besides, it seems impossible, after all these weeks, that Willow has survived. It's growing cold on the island, the first flimsy snow has fallen, and Clem's heart is as frigid as the winter.

Of seven Ward sisters, only four remain.

Clem turns sixteen and no one even notices.

Juniper owns the island, the house, and the land, by the strange mercy of inheritance laws. The deed is hers. The house, with its bones of rotting wood and weeping mortar. The forest, with its secrets, and its bodies. Even Ernest's sagging shack, and the rusted tools that hang like relics from the shed walls.

Since they were taken, Juniper has not stepped off Beltane. Not once. Not even when informed that Clem, Hazel, and Ivy are being taken into foster care.

Juniper is tied to Beltane in ways that Clem can't understand.

Or forgive.

The year that follows is a slow drowning.

Clem, Hazel, and Ivy are placed together in a group home—a gray place that smells of bleach and boiled cabbage, with walls that seem too thin to keep their secrets safely inside. During this time, none of them speak a word of English. Not to the carers, not to the other children, not to the officials who come and go like shadows at the door. Not even to each other.

Hazel has not spoken a word to Clementine at all, not since the night of the knife, and Clem can't bring herself to feel much of anything, let alone despair. The silence between them is wide and deep as an ocean. When words do pass between them, they're in the secret tongue of their childhood—Hazel to Ivy, Ivy to Clem—a thread of connection stretched thin, but unbroken.

Bullies come with fists and cruel names, then with threats and bribes. The Ward sisters endure. Punishments rain down like hailstones, but they don't bend. They have lived in the shadow of giants taller than these and will not be broken.

And then Hazel ages out of the system.

She walks away from the group home with nothing but a battered bag and the scars on her face, her beauty carved into something hard and unfamiliar. But she is free.

Juniper petitions, from Beltane, by excruciatingly slow letter, to adopt the younger girls, but an investigation still hangs over Beltane like a curse. The law says no. Hazel tries, too, but what court will grant custody to a girl barely out of care herself and with no roof of her own?

Clem clings to Ivy with desperate fingers, determined to keep what's left of her family whole. But six months after Hazel walks away, the system pries them apart. Clem is sent to strangers, shuffled from family to family, group home to group home. She doesn't know what happens to Ivy, who is placed elsewhere, and Clem feels the last of the island's warmth leave her bones.

And on a night she can barely remember, she removes Henry's button bracelet and throws it away.

A year later, Clem, too, ages out. She fights tooth and claw, with everything left in her, to have Ivy put into her care. But with no job and no qualifications, she fails—and breaks apart entirely.

The spiral comes fast. A string of arrests for drunkenness. Nights in cells. Then rehab, where she meets a boy with hollow eyes and trembling hands who speaks of London like a promised land. A flat to share. A chance to get clean.

Clem locks up her heart, forces herself to forget about Henry and to compartmentalize the yawning gulf of everything that happened at Beltane, and her role in her parents' deaths, and boards a plane with a one-way ticket, the last bridge to Ivy burning behind her.

Ivy endures.

She spends almost four years in foster care, small and quiet and determined. She works hard, keeps her head down, and earns a scholarship to a community college in Chicago, where she devotes herself to math. Numbers are predictable. Numbers are safe. Numbers are always the same.

She learns to make herself invisible in the crowd.

The years turn. The world moves on.

A decade or two down the road, each remaining Ward will receive a letter in the mail, delivered by hand. It will be carried by a boy they used to know, who grew into a man they don't.

A single juniper berry will summon them home.

# 39

***September 2024***

The moon is high in the sky when the shot rings out, followed by the crash of the front door.

It cracks the silence open like a skull. Echoes off the stone, the timbers, the black sea beyond Beltane's edges. And then comes the crash as the door is ripped from its hinges, or maybe only flung open so hard it feels like the house itself shudders.

I jerk back from the window, breath knocked clean from my lungs. My heart stumbles, then gallops. I lift my hand, trembling, and press a finger to my lips, the silent command for my sisters clear: Make no sound.

With dawning horror, I realize someone shot the bolts off the front door.

And then we hear it.

Boots.

Wet, heavy, each step stalking across the floor. A predator listening for the rustle of prey. The tread of them spreads out, fills the house, the wet slap of mud, the creak of the old floorboards under heavy weight.

I don't breathe. I don't dare.

The boots pause. The air strains, taut as a wire. And then they move again, slow and measured, away from us, toward the other side of the house.

I inch toward the living room door, every nerve in my body thrumming. My fingers find the key in my pocket, cold as death. I put it carefully in the cylinder and turn, so slowly I can feel each tooth of the lock catch and release. The door gives, creaking open as if the house itself is protesting.

I hold my breath, waiting to see if the intruder has heard, then glance back at my sisters. Their faces are drawn, ghost lit in the moonlight.

"Quickly," I mouth. My hand flutters, urging them on.

But the boots are coming back. Faster now. Heavy. Sure.

Juniper freezes. And then she screams—just as Ernest rounds the corner, a shotgun raised at chest level. His eyes are wide, irises black as pitch, and when he spots us, he leers.

"*Je vous tiens,*" he mutters, his grin wide, stretching taut those thin, scowling lips.

He raises his shotgun directly at Juniper. She ducks, and a shot fires out, cutting through the silence like a snapped bone and splintering the wall behind us. Pain explodes in my head as a sharp pressure wave knocks into my face and chest, a brutal echo of sound smashing rapidly between walls.

Smoke and dust litter the air, acrid stench of metal and tangy ozone.

*"Run!"* I don't hear my own scream through the ringing in my ears, but my sisters comply—heading toward the back of the house.

We tear down the hall, feet pounding. I expect Ernest to give chase, but he's out of shots. I hear him behind us, cursing, the *click-click* of him reloading, shells falling like spent teeth onto the floorboards.

I yank them toward the back, deeper into the house, the darkest parts of the shadows, toward *anywhere*, but there's nowhere to go. We slip into the gap, the place where the house's bones are crooked, where the inner and outer walls don't quite meet. A secret passage made by neglect. By rot. We squeeze through cobwebs and dust, to the other side.

Juniper presses through, lithe as a wraith. Hazel and I struggle. The wood claws at us. Our hips, our breasts scraping against joists. The air is thick with dust, cobwebs clinging like burial shrouds.

My mind reels.

Ernest.

Here.

All along.

I thought—God, I thought he'd gone with Henry. Didn't Henry say that? I can't remember. My thoughts are jagged, broken. He's here. He's *been* here, watching, waiting, the rot at the heart of this place.

Not Daudir . . . not Daudir at all.

We spill out from the wall's hollow belly, plastered gray with dust, trying not to cough. My ears strain—boots, again. Ernest's boots, following our path, slower now, deliberate, like he can taste our fear.

I pull us onward, toward the kitchen. The dining room looms, its table like a carcass in the dark. The window is still covered, and somehow the sight chills me more.

Blind. Beltane is blind.

In the kitchen, my fingers scrabble for the cellar key, clumsy, slick with sweat. I fumble for the lock, breath choking my throat.

Ernest's voice rips through the house—he's closer than I thought—and his footsteps rattle as he runs back the way he came, picking up speed.

"You should 'ave done it!" he roars. "Should 'ave done it yourself and spared me zis!"

He sounds drunk. Or mad. Or both.

"Want to take ze island away from me?" Another gunshot, a door smashed open. "I know zat look in your eye."

I think we're done for, my heart pulsing in my mouth, but Ernest takes the stairs. We hear him pounding up them, maybe two at a time, maybe three, and then stalking through the corridor.

We spill down into the cellar. I twist the key, lock the door behind us, hands shaking. The dark swallows us whole. All that stands between us and death is a flimsy pantry door.

Above, he rages.

"You just 'ad to come back, sniffing your noses into my business!" Bang. "You couldn't leave 'er to rot?" Bang. "You couldn't let 'er fade into madness and leave me in peace?"

Each shot makes me flinch, ears ringing, the wood trembling.

A small pause, reloading, and then more raging. He seems only to be talking to Juniper.

"I know Alys told you. I could see it! I paid my dues for decades!" he bellows. "And you knew she 'ad me trapped, *knew* I would do anything to stay out of prison. A refuge, she said. A secret island. But you—you *drag out my debt*! Blood tithe, zat's what it is. Blood for blood!"

Hazel leans in, hissing, "He's raving."

But I'm not so sure.

Pieces of things Henry said to me years ago jigsaw themselves together.

*My father doesn't like people to know where he is.* And when I had asked him why Ernest didn't go to him in Toronto: *He doesn't want to leave the island. It's remote. He likes not being found.*

*He wasn't made to be a husband. He's better in the wild.*

The bang of a second bedroom door.

Silence falls, heavy and suffocating. A silence that throbs with threat. Then another bang.

A voice floats past my left ear.

*What could we give . . .*

My voice. My words.

My head snaps left. Nothing there but shadow.

The same voice, from the right: *. . . to buy our freedom . . . ?*

Above us, Ernest continues to rave, to smash open our doors, stalking onward like the killer he is.

And here is my answer. I feel it blooming in my bones, mushrooms on marrow. Conviction, like a blanket, settles on my shoulders.

Warmth spreads through me. Sweet. Thick. Like honey on the tongue. Like Granny Alys's embrace. Safety. A safety so complete I could weep for it.

I swallow hard. My hands stop shaking. I know that Daudir has answered.

"We have to kill him."

I expect to have to tell them why, to have to explain. But my sisters don't flinch. Don't argue.

Something is happening in this cellar. Something moving between us in the dark. A knowing. A rising force, raw and old and waiting. Beltane hums with it, or maybe it's only us, our blood, our bones, tuned to the same dread frequency, the same odd infection.

The power swells.

It is feral. It is intoxicating.

Unlike the night Holly died, when my sisters shared one unified thought—a life for a life—this time, I share it too. It was the answer all along. The only answer.

I am the first to strip off my shoes, my clothes, my hair tumbling loose in a pale curtain.

I am not the last.

Spores settle on our skin, cold and fine.

We are Ward blood.

We are the island's daughters.

# 40

***September 2024***

We work together, using childhood skills, never forgotten, to lead Ernest into the woods.

The storm doors yawn wide behind us, a mouth drinking in the deepening night. We leave our mark where we want him to see it: footprints in the mud, deliberate as runes, the path baited with our flight. The night air clings wet and cold, the rain tastes of iron.

Into the woods we slip, as we did when we were girls. As we did when we wore skins and antlers and wood in our hair. I feel them now, the phantom weight of that bone bracelet tight on my wrist, the remembered pelt heavy across my shoulders. We are Ward daughters.

The trees remember.

Their shadows open to let us pass, and then close right back up behind us. We move barefoot, silent, breath low, hearts drumming slow and steady, tuned to the dark. The air is thick with petrichor, moss and earthy rot, the kind that stains teeth green and creeps under fingernails. This is the scent of home.

We lather mud, icy, onto our bodies, over arms, bellies, cheeks, and hair, until *we* are of the earth. Hazel smears a streak across her brow, a hunter's mark.

I touch my fingers to my lips and lift them skyward, a silent kiss. *Daudir,* I think. Keeper of the rain, of the root, of the silent hunt. He's watching. The forest is watching.

We make ourselves prey. We let him taste our fear. See it. The broken branches, the scuffed prints, each step a lie.

And Ernest follows.

We hear him before we see him. Boots sucking at the mud. The rasp of his breath, ragged with drink, with the chase. His anger leaks out of him in mutters and curses. His steps, once cocky, pound slower now. Unsure.

Hazel flashes her teeth at me in the dark. A wolf's grin.

Ernest wants us scared. So we give him scared.

Then

we vanish.

Blending into the night, into the trees, into the shadows, like we've never been.

We vanish, and we watch.

Ernest stumbles into the clearing where we were, shotgun up, turning in circles, confused. The barrel scrapes bark as he spins. The click of the hammer pulled back echoes too loud. His finger twitches on the trigger—*bang!* The flash splits the dark.

But we're gone.

Flat to the ground, bellies to the soil, hands sunk in the loam, part of the island. We slide between the ferns, the nettles, the moss. Fingers closing slow around the rough braid of roots, the soft fall of pine needles. Juniper moves like water at my side.

We climb when we must, slow, careful, hands finding the grooved bark, feet silent as mist.

He blunders. He has no idea we're corralling him, folding the woods tight around him like a snare.

He doesn't hear us, but we hear it all.

His labored breath, the wet gasp of his lungs. The rhythm of his boots, slow now, uncertain. The scrape of his gun barrel against another tree as he turns in a circle, confused.

"Come out!" he yells, voice cracking. He is thick with an anger he's trying to drown. An anger he's choking on. "I'll make it quick!"

Liar.

Hazel circles wide. She's already gone full shadow. She lets a branch snap underfoot, just loud enough. Ernest jerks toward it, staggers after her phantom.

Juniper waits, breathing calm and deep, the night wrapped tight around her. I feel the air change between us. We've done this before. We remember the shape of the hunt. We remember what it means to track something that can kill you back.

We've done this before. We've hunted things. Things with teeth. With horns. Things that screamed.

And, once . . . with Henry.

I give Juniper a signal. She moves, breaking cover, her steps deliberate, loud. A rabbit bolting from the brush.

Ernest takes the bait. His boots crash after her, too slow, too heavy. The woods fight him with every step. A root snags his ankle, sends him sprawling. His shotgun hits the ground with a thud.

He curses, scrambling, and I let him retrieve it. He doesn't know it's useless.

We lead him where we want him, where the trees grow in a ring like old gods watching. To Daudir's place. The big-leaf maple rises in the center, at least fifty feet taller than I remember, the moonlight silvering its branches.

Ernest bursts into the clearing, panting, wide-eyed, spinning.

"Come!" he roars, voice breaking, throat raw. "Out!"

I am done running.

Done losing.

The blood hums in me now. The woods hum too. Daudir lives in my veins.

I'm ready to face *myself.*

I shift, just enough. The tiniest rustle. Just enough for him to step back, right into the loop of wire.

# 41

***September 2024***

He steps back.

The wire loop brushes his ankle, just a whisper against skin, but as he panics and tries to jump away, it constricts. The snare bites down, clean and merciless. It yanks his foot from under him, sends him sprawling into the leaf rot and mud.

He screams, dropping the shotgun, scrabbling at his leg.

But I am good with snares, and the tree he's tethered to is older and stronger than he is. I watch him writhe, and the strange clarity of the moment settles over me like a second skin. I understand now why I felt that pull, that need to set the snare before we even began the chase. Why my hands chose the wire, strong and unyielding, not the soft cord we used for rabbits. It wasn't just instinct. It was inheritance.

We step out of the trees as one, and Ernest doesn't even notice. Too busy yanking at the wire that only grows tighter as he works. He is all frothing sputum, French curses, helpless rage.

Above us, the clouds unspool, slow and spectral, revealing a hard, cold moon. The light spills through the maple's canopy, dappling the ground in pale coins. The clearing glitters like something enchanted or cursed.

And finally, Ernest sees us.

He goes very still. His eyes find us, three figures risen from the earth itself.

Panicked, he reaches for the shotgun, but I'm faster. My foot lashes out, sends it skittering across the clearing, lost to him now. He lunges, tries to catch my ankle, tries to drag me down with him, but his hands close on nothing but air.

We are not little girls anymore.

We are not women either.

We are Wards.

Thirst.

Hunger.

Memory.

Obligation.

Honor.

Loyalty.

We are feral compulsion.

We are a debt repaid.

We are rot, and root, and revenge.

And we are *done* running.

The knife is in my hand, as natural as breath. The blade isn't what it was, its edge dulled, its spine nicked, but it will do. It always does, faithful companion. Juniper kept it safe, hidden in the cellar, waiting for me to come home, humming to me in the dark.

The wood of the handle is worn smooth, intimate from my grip all those years ago. My hand is bigger now. Stronger. An Effigist is nothing without her knife.

Ernest thrashes as I approach, kicking, cursing, pleading all at once. I dance around him, fast, light. The blade flickers in the moonlight as I draw it along his flesh, shallow cuts, ribbons of red rising in its wake. Playful little slices that draw scream after scream.

He promises vengeance. Promises pain. Then bargains. Then begs. Then finally, when no mercy comes, he folds in on himself, bitter and small, all that bluster ground to dust.

"*Sales garces,*" he spits, hate thick as bile. "Should 'ave drowned you zat first day."

Hazel's smile is terrible, luminous. Teeth flash, white as bone. "Oh. Beltane would never have allowed that, Mr. d'Aboville."

His eyes roll wild, searching for any way out.

I meet my sisters' gazes. The moon glints in Juniper's eye. With a nod from my sisters and a nudge from Beltane, I make one quick lunge.

Blade parts flesh almost as smooth as butter. Perhaps with a little tearing. The right thigh. Deep. The way Holly bled when she fell.

Ernest howls, clawing at his crotch, at the wire, at the air itself. He swears, sobs, chokes on his fury.

But it's slow.

Too slow.

I step close enough to see the glisten of sweat on his brow, the terrible dilation of his pupils, even as he spits in defiance. The last scrap of a man who knows he's lost.

*"Va te faire fout—argh!"*

I drive the blade into his throat.

The forest swallows the sound.

Behind me, a voice—raw, broken, familiar—rips through the night.

"Stop!"

# 42

***September 2024***

Henry falls to his knees. He is making noises, guttural noises, deep in his body.

I go over to him and touch a gentle hand to his cheek. His grief, his horror—it's just another sound of the forest now, like the wind moving low through the needles, like the creak in the distance.

He is part of Beltane. Ever since he drank corpse-mushroom water mixed with blood, he is a part of us. It's why he never left. Why he can't.

And he knows this isn't about him.

A payment was due.

And it was ours to make.

We kneel in the clearing, our bodies slick with sweat, with blood, with something older than either. Ernest lies where we left him, sprawled like a broken thing, his mouth frozen wide, lips curled mid-curse. His blood seeps into the moss, dark as spilled ink, slow as a promise kept at last.

The trees lean closer.

We strip our sacrifice naked, and I free his leg from my wire, slow, reverent. The flesh beneath is ragged, white bone grinning through the ruin. He fought hard. That was his gift.

Henry sobs again, loud, useless. I barely register it.

Hazel, Alchemist, dips her finger into the blood pooling at Ernest's side, draws a slow and deliberate *W* on his chest.

A Ward debt paid. An offer. A plea.

"Daudir," Juniper breathes, voice breaking, lifting to a cry. "Daudir!"

"Daudir!" Hazel echoes, low, sure.

I draw in a breath thick with the sweet rot of mulch in rain, and scream: *"DAUDIR!"*

And the forest moves.

Not an animal. Not the wind. A presence.

A shift. A growl deep beneath the roots. The trees part with a groan like old bones, shifting, like cartilage popping.

He is as tall as the pines. Antlers like branches heavy with draping Spanish moss, speckled with ancient lichen. Eyes that are the hollow abyss of the long-dead elk skull, deep as still water, vast as the midnight sky. They drink in the night and give nothing back.

And I am undone.

My breath catches, and I am flooded by a love so profound, so pure, so terrible that it collapses me, breaks me open. I am no more, and I am everything.

His hair is the soft, smooth of pale silk, silver under starlight, falling in the hollows of twisted bark and bone. His skin, mottled, gray, and somehow luminous, swells with fungus and rot around nails I drove in myself. Tiny palms and little forearms. Behind Him, rib bones flare wide, angel wings.

We have whispered His name in the dark since we were children. Built shrines and effigies of pine cones, roots, and feathers. Of buttons and beetles and ribbon. Of wood and moss and bone. Left dollops of honey on stone, burned hair and fingernails for His honor. Swore we felt Him in the dark eye of His window looking in, in the roots beneath the ground, the earth beneath our feet, pulsing like a heart.

There is no need for belief anymore.

He is here.

Daudir. Forgotten God of the Wood.

He towers over us, awesome, terrible, magnified by a hundred degrees, the air humming with ancient power we can barely comprehend.

For a long moment, He regards us, antlers towering like a crown. Then He crouches, the stumps of His legs folding into the earth, gathering our offering into His arms as a father might lift a sleeping child.

Gentle as a babe.

Final as a death knell.

We don't bow. We don't look away. We kneel, heads tilted back, faces upturned in wonder, like children once more, devotion and adoration and unwavering faith.

And in that moment, I feel them defer to me. My sisters. Me, who once had faith enough for them all, and who doubted hardest.

Daudir's regard burns bright over my body.

Hazel's gaze flicks to mine, waiting.

Juniper's breath catches when I lift my chin, His Effigist reborn.

*Daughters of the Wood,* the forest whispers.

I see it, clear as moonlight on water. He is so beautiful, and at His center: The heart piece missing from our core. Our bright jewel. Our thread of love, of hope, and of joy. The one we endured for.

Her name, brilliant, sacred, blazes into my mind. Her bright, smiling face, her ruddy, happy cheeks.

Poppy.

Our seventh sister.

She is with Daudir now.

She *is* Daudir now.

And so is Granny Alys.

And so, in time, shall we be.

A knowing blooms in my chest, ancient and quiet, like a seed unfurling after a long, brutal winter.

"I believe," I whisper.

And somehow, it is enough.

Daudir turns, slow as winter's thaw, vast as thunder held in breath, and walks back into the waiting trees, the earth thundering, pulsing beneath Him. Ernest hangs in His arms, small and slack, his life spent for our deliverance.

A price paid. A promise kept.

Freedom stirs around us, not loud or grand, but deep.

Freedom from doubt.

From the world beyond Beltane.

From the shadows and fears that once clung to our names.

The forest will always protect Ward blood. If we follow the rules laid out, then we will always have a place at Beltane.

This is not myth. Not metaphor. It is memory. Bone-deep truth. Ward blood belongs to the forest.

And the forest, when honored, belongs to us.

If we give as we take, if we keep the rhythm, the rites, the reverence, then we are never alone.

We are never lost.

We are never forgotten.

The trees reach reverently toward Daudir's antlers, swaying against His side like kin. Root and sky bend and warp as He passes, bending to His shape, until they fold back in on themselves, swallowing Him whole.

As if He had never been.

As if He always was.

And Beltane breathes again.

Finally, I understand.

Not all gods wear crowns of gold.

Some come with root and rot and bone.

Some are made of forest and flame and forgetting.

And some are made from *us*.

Daudir, the Forgotten God of the Wood, has come at last.

And somewhere with Him, the seventh sister moves through the turning of the trees, as we shall, in time.

# ACKNOWLEDGMENTS

A book is a forest, is a house, is a whole world. Without these people, Clem and her sisters would have no shelter.

To my husband, my steadfast hearthfire. Without you, none of this would be possible. I love you dearly, I cherish you deeply, and I am grateful for you every day. To my mum, who always cheers on my bookish rituals and incantations, even when they involve . . . well, the very horrors you've just read. 😈

To Victoria Marini, my fierce and passionate agent; Jessica Tribble-Wells, who saw the wood for the trees; Charlotte Herscher, who helped me shape these word effigies into something alive; and Jenna Justice, whose copyedits (as ever) are as sharp as a blade and as vital as breath. Thank you also to Rachel McClure for meticulously picking off the mushrooms and stray maggots from these walls. To Miranda Gardner for shepherding the book through production, and to the entire Thomas & Mercer team: Your unseen work is the strong foundation of this rotten forest house, and I am truly thankful.

To my friends Claire D., Kat Ellis, Ann Dávila Cardinal, Twin, Vickie R., and to Mel T., who offered a line of dialogue I pressed like a wildflower into Granny Alys's heart ("all the best houses have strong personalities"). Thank you for your companionship on this crooked path.

To early readers: Angela Slatter, Tatiana Sclote-Bonne, Clay McLeod Chapman, Susan Dennard, Sadie Hartmann, Joshua Winning, Kat Ellis, Ann Dávila Cardinal, Viggy Parr Hampton, Kathryn Foxfield, and Hannah Whitten, thank you for letting your eyes wander these mossy pages.

To the bloggers and reviewers who speak of my work with such generosity: Your words are torches in the dark, guiding readers (and me) through the brambles.

To everyone who touched this book in ways I may have forgotten to name, you are here, too, woven into its fabric.

And to you, dear reader, who picked up this story and stepped into the house at Beltane: I hope you carried something away with you. A shadow, a whisper, a secret pressed into your pocket.

All hail Daudir.

*Dawn Kurtagich*
August 2025

## WARD SECRET LANGUAGE KEY

## THE WARD TONGUE

A = HA
B = CH
C = BU
D = DIR
E = EM
F = JI
G = D
H = GI
I = JA
J = IP
K = K
L = KLO
M = MON
N = NI
O = AU
P = PRU
Q = KIR
R = RES
S = SHE
T = TAU

U = JOPO
V = V
W = WEN
X = ZEB
Y = DOS
Z = ZERA
TH = G'
CH = THR

# A TECHNICAL NOTE ON THE WARD TONGUE

The Ward sisters forged a language of their own, as children do when the world will not understand them. Each letter, or pair of letters, was given a sound, a shape, a soul. Together, these fragments wove into words, part code, part charm, part secret song.

But the Ward tongue is a jealous one. When two vowels meet, their voices clash and knot. To keep them from devouring each other, the sisters cut a small seam between them: an apostrophe, a mark of separation, a breath held in the dark.

So the simple word *die* becomes *dirja'em*:

- D = Dir
- I = Ja
- E = Em

The mark between *a* and *e* preserves their voices, keeping the word whole.

Remember this rule, and the Ward tongue will open itself to you. Forget it, and the words may twist into something unrecognizable.

# ABOUT THE AUTHOR

Dawn Kurtagich is the award-winning author of several YA horror novels, including her acclaimed debut *The Dead House*, *And the Trees Crept In* (*The Creeper Man*), *Teeth in the Mist*, and *Blood on the Wind*. *The Madness* and *The Thorns* are her first books for adults.

The daughter of a British globe-trotter, Kurtagich grew up all over the world, but her formative years were spent in Africa—on a mission, in the bush, in the city, and in the desert. She leaves her North Wales crypt after midnight during blood moons. The rest of the time, she exists somewhere between mushrooms, maggots, and mold.

You can always find the author on her website at www.dawnkurtagich.com.